Two Old Ladies and a Secret Child

by
Suzanne Shearing

Grosvenor House
Publishing Limited

This book is published by
Grosvenor House Publishing Ltd
Link House
140 The Broadway, Tolworth, Surrey, KT6 7HT.
www.grosvenorhousepublishing.co.uk

This book is a work of fiction. Any resemblance to
people or events, past or present, is purely coincidental.

A CIP record for this book
is available from the British Library

ISBN 978-1-83975-335-0

To Mark

Acknowledgements

First of all many thanks to the friendly team at Grosvenor House Publishing, including Tanis Eve, Becky Banning, Máire McAvinchey and Jenny Warren, all of whom have been a pleasure to work with.

I'm grateful to Verity Savage and Vanessa Mendozzi for helping me to bring my cover design to fruition, and John Harwood-Bee for his knowledge about catamarans!

Many thanks to Chris West and the Cottered Writers group, and all members of the Buntingford Writers group for their encouragement and critiques.

And my special thanks go to my friends and family who were press-ganged into reading the book, and especially those who found themselves named or portrayed within the pages!

I'm thrilled with the reviews from those who read the manuscript before publication: Mary Godfrey, Brian and Lin Emsley, Becky Manning, Christine Green, Helen Byrne, Shirley Holmes, Jenny Warren, Richard Wood and Jonathan Miller. Your words are greatly appreciated.

Last but not least, thank you for reading my debut novel!

Chapter one

Ria was hanging out the washing.

She was on autopilot, as she always was when doing mindless, repetitive jobs. She shuffled back into the kitchen of her country house. She knew she was shuffling. She remembered watching her mother shuffle around her family home many years ago. She had even asked her why she did it. Her mother gave her a withering look and told her that she would find out one day.

That day had come. But she wasn't sure why she shuffled. Or why her shoulders were bent or her skin lined. Her shell was crumbling, day by day, but Ria was still in there somewhere. She was still the same girl that went to music festivals and danced the night away. She was still the woman who was commended for her bravery by the police force. Still the woman who made others laugh with her sharp wit and funny stories.

They were all still in there somewhere, but that was not how others saw her these days. Even Ria had difficulty locating her real self. Now, there was no one to amuse, no one to help, no one to dance with, even if her old legs would let her.

She made a cup of tea and sat at her kitchen table. The place was silent. Even her spaniel Roxy had settled down for a nap. Ria looked out of the window. Nothing to see but her washing, hanging limply, without so much as a breeze to dry it. She picked up her tea and mooched into the sitting room. She looked out of the front window onto the lane. Nothing to see.

It had now been 10 years since she'd retired, and gradually she had lost touch with old friends and work colleagues who had moved away or died. Her only child, a son, had moved to Canada, and apart from a phone call on her birthday and at Christmas, she didn't hear from him. Ria had never married the abusive man who had fathered her child.

What was she to do with what was left of her life?

The doorbell rang. Ria was shocked into the moment. Few people ever knocked at her door. Roxy leapt to her feet, and ran to the door, barking. Ria peered out of the window and saw a woman standing on her doorstep. She grabbed Roxy's collar, and gingerly opened the door. The woman was about her age and had a friendly face.

'Sorry to bother you,' she said, smiling. 'I've just come to introduce myself. I've just moved in two doors down… into Lavender Cottage.' She thrust a bunch of daffodils into Ria's hand. 'I thought you might like these. They were growing in the garden.'

There was something familiar about the woman's voice. Ria didn't know what to do. She wanted to be friendly. How wonderful it would be to have a new friend in the lane, but the woman could be anyone. You had to be careful nowadays.

There was a pause. 'I'm Amanda by the way. Most people call me Mandy.'

Ria stared hard at her. 'Yes, they do!' she exclaimed, 'Mandy Anderson as I live and breathe!'

Mandy was startled and stared at Ria. 'Oh, wow, do I know you?' she began.

'Mount Grace School, it's me, Ria!'

'Ria Radcliffe! I can't believe it, how wonderful to see you.'

'Well, don't stand on the doorstep. Come on in. Don't mind Roxy, she's harmless.'

The two old friends had nearly 60 years to catch up on.

Mandy had never found her soulmate and also lived alone. She had travelled the world as a theatrical agent, but it wasn't anywhere near as exciting as some would believe.

'Who was that awful boy that we both thought we were in love with?' laughed Mandy.

'Oh, don't talk about him,' said Ria, thinking of the frightening day when she was 16 and was told that she was pregnant.

'OK,' said Mandy, 'What about our gang. Did you keep in touch with any of them?'

'For a little while. But my parents moved us to this area for my dad's work, so it fizzled out after that. You?'

'Same thing really. We saw each other for a little while, but then some went off to uni, others moved or got married, and we all went our separate ways. Shame really. Oh, Ria, I'm so glad you're my neighbour! I thought I might go stir crazy in that little cottage on my own.'

'What brought you here?' Ria asked.

'I had to downsize. Not much left in the kitty, so I decided to move to this lovely village. Do you like it here?'

'It's very quiet,' offered Ria.

'Won't be now I'm here!' laughed Mandy.

The two women chatted on into the evening. They had found their teenage selves again.

It was exhausting but thrilling.

The next day Ria was invited for a guided tour of Lavender Cottage, and to have lunch.

She had never really looked at the place before, as her dog walks always took her in the opposite direction. Now she stood at the gate and took in the old building. It was looking a bit tired but had been a chocolate box cottage in its day. It was nothing that her old friend couldn't put right. A lick of paint on the picket fence and the front door would make the world of difference. The thatched roof was in great condition, although climbing ivy was threatening to envelop it. A tempting smell of baking hung in the air, mingling with the fragrance of the lavender, growing wild in the garden.

'Don't just stand there, come on in,' said Mandy from her doorstep. She was wiping flour from her hands with a tea towel.

Ria presented her with a bunch of asparagus that she had picked from her garden that morning.

They settled down to their lunch of homemade soup and crusty bread, followed by a piece of hastily made Victoria sponge. There was no shortage of conversation. The pair chatted happily until late afternoon. But although they were delighted to see each other, it soon transpired that neither of them was very happy with their lives. They were lonely, rudderless and lost. Unemployable but capable, fun to be with, but ignored. Derided for their ailing bodies, but full of wisdom and experience. They had become sad and accepting of their lot. They had given up. All that talent wasted.

But now there was a new spark. An awakening of lost spirits.

There was still a lot of unpacking to do, so they picked a box each and started to empty the contents onto any available surface.

'I see you like a good crime story,' said Ria as she carefully unpacked a box of books.

'Yes, always have,' said Mandy. 'I even tried to write one once. Could have done with your police knowledge back then.' She laughed.

'Wow, I'm impressed.'

'It's all about tech nowadays,' Mandy continued. 'That's when I packed up. Technology overtook me years ago.'

'Me too,' Ria agreed. 'But you should have another crack at that book.'

'Need an unusual idea. Did you come across any interesting cases in your career?'

'Not really. I was at the bottom of the food chain. Mainly shoplifters and domestics. What about you?'

'I've spent most of my life dealing with actors. I wanted to be one myself once, like most agents. We imagined that we would get the pick of the jobs as they came in, but it doesn't work like that. And all actors want to play the bad guy parts! We live and learn.'

'Can you imagine us as villains?' laughed Ria. 'Old fogey pillars of the community. I know all the ropes, and you're an actress... well, sort of!'

'What fun!' agreed Mandy.

Ria fell into bed exhausted that night. They had made a good start on the unpacking, but they would have another crack at it tomorrow.

Apart from the grey hair and the obvious physical signs of ageing, Mandy hadn't changed a bit, she thought. She was still bright and funny, and great company. Things were looking up for them both.

The next day Ria made lasagne and a bowl of salad and took it to Lavender Cottage for lunch.

'Ooh, real cooking!' said Mandy. 'What a treat. I seem to live on sandwiches and soup.'

There were still a dozen boxes to unpack, so after lunch they set to. It was fascinating for Ria to rummage through Mandy's things, it satisfied her nosy streak. Mandy was less than enthusiastic. She slumped onto a chair.

'Why don't we just leave this lot and clear off?' she said.

'Clear off where?' Ria was startled.

'Anywhere. Go on a road trip. Do something exciting.'

'But you've only just moved in, and we're hardly Thelma and Louise!'

'Where's your sense of adventure?'

'Are you serious?'

'Totally. What else are we going to do? Bury ourselves in the middle of nowhere and wait to die?'

'Mandy, you are a nutter!' laughed Ria. 'I haven't got the money for a road trip.'

'Details, details. Come on, Ria, you never used to be a stick in the mud.'

'I think you must have been watching too many movies... maybe I should start calling you Shirley Valentine.'

'Yes, great! She had the right idea. I'm not ready to be old, Ria. I've wasted too much time already.'

'But I have a dog,' Ria retorted.

'Bring her. She'll love it!'

And that was how, against her better judgement, Ria found herself packing a suitcase the following morning. Roxy was watching with interest. 'I must be mad,' her owner said. 'I have absolutely no idea where we're going, or even where we'll stay tonight.' But Ria felt excited, for the first time in years.

It was a perfect morning. The spring sunshine illuminated the daffodils and primroses along the lane as Ria dragged her suitcase and an excited Roxy to Lavender Cottage.

Mandy's Land Rover stood on the drive with its tailgate open. The boot was stuffed with luggage. The front door of the cottage was open. Ria poked her head inside. 'Are you ready Shirley Valentine?' she called.

'Coming,' replied Mandy. 'Get yourself in the car, and I'll be right with you.'

Ria climbed into the front seat with Roxy. She had planned to put her in the boot, but there was no room.

Then Mandy emerged from the cottage carrying yet another box, which she carefully placed on the back seat. She locked the front door, and off they went.

Ria could scarcely believe that this was happening but felt a huge relief that she was getting out of her house and into the world, and better still, with a good friend and her beloved Roxy.

Mandy seemed quiet, but Ria let her concentrate on the driving.

They soon left the country lanes and hit the motorway. 'Any idea where we're going?' ventured Ria.

Mandy glanced at her and smiled, 'Yes, I know exactly where we're going. We'll be there in about two hours. You'll love it.'

'Do tell,' said Ria.

Mandy just tapped the side of her nose and drove on. 'It's a surprise,' she said.

Ria had not realised how tired she was and soon dozed off. Eventually, the car stopped, and she awoke to the sound of a baby crying.

Mandy was getting out of the car. Ria looked around. They were parked beside a mobile home in a holiday park. Mandy reached into the back of the car and took the box from the back seat. The baby stopped crying. What? Surely not...

Mandy put the box on the mobile home steps and opened the door. She then carefully lifted the box and disappeared inside.

Ria was still half asleep and totally confused. Roxy started jumping about excitedly and demanding her attention. Ria and Roxy followed Mandy into the mobile home.

Mandy was sitting on the sofa, cradling a baby.

'What on earth... where did the baby come from?' asked Ria.

'OK, I'll tell you, if you promise to just listen,' said Mandy defensively.

Ria sat at the small table and stared at the baby. 'I'm listening,' she said. Roxy was fascinated with the new arrival and sniffed her approval.

'Yesterday,' Mandy began, 'I was in and out of the cottage packing the car when I spotted another box on the doorstep. At first I thought it was a delivery.'

'From Sainsbury's, I suppose.'

'Well, if you're going to be sarky.'

'Go on.'

'OK, well when I looked closely, I could see it was a baby wrapped in a blanket. It hadn't made a sound. I looked around, but there was nobody about. I took her indoors, she's a little girl, and Ria she is so gorgeous, I'm totally in love with her.'

'So, you called the police?'

'Well no… hang on… not yet. I thought the mother might come back. Maybe a young girl who panicked.'

'But why your house? Nobody knows you?'

'I have no idea. Maybe she knew the people who were in Lavender Cottage before me.'

'So why have you brought her here?'

'Ria, listen to me. I have always wanted a child, but it never happened for me. It's OK for you. You have a son. This child needs—'

'Have you listened to yourself, Mandy? This is madness. You cannot keep this baby. She has a mother and a father.'

'Who don't want her!' shouted Mandy.

Ria softened her tone. 'Mandy, you are old enough to be her great-grandmother.'

'Maybe, but I reckon I still have a good 15 or 20 years in me. Plenty of time to give her a fantastic start in life.'

'We have to tell social services and the police.'

'And what will they do? Put her in a foster home until she can be adopted by God knows who. And she could be pushed from pillar to post for years before that happens. You know what the system is like. Or they might find the teenage mother and her spotty drug addict boyfriend and hand her back to them. No, she's better off with me.'

Ria got up and put the kettle on. She knew that Mandy was right. She had seen children put through the system and the resulting dysfunctional adolescents that emerged at the other end. There was so much red tape that adoptions took forever.

Maybe Mandy could foster the baby legally? No, she was not an approved foster parent, and would probably be considered too old. And then she would have the heartbreak of having to part with her.

'You're quiet,' said Mandy. 'Are you angry?'

'No, just thinking,' replied Ria as she searched for tea bags and mugs.

After a couple of trips to the car, she finished making the tea and found some ginger biscuits.

Mandy put the sleeping child back in her box cot and came and sat at the table.

'So that's why you were in such a hurry to clear off?' said Ria.

'I was scared that I would have to give her back, that the police would come, I don't know. Ria, this could be the start of something great. We could both sell our houses and buy a beautiful place by the sea. The two of us could have great fun, and bring up the baby together, and Roxy would love it.'

Mandy certainly painted an attractive picture. Ria would love to share a seaside home with her best friend and a little girl and her dog. It would feel like the real family she never had. She couldn't believe that she was even considering it. They would end up in jail.

'Who would ever know?' Mandy continued.

'Well, if the person who abandoned her changed her mind and told the police, it wouldn't be rocket science to find out that you owned the house and had disappeared. They would find you, make no mistake about that.'

'The mother either didn't want her or couldn't cope. She may have kept the pregnancy a secret from her family. She's not likely to go to the police, is she?' Mandy retorted.

'Maybe not, but we don't know. You can't be looking over your shoulder forever.'

That night, Ria lay in bed, mulling it all over. She had come across one or two cases of abandoned babies during her working years. She remembered being told that some 50 babies a year were abandoned. Great efforts were made to find the mothers, but in most cases, they were never traced. Both Ria and Mandy had become besotted with the baby girl with silky blonde wisps of hair and blue eyes.

They located a department store with a baby section eight miles from their holiday home, and Ria felt a wave of excitement as they made their way through the store.

When she had had her child, it had been a different story. She was alone and penniless with a tiny baby at the age of 16. And it was at a time when it was almost a hangable offence to have a baby 'out of wedlock'. Only for the girls of course. The men usually turned their backs and were happy to label the single mums as slags and worse. Ria had been taken to a mother and baby home, where her parents' plan was to have the baby adopted at the age of six weeks. Then the whole sorry saga would be forgotten about.

But Ria was feisty and had always loved babies. Nobody was going to force her to give her child away.

Her memories of her baby were bittersweet. She managed to get a job and a flat, and a couple of childminders. But it was not easy. It didn't stop her from adoring her child, just like any other new mum, and her youth made her fit enough to cope. She had to manage with a second-hand pram, and baby clothes from jumble sales. How lucky this little girl would be.

Mandy wandered around looking in awe at everything that was available for babies. Over the years, though, she had failed to notice that big springy prams had been replaced by pushchairs that would fit into car boots. And the price! What a shock. The young assistant made a beeline for the women and the baby that was snuggled in Mandy's arms.

'Ooh, what a gorgeous baby,' she cooed. 'Is it a girl? She looks so pretty.'

'Yes,' replied the proud new 'mum'.

'What's her name?'

Mandy looked at Ria. Her name? She really hadn't thought about a name.

'It's Matilda,' said Ria. Mandy looked shocked.

'Yes, Matilda,' Mandy improvised.

'That was my mother's name.'

Soon Matilda was tucked up in her new buggy, and both women were loaded down with bags full of clothes, nappies, toys and baby milk.

Back at the mobile home site, they managed to hire a cot and were soon organised.

Despite her better judgement, Ria was enjoying herself. She told herself that she had been sensible all her life, and maybe now in her golden years she had earned the right to live for each happy day. Who was she hurting?

The little family started to relax into a routine, and the days flew by. The mobile home, which Mandy insisted on calling a caravan, had been booked for two weeks, and already a week had passed.

'So, what's the plan?' asked Ria over breakfast.

'Plan?' said Mandy as she demolished her third piece of toast, with Matilda at last sound asleep in her cot.

'Yes, we'll have to leave here in a few days.'

'Oh, that plan. Yes, well, I can't go back to Lavender Cottage with Matilda. You'll have to go back and put our houses on the market, while I look for something near the sea.'

'Seriously? You really want to do this?' Ria was wavering.

'Yes, Ria, seriously. Why not? If it makes three people and a dog happy, and it's not bothering anyone else, why not?'

Ria was surprised to find that she couldn't find a worthwhile argument against that logic, and she was not looking forward to going back to her lonely, useless existence in her large house.

Mandy managed to book the caravan for another two weeks, and Ria set off with Roxy to sort out things at home. Mandy and Matilda would have to manage without the car until she returned.

Chapter two

Ria was tired after her long drive. As she and Roxy settled down for a rest in the sitting room, she felt that the last week had been some sort of weird dream. This was her reality. This house, this recliner, this room. There were a couple of letters. A phone bill and a handwritten letter. She loved real letters, so much more personal than emails. She put on her glasses, and her tired old fingers tore open the envelope.

It read:

Mother

I hope you got my last letter? I didn't want to discuss this on the phone, and I don't have your email.

I was worried as I hadn't heard from you. Maybe you're angry?

Please don't be. You are the only one I can turn to. To repeat, I had an affair (stupid, I know) with a girl who was on a training scheme at the embassy where I work. She got pregnant. I could not let my wife know, and it turns out that the girl is some sort of Scandinavian royalty (quite low in the pecking order, but nevertheless). She went to England to have the baby secretly as she is due to marry some bigwig later this year.

I asked my old school friend Tony, remember him? to leave the child with you, as you would know what to do. But not a word to anyone, Mother! My marriage would be over, and the press would have a field day. Just say the baby is a foundling and please see it is adopted by a good couple. And, Mother, burn this letter, just in case. Please don't ring me. I can't talk at home or at work about this.

I hope you are well.

Talk soon

C x

Ria's mouth dropped open. So, Matilda was supposed to be left on *her* doorstep, not Lavender Cottage. This was her grandchild! And her son referred to his daughter as 'it'. Her head was swimming. Now she knew she must keep this child, royalty or not.

Royalty!

She needed time to process this staggering turn of events. Her first instinct was to call Mandy, but she was suddenly nervous about telling her on the phone. She would show her the letter when she got back. But no, Charles told her to burn it. And she wasn't proud of her son's behaviour. This needed a lot of thought.

Ria spent the next couple of days briefing estate agents about her home, and Lavender Cottage.

They were more than a little surprised that Lavender Cottage was on the market again, so soon after completing the sale with Mandy.

Ria felt even more desperate to get away. As if her secret would stay here with the house. She had always preferred to be open about everything, but this was different. She couldn't let her son down; however stupid he'd been. And she couldn't risk losing her only grandchild.

On day three, she packed up the car, locked up both houses, making sure that the estate agents had keys, and she and Roxy left the house that had been home for almost 10 years. She hardly registered the drive back to the holiday park. She had too much to think about.

Mandy was delighted to see her. She had harboured a slight worry that once she got home, Ria would change her mind and decide to stay. But here she was. And Mandy couldn't wait to tell her some exciting news.

'So glad to see you,' she said as she hugged her friend. 'I have something fantastic to tell you!'

Ria didn't reply. How was she going to break *her* news?

'Are you OK, Ria? You're very quiet. Everything OK with the estate agents?'

Ria just couldn't find the right words. 'Let's have a cup of tea,' she said as if that would solve everything. 'I'm just a bit tired from all the driving.'

'Of course, sorry,' said Mandy as she put on the kettle, and grabbed a couple of mugs.

Ria went to the cot where Matilda was sleeping peacefully. She gently stroked her head.

'Don't wake her,' said Mandy, 'please, she's just dropped off.'

She put the mugs of tea on the table, and both women sat down. The atmosphere had become tense. Both knew that something was up.

Ria reached into her bag and pulled out an old black and white photograph. She handed it to Mandy. Mandy was puzzled but took the picture and looked at it closely. It was of a baby. It looked like Matilda. Same shaped face, same wispy blonde hair.

Mandy looked at Ria. 'Who is this? Why are you showing it to me?'

'It's my son.'

'Oh, I see, yes he's a beautiful baby. This is all bringing back memories for you?'

'Can you see the likeness to Matilda?' asked Ria.

'Well, all babies look alike at this age, don't they?' laughed Mandy. 'Have a biscuit. I have some great news.'

Mandy had spent her time while Ria was away looking at houses along the coast. It was not always easy, the estate agent said, to find a front-line sea-view property, but there was something he wanted to show her.

In the prettiest bay stood a detached villa with its own small beach. It had four bedrooms, all with en suite, and four reception rooms. The views were stunning. Mandy fell in love with it immediately. She couldn't wait to show Ria.

'I have some important news, too,' said Ria, looking solemn.

'Oh no, what's the matter?' Mandy didn't want anything to burst her bubble.

Once more Ria rummaged in her bag and pulled out Charles's letter. 'Before you read this, I want you to solemnly promise that you will never tell a living soul.'

Mandy was shocked but intrigued. 'Blimey, what on earth is it?'

Ria handed her the letter. Mandy read it carefully.

'Dear God, this is not a joke, is it?'

'No, Mandy, it's genuine.'

'Matilda is royal?'

'Probably about tenth in line.'

'And she's your granddaughter.'

'Yes.'

'But I found her, I wanted her to be mine,' said Mandy, sounding like a whiny child. 'What a good job we didn't go to the police.'

There was a long pause while Mandy absorbed the information.

'Well, we can still both bring her up, can't we? I love her so much, Ria, and you have a right to have her now.'

Ria was deep in thought. Her son wanted his child to be adopted, but surely wouldn't object to his mother raising her. And the birth mother would never dare tell her secret. But how would she explain the tot to her daughter-in-law if she and Charles were to visit?

Or anyone else for that matter. Would the birth have to be registered to enable Matilda to go to school or get medical treatment? So many questions.

'Ria?'

'Sorry, just thinking.'

'Well, I have something I want to show you,' Mandy enthused.

'Now?'

'Yes, why not.'

Ria stuffed the letter into her jacket pocket, and they all made their way to the seaside villa.

Mandy stopped the car at the front of the house and was mortified to see the agent showing some people around. She jumped out and hurried to the agent, who was standing with a middle-aged couple. Ria followed her with Matilda in her arms.

'Excuse me, sorry, I just, could I have a word with you, please?' Mandy pleaded.

The agent, a smart woman in her thirties, suggested that the couple who were viewing continue without her for a few minutes, and turned to Mandy and Ria. 'Ah, it's Mrs... er, Mandy, isn't it?'

'Yes, I viewed this house the other day. This is my friend Ria... you remember I was waiting for her to see it.'

'Yes, but you really should have made an appointment. As you can see, I'm in the middle of a viewing.'

'Please let her look, as you're here. I think we'll put in an offer today.' Mandy glanced at Ria, who looked startled.

The agent smiled and led them into the sitting room. 'I'll need to attend to the other couple. As you've been here before maybe you could show your friend around?'

'Yes, great, thanks, that's fine.' Mandy was delighted.

Ria passed the sleeping infant to Mandy and walked to the French doors at the back.

The view was stunning. The sparkling blue sea, soft yellow sand and the hills and rocks that made up the surrounding cove. She felt she had come home, and to her surprise, tears sprang to her eyes. She pulled a tissue from her pocket and gave her nose a blow.

They went upstairs, admiring the spacious bedrooms and modern bathrooms, and then inspected the whole property, including the wonderful private beach. When they came back into the sitting room, the other couple were having a final look before having a quiet word with the agent in the hall, and then leaving.

Ria prayed that they hadn't made an offer.

Mandy and Ria looked at each other. Mandy laughed. 'I do believe you're going all emotional on me.'

Ria smiled and dabbed her eyes. Could all this really be happening?

The agent returned. 'So, what do you think?' she said.

'Well, Ria's in tears already, so I'll take that as a yes,' laughed Mandy. 'Are the other couple making an offer?'

'It looks likely. He's a journalist, and they want a second home by the sea. They seemed to like it.'

'Well, we'd like to offer the asking price,' said Mandy.

Ria was stunned. 'The asking price?' she said.

'Yes, we don't want to lose it.'

So, all they had to do now was sell two houses.

So their course was set, and although they had a lot of work in front of them, for now they could relax. The holiday site had allowed them a block booking for six months. It was not cheap, but they were coming into the summer season, so were lucky to get anything.

So, for a few lazy days there were walks along the seafront, sitting watching the world go by on pavement cafes, and reading newspapers and trashy novels.

Ria realised that she hadn't answered her son's letter, but she would have to word her reply carefully in case his wife had sight of it.

Dear Charles

Thank you for your letter and package, which arrived safely, although first delivered to the wrong address! What a surprise!

Rest assured that all is well here, and I will hang on to the package for safekeeping.

I will be moving soon and will keep you posted.
Take care.
Love to Anna
Mum xx

She took a stroll to the park shop where there was a post box, and she needed some milk and a paper. The sun was shining again, and a wave of happiness engulfed her. She hadn't felt this good for years. For once, the future was looking rosy. She didn't think she would ever have a grandchild, as her daughter-in-law, Anna, was unable to conceive. Now she had a beautiful granddaughter, a seafront villa very soon, and a lovely friend to share it all with. And to think that just a few weeks ago she had succumbed to being a lonely old lady waiting for God.

She popped the letter in the post box and then noticed the newspaper placard by the front door of the shop. 'ROYAL BABY KIDNAPPED' screamed the headline, and underneath, 'Princess cancels wedding as scandal unfolds'.

Ria staggered back against the post box. Her head was swimming. She heard a voice saying, 'Are you alright, love?' As she focused, a small group was gathering around her. Voices: 'Get her some water,' 'It's probably the heat,' 'Should I call an ambulance?'

'No, no, I'm fine,' she managed. 'Please don't fuss, I'm OK, really.'

She sipped the water that someone had offered her, picked up a paper, and started back to the caravan.

'Here, she didn't pay for that,' came a voice, and another, 'She's not well, bless her, leave it.'

Mandy was sitting on the sofa cradling Matilda. 'Whatever's the matter. You look ill!'

Ria handed her the paper and slumped onto the chair. 'I only saw the headlines; I haven't read the story yet. How the hell did this get out?'

Mandy read aloud, '*A scandal is unfolding, as an unnamed Scandinavian princess has called off her wedding, as it is claimed that she secretly had a baby to another man. The princess was due to marry a 'European aristocrat' in October, according to a source. The source claims that the child, who was born in England, was then kidnapped when less than a week old. There is a lot of speculation about which royal family is involved. Norway, Sweden and Denmark all have young princesses, but all are denying any knowledge. There has not been a public announcement of a wedding in October, or a cancellation, but this newspaper has evidence from a reliable source that the child was born and is no longer with her mother. The police say they have no knowledge of a kidnapping, but these matters would be dealt with by Special Branch, MI5 and MI6.'*

'Special Branch, MI5, you really must get rid of that letter now, Ria!'

'God, yes. I'll burn it now,' said Ria as she reached into the jacket pocket that was hanging on the back of her chair. She felt in one pocket, and then the other. Nothing but a tissue. She looked on the floor and then started to panic. She looked everywhere in the caravan and then took her frantic search to the car. The pair of them searched every corner of the caravan, but it just wasn't there.

'What the hell have you done with it?' raged Mandy.

'Don't yell at me. It was in my pocket...'

'Well think, where could it have fallen out?'

Matilda started crying at the raised voices. This made Roxy bark.

'The last time I wore it,' Ria shouted above the noise, 'was when we went to view the seaside villa.'

'Oh no,' she continued, 'I did pull a tissue from my pocket when I got emotional. We were in the sitting room. Maybe it dropped out then.'

'Do you suppose the agent picked it up?' asked Mandy.

'Maybe, but surely she would have given it back.'

'Unless she thought it belonged to the other couple who were viewing,' Mandy continued. 'You know the journ... Oh no, he was a journalist! For God's sake, Ria, he was a journalist!'

Ria looked nervously out of the window, as though expecting the riot squad to appear.

'Nobody knows we're here,' said Mandy.

'What about the estate agent?' Ria was panicking.

'I didn't give the estate agent this address. I thought she might worry that we couldn't afford the villa. I told her we were staying at a hotel while we viewed a few places. She wants us to go into her office to give her all the details, but she knows we have properties to sell, and she said the vendors would wait for us as we were offering the asking price and they're not in a hurry.'

Ria picked up Matilda and gave her a hug. Surely no one would accuse them of kidnapping?

Suddenly she was angry. 'That bastard! Going to the press! Good job the letter was not in the envelope addressed to me. They can't know who we are.'

'Unless the estate agent tells them.'

'No, client confidentiality and all that,' Ria continued. 'We'll be OK here for a while.'

The speculation about the princess and her baby continued in the press and spread to all the news media channels. It didn't take them long to discover that the young lady in question was 23-year-old Princess Tindra, who had been on secondment in Canada for a year. Her child was born in a London hospital and was subsequently 'stolen' by a man who was seen on CCTV, and described as middle-aged, and wearing a hoodie. He disappeared into the back streets and had not been traced. Could he have been the mystery father? The baby would be tenth in line for the Swedish throne. The palace confirmed that the wedding to German aristocrat Stefan Von Hechingan had been 'postponed'.

'What a bloody mess,' said Ria, as she read the latest instalment. 'All because my dear son couldn't keep it in his pants. What was he doing with a 23-year-old for crying out loud? He's 54!'

'Well, he's given you a grandchild, so be grateful,' laughed Mandy, who was now beginning to take it all with a pinch of salt. It would blow over soon enough.

Ria's phone rang. 'Speak of the devil,' she said. 'Hello, Charles. I thought you didn't want to speak on the phone.'

'I'm at your house. Where are you?' His tone was angry and impatient.

'I told you I was moving.'

'I thought I could trust my own mother. Now everything is on the line, my marriage, my career... and all because you couldn't keep your mouth shut. I need to come and get the kid and put it in an orphanage or a convent or wherever they take unwanted babies these days... somewhere where it can't be tracked back to me.'

Ria saw red. 'IT is very happy with me, her grandmother, thank you very much, and she isn't going anywhere. She is not a parcel you can just throw out. This is what you get for being unfaithful to your lovely wife and taking advantage of a young girl away from home. Go back home and keep your head down. And for the record, I didn't tell anyone.'

With that, she cut off the call. Almost immediately a text arrived: 'I will find you, Mother, and that kid is coming with me.'

Ria couldn't hold back the tears. She didn't have much contact with her son, but she couldn't bear to be on bad terms with him. Now she was afraid of him, just as she had been of his father.

Mandy gave her a hug. 'Come on,' she said, 'let's get a takeaway and watch a film. Things will seem brighter in the morning.'

The next morning was certainly sunny, but the two women were tired after a sleepless night with a restless baby. Mandy made some coffee and toast, and sat at the table, as Ria fed Matilda. There was a knock at the door. Both women jumped, their nerves in shreds.

'Who is it?' called Mandy. 'God, I hope it's not Charles.'

She looked out of the window. The man looked familiar, but it was not Charles. Ria had shown her several photos of him. She gingerly opened the door.

The man was smiling. 'Remember me?' he asked. 'From the beach house?'

Bloody hell, it was the journalist! The brass neck of him!

'What do you want?' she spat.

'That's not very friendly,' he said. 'Shall we talk out here or can I come in?'

'I have nothing to talk to you about.'

'Oh, I think you do. Can I smell coffee?'

Mandy glanced at Ria. 'Let him in,' she said wearily.

'Thank you,' said Tom Delaney as he stepped inside.

For a moment, nobody said anything.

Tom reached out to stroke the baby's head. 'Hello, princess.'

Ria pulled her away. 'What do you want?'

'OK, look, cards on the table,' he began. 'Obviously, you will know that I found your letter. There is not a journalist on earth who would not have sold the story. It might have occurred to me to talk to you first, but I was angry that you had snatched the beach house from me after our second viewing. I offered the vendors more money, but they had agreed to take your offer. Anyway, here's the deal. You let me have the beach house, and I'll keep quiet about where you and the baby are.'

Ria put Matilda in her cot. 'I can't understand why you didn't already give us away when you sold the story,' she said.

'I didn't know who you were or where you were. And in any case, I might have another bite of the cherry this way.'

'So how did you find us?' asked Mandy.

'I'm a journalist,' said Tom. 'It's what I do. So, how about it?'

Ria saw all her dreams going out of the window. 'No,' she snapped. 'You're not having the beach house. You would still be back for money or something else later.'

'It's blackmail,' put in Mandy.

'OK,' said Tom, reaching for the door. 'Your choice. Expect some visitors.'

With that, he left.

Mandy grabbed her suitcase and started packing. 'We have to get out of here *now*. If he goes to the police, they could be here in minutes.'

'I think he's more likely to go to the papers first, but, yeah, we need to move fast,' Ria agreed.

It was getting dark, and they had no idea where they were going, but the important thing was to put some space between them and the park site. They were packed and in the car within five frantic minutes. They took off into the dark lanes.

And so did Tom Delaney, at a discreet distance.

Chapter three

They turned onto the coast road, which was better lit, and drove for 20 minutes before anyone spoke. 'He could have taken our car number,' ventured Mandy. 'Almost certain to,' said Ria, who was sitting in the back seat cuddling her granddaughter. Roxy was snoozing on the floor.

'How much further are we going?' Ria continued, 'If we leave it too late, we won't get anywhere to stay tonight.'

So far there had not been an obvious place to stop. They needed a B&B or a cheap hotel. They were still driving an hour later, which was bad luck for Tom Delaney who had had to stop for petrol and then lost them.

They had turned off the main road into a boatyard that overlooked a harbour. There was a restaurant right on the waterfront, and they were hungry.

'Come on,' said Mandy, 'Let's get a bite to eat. We'll have to leave Roxy in the car, but she'll be fine.'

Ria didn't need asking twice. She was starving. She just hoped Matilda would stay asleep and not make a racket.

There were only a few people in the restaurant. A young couple eating burgers, a family group, and a man sitting at the bar enjoying a pint. Ria passed Matilda carefully to Mandy and went to the bar to order drinks. The man looked at her and smiled. 'On holiday?' he asked cheerfully.

'Sort of, well, yes,' Ria replied. 'But the B&B that we had planned to go to tonight has double booked. You wouldn't know of anywhere near here, would you?' Ria had always been good at thinking on her feet and telling the odd porky where necessary. 'I'll give it some thought,' he said.

The two tired, elderly friends quietly ate a meal of fish pie and vegetables, followed by crème brûlée and coffee. It was the best meal they had had for days. Luckily, although Matilda had woken, she was quiet and gurgling happily.

They were about to leave when the man at the bar pulled up a chair beside them.

'Look, I might be able to help you. I hope you don't think I'm being... well, you might not like the idea, and you can say no, but...'

Mandy laughed. 'Spit it out, man,' she said. He seemed a genuinely nice guy. He was about 50, and well-built with laugh lines and smiley eyes.

'Sorry,' he laughed. 'I'm Jack by the way. Anyway, what I'm trying to say is that I have a catamaran moored here... you can just about see it from here when it's light. It can sleep four. You're welcome to stay in it tonight. It has all mod cons.

But I will be leaving for France in the morning, so you'd need to go by 10. I won't be there tonight. I live just down the road, but you could phone me if there are any problems.'

'Do we sleep in hammocks?' laughed Mandy.

'That would be fantastic. Thank you so much,' said Ria. 'But we also have a dog. She's in the car.'

'So do I,' said Jack, smiling. 'That's fine as long as she's well behaved.'

'Oh, she is,' the women chorused.

Ria glanced over to the barman who was wiping some glasses and could hear everything. She looked at him for reassurance. He gave her a smile and a nod that said, *this guy's alright. He's a regular.*

Jack took the little party down a long jetty, past yachts and boats of all shapes and sizes until they got to the very end, where the enormous catamaran was berthed.

He helped them to climb aboard. Ria didn't know what she was expecting but she was amazed to see what looked like a luxury yacht. There was a sitting room and a fully fitted kitchen, and two bedrooms, each with double beds and a luxury bathroom.

'Wow,' said Mandy. 'Are you sure about this? Can we pay you something?'

Jack grinned. 'If I'm helping two, or should I say four, damsels in distress, then that's reward enough for me. But don't forget, I'll be back at 9.30am to leave here at 10. Have a good night.'

'What a fantastic guy, so trusting,' said Ria as she filled the kettle.

'Wow, how the other half live!' Mandy agreed. 'But we need to sit down and work out what to do next. I think we're safe enough here for tonight.'

Ria was thoughtful. 'We can hide for the next few months, but what happens when we move into the beach house? We'll be easy to find there.'

'Well, hopefully,' Mandy began, 'all the press interest will have blown over by then, and Charles will have given up and gone back to Canada.'

'But what about the special forces? I doubt if they'll give up and go away. And they are the ones with all the resources.'

'But we haven't done anything wrong,' said Mandy as she rummaged in a cupboard for teabags. 'You surely can't kidnap your own grandchild if the parents don't want to know.'

'The only proof I had was the letter,' replied Ria. 'And I wouldn't be able to say my son is the father.'

They drank their tea in silence, and then went to bed. The catamaran rocked gently, which both women found very soothing, and even Matilda and Roxy slept through the night.

They were up early to make sure that they didn't delay Jack's departure. By 9am, they were ready to leave and looking forward to some breakfast. They didn't want to use more than the boat's teabags. It was yet another beautiful day, and they went onto the deck to admire the view. Mandy looked back along the harbour to the boatyard where she had parked her car. At least it was still there! But wait. She did a double-take. Someone was looking in her car windows. 'Ria, look.'

Even at this distance, there was no mistaking him. It was Tom Delaney.

The women ducked down and went straight back inside the galley. They looked at each other in horror. There was no way he would go now that he had found their car.

Soon Jack appeared with a bag of croissants and some fresh milk. 'I came a bit early so we could all have some breakfast.' He smiled. Noting their expressions, he put the food on the table and looked hard at them. 'Is something wrong?'

This time it was Mandy's turn to be creative. 'The thing is,' she began, 'we are trying to get away from my violent ex-husband. And we've just seen him looking at my car!'

Jack went on deck to see for himself. 'Yes, he's still there,' he said when he returned. 'Shall I call the police?'

'No, no,' said Ria. 'But he won't go while the car is still there.'

'We're really sorry about this.'

Jack looked worried and looked at his watch.

'I have an idea,' said Mandy as brightly as she could. 'Please could we go to France with you?'

He looked stunned. 'Well I suppose... have you got passports?'

'Yes,' said Ria. The women had not expected to go abroad, but both had brought their important documents in case they needed ID.

'OK, why not,' said Jack. 'If you're sure you want to come, it will be great to have company.'

So, within a few minutes, they had set sail and left their nemesis standing on the quayside.

Jack told them it would take about six hours to make the crossing. There were shorter routes, but they were too busy and dangerous. About halfway across, Jack, who had been in a jovial mood, suddenly said, 'Just had a thought. You do have passports for the baby and the dog I suppose?'

'The dog?' Ria was alarmed.

'Yes, these days all animals have passports. All to do with rabies and vaccinations and stuff I suppose.' There was silence. 'They won't let you in without passports for everyone.'

This was a new and dire problem. 'I won't be sailing back to England for weeks,' said Jack. 'So I can't take you back I'm afraid.'

Seeing these ladies of a certain age looking worried, he said, 'Look, there is something I can do. You'll get me shot, but as this is a catamaran it can beach on sandbanks. You could get off there, away from prying eyes.'

'Sounds good to me,' said Mandy.

'Just add illegal immigrants to our rap list,' muttered Ria.

So, by 4pm they were waving Jack goodbye. 'Are you sure you'll be alright?' he shouted. 'Just phone that number I gave you. Pierre speaks perfect English and I've asked him to help you.'

'Thank you so much, Jack, we will.'

'Just thought,' said Mandy. 'Charles has your phone number, right?'

'Yes, you know he does.'

'Well, he can trace you with that!'

Ria took the phone out of her pocket, and the battery out of another pocket and held them up for Mandy to inspect. 'I wasn't born yesterday,' she snapped. She didn't want to admit that she had only thought to do it last night at the boatyard.

'Sorry, just a thought. We'll use my phone then.'

Between them they dragged Matilda's buggy along the beach to the road, with Roxy running free and having a whale of a time. The place was deserted. Jack had chosen a good spot. But they needed nappies and baby milk, not to mention dog food and food for themselves.

Finally, they found a bench and sat down to phone Pierre.

'Yes, beautiful ladies, I have been expecting you to call,' he said. 'I know where you are. I will come and get you now. Please wait. Maybe 15 minutes.'

Charles walked into the boatyard restaurant. He went straight to the barman.

'I'm looking for my mother,' he began. 'Old woman, probably with a baby.'

'There were two women and a baby in here last night,' he said. 'They seem to be in demand. That guy over there was asking after them.' He nodded towards a man sitting alone with a laptop on the table and surrounded by empty glasses.

Charles glanced over at him. 'Who is he?'

The barman shrugged.

'Do you know where the women went?' Charles persisted.

'They had nowhere to go, so Jack let them stay on his catamaran for the night. But they had gone when I got in this morning, so I have no idea where they are now.'

Charles bought a coffee and moved towards the mystery man.

'But they'll be back,' called the barman. 'Their car is still in the car park.'

Matilda was crying. She was hungry and needed a nappy change. This was not going to be a good introduction to Pierre. The women had no idea who this man was or how he was going to help them. But they trusted Jack and had no other ideas. They remembered little of the French language from school, and although Mandy was well travelled, she had never spent more than a day or two in France.

A large black Mercedes pulled up alongside them. A good-looking man in his fifties jumped out. He was casually, but expensively dressed and full of energy and enthusiasm. He bounded over to them. 'You are my beautiful English ladies, and this poor petit bébé … I am Pierre, I expect you know.'

'I'm Ria, and this is Mandy,' said Ria, 'and the baby is Matilda, and the dog is Roxy.'

'All very beautiful,' he said, 'I will take you now. Please get in the car; I will put the poussette in the boot.'

Having installed the buggy and their luggage in the boot, they took off at speed.

'Where are we going?' ventured Ria as she cradled Matilda, who was whimpering.

Charles took his coffee and looked out of the picture windows into the car park. There were only a few cars. He would ask the barman which was his mother's car in a minute. First, he wanted to know who the man with the laptop was.

But he needed to think about this. He sat at a table by the window. The story had been all over the papers, but as far as he knew there had been no connection made with his mother. Or with him. He had to make sure it stayed that way. The man may have heard him asking the barman about his mother. But what was his interest?

Before he could finish his train of thought, Tom Delaney picked up his laptop and pint and put them down on Charles's table.

***

The black Mercedes sped on through the countryside and small towns, with Pierre chattering away, asking them about themselves, sometimes throwing in the odd French word. Mandy smiled to herself. Sometimes he sounded like Del Boy from *Only Fools and Horses*.

'I am taking you to Paris,' said Pierre, 'to my father's house. He lives alone and loves company. You can stay there, and he doesn't want any euros. Maybe you can help him with, maybe laundry or cooking?'

The women looked at each other. 'Yes,' ventured Ria, 'of course.'

Mandy's phone rang. It was the estate agent in England. He had a buyer for Lavender Cottage, he said. Could Mandy come into the office to sign some papers, and instruct a solicitor?

The usually confident Charles felt uneasy as this stranger plonked himself down beside him.

'I gather you've lost your mum?' said the stranger.

'And you are?' replied Charles.

'Tom Delaney. I'm guessing your name begins with C.'

'What?' said Charles.

'Your letter to your mum. You just signed it with a C.' He was slurring.

'What letter to my mum? I don't know what you're talking about!'

'Does your mum have another son?'

Silence.

'Um, I thought not. So, you must be the father of the little princess that you want to get rid of. Congratulations!'

Charles was on the ropes. 'Who *are* you?'

'Like I said, Tom Delaney. Journalist.'

Charles got up to leave.

'Don't rush off,' said Tom. 'Maybe we could help each other out.'

Charles slowly sat down again.

Tom continued, 'You want to find the baby to make sure that none of this comes back to you, right? I want to find the baby because it's a bloody good story. So let's join forces. Let's face it, it's with a couple of old ladies, no disrespect to your mum. It can't be too difficult to find them. Their bloody car's right outside!'

'And then what?'

'Well, come on, mate, we'll sort it out between us, to everyone's advantage. What *is* your name by the way?' Tom finished his pint and called for another.

Charles got up again. 'Do you think I'm stupid?'

'No, mate, maybe a bit naive. Your car's outside. I've got the number.'

'It's a hire car.'

'So you showed them your driving licence and ID?'

'Of course, but the Data Protection Act...'

'Naive.'

* * *

After more than an hour in the car, Ria and Mandy wondered if they should be trusting this complete stranger to be taking them somewhere safe. It all seemed a bit unreal.

And then the car pulled into a long drive. Before them was a magnificent 17th-century mill house, built beside the river Vacouler, just 45 minutes from Paris, according to Pierre. He told them it had seven bedrooms, four bathrooms, numerous receptions and no less than seven chimneys! It was set in acres of countryside.

They pulled up outside the huge double doors, and a golden Labrador ran out to greet them, followed by a mature, distinguished man who looked as though he'd just emerged from a 1930s movie. He wore a red smoking jacket and a yellow cravat. He was tall, and straight, and had the bearing of a military man. He had a charming smile.

The weary women climbed out of the car, Mandy clutching Matilda and Ria pulling a sleepy dog.

'Welcome dear ladies,' said their host. 'My name is Richard, and you've met my son Pierre. Do come on in.'

They followed him through the double doors and into a magnificent hallway with flagstone floors, beams and carved wood panels. He led them into a sitting room with large comfy sofas and a table set with a teapot, four cups and saucers, sugar and milk and a plate of biscuits.

He motioned them to sit down. 'Just a little refreshment to keep you going until dinner.' He smiled.

Somehow Ria had been expecting a little old man in a dusty cottage. She was speechless. Mandy was seldom speechless. 'This is so kind of you, Richard. What a beautiful place.'

'Thank you, my dear. Which one are you?'

'Sorry, I'm Mandy and this is Ria.'

'No need to be sorry, my dear, we Brits are always apologising.'

'You're English!' said Ria.

'Good Lord, woman, can't you tell?' he laughed. 'Harrow and Cambridge. Married a French student, Maria. My lovely wife for 45 years, sadly now passed.'

He glanced at a framed black and white photograph of a bride and groom on top of a grand piano.

'So, what brings you two here with babies, dogs and luggage?' he said, smiling. 'No, I mustn't pry. I think I heard that you were escaping from a violent partner? Some of these brutes give the rest of us men a bad name. But I hope he doesn't know you're coming here. I don't want any shenanigans.'

'Even we didn't know we were coming here,' laughed Mandy.

'Don't worry, girls,' he laughed. 'I'm just kidding. I'll sort the idiot out.'

Chapter four

Charles knew he had met his match. That damned letter! How had this guy managed to see it in the first place? Surely his mother would not have gone to the press. No, he knew her better than that. Obvious thing to do was ask. But the guy looked drunk.

'That letter you mentioned, supposedly from me. How did you come by it?'

Tom wasn't bothered about him knowing the truth. Maybe he would have done six drinks ago.

'It dropped out of your mother's pocket. She didn't notice, and I picked it up.'

'And it didn't occur to you to give it back to her?'

'Not once I'd read it. Pure gold!'

'Would you give it to me?'

'Why would I do that? You said it's nothing to do with you.' Tom smirked. 'Anyway, there are too many copies floating around now.'

'Look, be reasonable, man. I stand to lose my wife, my career, my reputation, everything I have ever worked for. For one lousy story! How much are they paying you? I'll match it.'

'Too late, it's already all over the papers.' He laughed.

'Yes, but nobody has identified me. And the princess, whatever her name is, won't tell anyone. There are only two people who know, the princess and you... and my mother of course.'

'You are a very silly boy,' Tom mumbled, reaching into his breast pocket. 'I have all that on tape. When will you people ever learn?'

Richard cooked a mean roast dinner but had never got the hang of French cooking since his wife died, so they all sat down for roast beef and Yorkshire pudding.

After a comfortable night's sleep in the spacious bedrooms, Richard took Ria to the nearest shops to stock up on nappies, baby milk, dog food and toiletries.

Mandy unpacked and settled in before taking Matilda and Roxy for a walk around the grounds. Richard's dog, Mufti, was delighted to have a playmate and the two of them ran around like lunatics and had play fights.

Mandy began to relax. It was an idyllic setting, and the weather was glorious. She walked to the river and sat on a log bench, admiring the rippling water and the sounds of the birds. The phone rang. It was the estate agent from the beach house. 'Hi Mandy. I hope you don't mind me calling. I just wondered why you had changed your mind about the beach house? Is there a problem? Anything I can do to help?'

'What, no I haven't, we haven't changed our minds. I've even got a buyer now for Lavender Cottage.'

'Oh, that's strange,' said the agent, 'only someone rang up and said that you had changed your mind. I was on the verge of offering it to the other couple who viewed, but I thought I'd just check with you first.'

'Thank goodness you did!' Mandy was furious. 'Who rang up?'

'I don't know; my colleague took the call. Is everything alright?'

'Yes, yes, no problem. Do you want me to send a deposit to hold it?'

'We will do soon, but no rush. Your word is good enough for me.'

The call ended. That bastard was still trying to get the beach house. Did he never give up?

Charles was mortified. How had he been so stupid? This man could splash his name all over the papers. There would be a huge scandal. *Married Embassy worker fathers a royal baby and then has her kidnapped to cover his tracks.*

He stood up, his face red with fury, and left the restaurant. He walked the few yards to the waterfront.

Where the hell was his mother? Was she still on one of these boats?

The restaurant was closing. The staff were leaving, and the only cars left in the car park were his, and two others, presumably Tom's and his mother's.

So, Tom was still lurking about.

Suddenly there were footsteps behind him.

Ria and Richard came back with everything a baby could ever need, and a new dog bed. Richard had been very generous, which Ria found a bit worrying. How long did he expect them to stay?

Later Richard went out with the dogs, and Ria and Mandy had a chance to catch up over a cup of tea in the kitchen.

'I think Richard thinks we're here for life,' said Ria. 'What *is* our plan?'

'Well, if he lets us, we could stay here until the houses are sold,' said Mandy. 'It could be months of course, but what else can we do?'

'I don't think Charles could find us here,' said Ria, 'but you never know with that loathsome reporter or the police for that matter.'

'Did I hear you say police?' said Richard as he entered the room, followed by two panting dogs.

Charles swung round to see Tom staggering towards him. 'Had time to think, silly boy?' he stammered.

He lurched towards Charles, who stepped briskly out of the way. Tom tripped and fell headlong into the harbour. For a moment there wasn't a sound, then his head emerged from the murky water, and he shouted, 'Get me out of here, get me...' Then he disappeared again only to reappear moments later. 'Help me!'

Charles looked around. There was no one about. Could this be his chance to rid himself of all his worries? He watched Tom Delaney go under for a third time, turned and walked away.

In an MI5 office somewhere in London, Inspector Morris had called a meeting of his officers and one or two from MI6 and Special Branch.

'Will someone bring me up to speed on this royal baby fiasco,' he started.

Sergeant Gill stepped up. 'The last anyone saw was the hooded man leaving the hospital and walking down the road. CCTV only covers one road after that, and we lost him. We've traced all mobile phones that were in the area and it would appear that he didn't have one. Not that was switched on anyway, sir. We got ANPR on vehicles leaving the area, and they are all being checked.'

'A baby can't just vanish.' The inspector was flustered and under great pressure from upstairs. 'What about the journalist who broke this story. Have you spoken to him?'

'No, sir, he's a freelance. We've left messages for him, but he hasn't come back to us.'

'Well, get him in for God's sake! Have you spoken to the princess?'

'We did interview her, sir, but she refused to name the father. After that, the lawyers got involved and we couldn't get near her.'

'She'd been living in Canada, hadn't she?'

'Yes, sir.'

'Well, find out who her friends and work colleagues were. Someone must know who she was seeing.'

'Do you think the father was involved in the kidnapping, sir?' asked the sergeant.

The inspector sidestepped the question. 'Have there been any ransom demands?'

'Just a couple of hoax nutters, but not a genuine one, no.'

The inspector was thoughtful. 'I think maybe it's time to go public with this, now that the whole world wants to know what has happened to a royal baby. Call a press conference and ask people to let us know of any unexpected new baby arriving in their neighbourhood.'

'We'll be inundated, sir.'

'Then you'd better be prepared for a few late nights, sergeant!'

Charles took to the road while he thought about what to do next. He couldn't wait by his mother's car for her return because it was next to the harbour restaurant and he was the last one to be seen with Tom Delaney. He didn't want to be around when the body was found. Questions would be asked. He just hoped that the recording of his conversation had been wiped and lost in the muddy water.

He put the radio on for the news. To his horror, there was an appeal for anyone who had unexpectedly turned up with a new baby to be reported to the police. The enquiry had been stepped up. He suddenly realised with a pang of panic that there was someone else who could involve him. His old friend Tony, the hooded kidnapper. He may be a friend, but would he crack under this sort of pressure?

Richard was unsettled. 'What was that about the police?' he asked.

Ria began, 'Well we were just saying—'

Richard interrupted her, 'Now, my dear girl, I don't deserve to be lied to. What's going on here?'

The women looked at each other.

Mandy said, 'I think we should tell him the truth.'

Ria's instinct was to trust Richard, but he was a virtual stranger.

'OK,' she agreed. 'But Richard, would you please promise to tell no one.'

'Now you've got me intrigued,' he said. 'Go on.'

So, between them they told him the whole story. He poured himself a whisky.

'You mean this child,' indicating Matilda who was snuggled up in a blanket on the sofa, 'is the missing royal baby that has been all over the TV and newspapers?' Ria and Mandy nodded.

He paced about the room, wondering what to do. 'Do Jack and Pierre know about this?' he asked.

'No,' said Ria, 'you're the only one we've told.'

'So there was no violent partner?'

'No,' the women chorused.

'So, the world's media, the special services and the child's father, your son, Ria, are all looking for this baby.' It was a statement, not a question.

'But what will they do with her when they find her?' he continued, more to himself than to the women. 'Her parents don't want her. Surely as the grandmother you would have a claim on her?'

Ria replied, 'If I say I am the grandmother, I would be betraying my son. I know he's been a fool, but I can't see him lose his marriage and his career.'

'Um, I see the problem. Let's all sleep on it for now. You're safe enough here for the moment.'

Tony was watching the TV news with his wife, Tina, when on came an appeal to find the lost royal baby.

He'd been following the news with interest and increasing fear and foreboding. It was one thing doing a favour for a friend, but he had no idea that the repercussions would be so great. Supposing someone had seen him taking the baby? He never even thought to look for CCTV cameras. He had promised not to make contact with Charles, but he was desperate to talk to someone about it all. He hadn't told Tina. She would have stopped him. She always was the sensible one.

They were calling him a kidnapper. He was nothing of the sort. He had just taken a tot from her mum, who didn't want her, to her grandma's at the request of her dad. What was wrong with that? So why was he so frightened? He jumped every time the doorbell rang. He was ratty with Tina. He couldn't tell her. It wouldn't be fair to involve her. He'd have to just keep his head down and go to work in the factory every day as normal.

Charles now knew that his mother had not deliberately betrayed him. She had been careless, but not disloyal. He felt a surge of anger. He had told her to burn the letter. If she had done as she was told there would not be a problem. He knew in his heart that, however mad his mother was at him, she would never betray him. He thought back over his childhood days, how she had loved him, always put him first, worked hard to ensure that he had a good education. And she did it all by herself. Nevertheless, he had always managed to blame her for everything. He had taken her for granted.

A tear escaped from his eye as he realised how much he really loved her and missed her. But the new threat was that she would bond with her grandchild and refuse to part with her. That was pretty much a given. And it would be awful to have to wrench the child away. It would almost certainly finish the relationship with his mother. But his mother would have no way of explaining the baby away when the whole world was looking for her. Where the hell had she disappeared to?

Richard and his new guests were beginning to relax with each other now that the truth was out in the open. After the initial shock of the news, Richard seemed to be excited that his otherwise humdrum life had been spiced up with a new drama.

The women were curious about him.

'How do you know Jack the catamaran man?' asked Ria over lunch one day.

'Oh, that's easy. Pierre has a catamaran too, and their paths cross from time to time. They belong to some owners' club or something,' explained Richard.

Mandy wanted to know whether Jack came to France for business or pleasure, and how he could afford to swan about on such a luxurious boat. It was an impertinent question, but now that everything was known about her, she felt she had a right to ask.

'Good question.' Richard smiled. 'Let's just say that doing that trip on a regular basis can be very lucrative.'

Ria gave him a flirty smile. 'How so?' she asked. She was warming to this man. He had an attractive dimply smile and intelligent eyes. They were about the same age, although he seemed to belong to a different era.

Richard smiled back. 'Who wants a cup of tea?' he said.

Princess Tindra had hardly left her room since the birth. She sat on her bed looking at the one and only picture she had of her daughter. She had tried so hard to keep her shameful secret and had almost succeeded. But now the truth was out for all the world to know. Her aristocratic fiancé had run for the hills, and her parents were hardly speaking to her. Her life was ruined at the age of 23. The only one showing her any sympathy was her brother Hugo who was two years her junior. A quiet, sensitive lad, he felt for his sister and gave her a shoulder to cry on.

They talked endlessly about what she should do. She could try to carry on as if nothing had happened. She could go abroad again, but where? What she really wanted was to have her firstborn child in her arms again. And why not, now that it was no longer a secret? And the father would not want to get involved. She would never tell anyone who he was, because, truth be known, she wasn't too sure herself. She had done a lot of partying in Canada.

The police and MI5 were indeed inundated with calls from people who had seen a young baby appear in their neighbourhood. It was bizarre. Surely they would have noticed the pregnant mums beforehand? Most of them had been registered and weren't too difficult to verify. Some calls were malicious. Some were hoaxes. There were some strange people out there. But each and every one had to be checked.

One woman phoned in and said that an elderly woman had moved into Lavender Cottage next door to her, and she had heard a baby cry. The woman had then disappeared, and the house was on the market again. Another neighbour had also disappeared, and her house was also up for sale. Just another report. It would take a week or two to get around to it.

Meanwhile, cars leaving the vicinity of the maternity hospital on the relevant day were checked again. Most were local, but a few had taken a long journey, and one had returned immediately. That car was owned by one Tony James Ellis. He would need a visit. It would be Sergeant Gill's job to try to match Ellis's journey with the reports of babies from the public.

Charles had stopped panicking about Tom Delaney. He had to go back to the boatyard. It was the only way he was likely to be able to find his mother and the baby. But he wouldn't go into the restaurant. He didn't want to face any questions or hear the gory details. He would wait for her to come back to the car that she had arrived in.

A thought suddenly struck him. What if something had happened to her? Her car had been in the car park for days. It wasn't like her. He had to stop this. He was getting neurotic. But what if she had abandoned the car? He could wait forever.

He knew she had spent the night on a catamaran that was heading to France the next day. So that must be it. She must have gone to France! But how could she have taken the baby without a passport? Maybe she had managed to get a passport for her somehow. He grabbed his phone and brought up a map of the area. Where in France would they have headed for? The restaurant staff would know, but he couldn't show his face in there again.

He tried to ring his mother for the umpteenth time. But her phone was dead. Dear God, was *she* dead? Was the baby dead?

Matilda was growing more beautiful every day. Her wispy blonde hair was growing into curls, and she was a happy little soul. Both women were in love with her. And Richard, whose own children had long since left home, and not produced grandchildren, was besotted. He was also just a little bit besotted with Ria. She was a fine, brave, caring woman. Not a bad looker for her age either.

All in all, he was enjoying having his new little family around him. But he had become afraid of losing them. He imagined them all being arrested, himself included for harbouring them. They would all end up in jail… but no, surely the elderly ladies would not be imprisoned. And come to think of it, *he* was an elderly man. But what would happen to that poor beautiful child? He shuddered.

He tried to think how they could be traced to his home. Jack and Pierre did not know their story, so he had no reason to distrust them. He was worrying for nothing. He would just enjoy their company, and maybe get to know Ria a little better.

Sergeant Gill had made a possible connection. The car driven from the vicinity of the maternity hospital in London to a village in Hertfordshire, and then immediately back to a London suburb was registered to Tony Ellis. They had also had a report from a woman in the Hertfordshire village that someone had moved into a neighbouring cottage for just a couple of days. They heard a baby crying. Then the elderly woman newcomer had left and put the cottage back on the market. She hadn't been seen since. Just a few doors away another woman had disappeared, also putting her house on the market.

Sgt Gill decided to pay the estate agent a visit.

John Barnes, of Barnes and Barnes, greeted him. 'How can I help you, sir?'

'What can you tell me about Lavender Cottage?' he asked.

'I'm afraid it's under offer, sir.'

Sgt Ellis took his warrant card from his pocket and showed it to John Barnes.

'Oh, I see. Well, of course, I'll help if I can.'

'Who owns the cottage at the moment?'

'I'm afraid I can't give out personal details. You know, Data Protection Act.'

'Mr Barnes, you can where a crime may have been committed. Had she been there longer, she would have been on the electoral roll. Now come on, a name please.'

'Well,' said John Barnes, 'it was rather strange. She loved the cottage and was determined to buy it, but within days of moving in, she said she wanted to sell it. There was no explanation. Then she left the house.'

'Her name.'

'Oh, sorry, yes it's Amanda Anderson.'

'Did she have a baby with her?'

'A baby? Not as far as I know. She's a pensioner.'

'Do you have a mobile phone number for her?'

'Yes, I'll get it.'

'Thank you. I'd also like to ask you about the house you have for sale in the same lane. The Gables. Who owns that?'

'That is another lady pensioner, Ria Radcliffe. She has lived there for years, but she also left, and we haven't been able to contact her directly, only through Miss Anderson.'

'So, the women are together?'

'It would seem so.'

John Barnes handed Sgt Gill a piece of paper with the requested phone numbers of the two women.

'Thank you. You have been very helpful,' said Sgt Gill. He felt he might be getting somewhere.

As soon as he got back in his car, he was tempted to call Miss Amanda Anderson, but decided that it would be better to track her location, and he didn't want to spook her.

John Barnes got there first. After all, this was his client. He called Mandy and confessed that he had had to give her number to the police.

Mandy was relaxing in the late spring sunshine when she took the call from John Barnes. Richard and Ria had taken Roxy for a walk, and Matilda was asleep in her cot.

'How dare you give them my number! What about client confidentiality?' she wailed.

'I'm really sorry,' he replied, 'but I had no choice.'

Mandy cut off the call in panic and took the battery out of her phone. Now the police would know where she was!

She ran indoors just as Richard and Ria returned from their walk. They were laughing and enjoying each other's company.

'We have to get out of here fast,' said Mandy, gathering up some of her things.

'Hold on, what's the panic?' said Richard.

'The bloody estate agent gave the police my phone number, so they can trace us here,' she said, running up the stairs to pack.

'Oh my God,' said Ria. 'Take the battery out of your phone.'

'I have,' came the answer, 'but they might have already tracked us.'

Ria looked at a distraught Richard. 'Can you get us out of here?'

Richard thought for a minute. 'Well, of course, but where will I take you?'

Charles sat in his car, next to his mother's car in the boatyard car park. There were a few people working on boats that had been lifted from the water and were expertly poised on wooden cradles so that they could have barnacles scraped from their hulls, and maybe be repainted. He watched a few boats leaving the harbour, and one or two arriving from their travels. And then for the first time, he saw a catamaran. It was huge, and superb, sailing into the harbour. It took a while to manoeuvre into its berth, and eventually a man emerged and walked along the boardwalk to the boatyard.

Charles jumped out of his car and went to meet him.

'Are you Jack?' he asked.

'Who's asking?' replied a wary Jack.

'Sorry, it's just that I heard that my mother had gone to France with you and I was worried about her. Her phone is dead.'

'Oh, which one is your mum? Poor ladies were trying to get away from a bloke... her ex, I think. He was hanging around by their car, so I took them with me.'

'Where did you take them?'

'France.'

'Yes, but where exactly?'

Jack suddenly realised that for all he knew he could be speaking to a customs guy or a cop.

'Cherbourg, I believe, yes, Cherbourg. Forgive me but I'm late for a meeting. Good luck.' And with that, he dashed off.

Charles wandered down to the waterfront and looked over the edge, where he had last seen the drowning, terrified, screaming face of Tom Delaney that he would never forget.

He half expected the face to still be there, taunting him. Or the remains of the rotting, floating and bloated body that he had seen in his nightmares.

A voice behind him made him jump. 'Looking for me, mate?'

Chapter five

At the Mill House, there was panic and pandemonium. Ria and Mandy were packing their suitcases, and Richard was bringing the car to the front of the house. As they packed the car, Ria called to Mandy, 'Will you bring Matilda. I'll get Roxy. Don't forget her food and nappies.'

Minutes later, Mandy called from the bedroom window, 'Where is Matilda? I thought you left her in the cot. Is she in the buggy downstairs?'

Ria froze. She *had* left her in the cot. She looked to Richard. He was shaky.

Ria and Richard hurried inside and upstairs, as fast as their old legs would carry them. 'She's not here,' exclaimed Mandy. 'I told you. She's not here!'

They started searching the house. They all knew it was ridiculous. The infant couldn't walk, or even crawl. But maybe whoever had taken her out of her cot had put her somewhere else in the house. They searched everywhere, and then searched the grounds.

Richard took charge. 'Look, girls. You need to go.'

'We can't go without Matilda!' cried Ria. 'Didn't you check on her, Mandy?'

'There's no point playing the blame game,' said Richard, his eyes full of unshed tears.

'Matilda has gone. We'll find her, but for now you need to leave before the gendarmes get here.'

'We need the gendarmes to look for her!' shouted Ria.

'No, you don't,' said Richard. 'If they know that you had her they will not believe that you somehow misplaced her. They will hold onto you and probably send you back to England, and you will have no chance to look for her. Now get in the car. I promise you we will sort this out later.'

Charles turned to face the angry voice.

It was Tom Delaney. He had a few cuts and bruises but was very much alive.

Charles paled.

'What's the matter, me old fruit? You look like you've seen a ghost,' said Tom.

Charles tried to move away, but Tom blocked his path.

They were both inches from the 20ft drop into the water. Charles could smell the alcohol on Tom's breath.

'You tried to kill me,' said Tom.

'No, you were drunk. You tripped.'

'You were happy to let me drown.'

Charles felt a sudden flash of anger. Yes, he was happy to let him drown. He thought he had got rid of this odious man and his threats to expose him.

Almost without any conscious effort, he grabbed the man's grubby lapels and pushed him into the harbour.

He glanced around. Nobody seemed to have noticed. There was a lot of hammering and noise from machinery in the boatyard. This time he would make sure Tom Delaney did not get out alive. Once again, his nightmare vision appeared before him. There was that face again, looking up at him, his body thrashing about. Charles looked about him. There was a loose brick on a low wall. He grabbed it with both hands and stood over the drowning man. When his head came up, Charles dropped the brick. With a 20ft drop, the brick had some gravity. It hit its target full on. With a last gasp, Tom Delaney met his maker.

Prince Hugo was worried about his sister. She was struggling to cope with the publicity surrounding her baby, and the shame that her parents were heaping upon her. She was under great pressure, both from her parents and from the media, to name the father. She was also embarrassed that her ex-colleagues at the embassy in Canada were being harassed by the press who wanted to know who she spent time with. All sorts of spurious stories were emerging, and she was also mourning the loss of her little daughter.

That little girl was Hugo's niece. He was an uncle. He wanted to meet her and put her back in the arms of her mother. He was on a gap year. Maybe he could do something to help her. He needed to have a straight talk with her. She was still in her bedroom where she spent most of her time. She was always pleased to see Hugo and gave him an unexpected hug.

'What was that for?' he laughed.

'Oh, just for being my best friend,' his sister replied.

'Will you be truthful with me?' he asked.

'What about?'

'About everything. You have been very secretive with everyone, and I want you to trust me.'

'I do trust you.'

'OK, will you tell me who the father of your baby is?'

'Oh, come on, Hugo, what difference does it make?'

'Tindra, it will come out sooner or later. You know it will. If you trust me, tell me.'

'OK, if you must know, I don't know!'

'What? What do you mean?'

'I slept with three men at about that time.'

Hugo was shocked. He had imagined that his sister was a virgin. 'THREE men!' he exclaimed.

'Oh, get off your high horse. How many girls have you had sex with?'

'It's different for men.' Hugo was more sheepish now.

'How so?' said an angry Tindra.

'OK, let's not get into that,' replied Hugo. 'Tell me about them.'

'Well, there's not much to tell really. I was being coerced into marrying Stefan who I had no feelings for, and I suppose I was trying to sabotage it.'

'Well, you did a good job. Go on.'

'One guy was called Jacob. He was mixed race and about the same age as me. We both got a bit drunk at a party. As you know, I wasn't used to drinking. It was a one-off.

'Another one was Swedish, William. Nice guy, but he was only out there for a few weeks, so that was that.'

'And the third guy? Tindra, I just can't believe all this.'

'I'm sorry,' said Tindra. 'This is why I didn't want to tell you. You'll judge me like the rest.'

'No I won't. I'm just surprised, that's all. So tell me about the third guy.'

'Well, he was an old bloke.'

'An OLD bloke?' Hugo couldn't help himself. 'How old?'

'Oh, probably about 50,' came the reply. 'He was English. His name was Charles. I called him Charlie, which he hated.'

'So why did you sleep with him?'

'He was actually quite charming. He was something important at the embassy where I worked.'

'Did you tell any of these guys you were pregnant?'

'No, well, only Charlie. When I started to show, I left for London. He took me to the airport. He had noticed and asked me straight. I told him it was his because I didn't want him to think I had been sleeping around. And anyway, he was married, so it wasn't going to come to anything anyway.'

'MARRIED?' Hugo was horrified.

'Yes, married. It does happen. Anyway, it came in useful because he was terrified his wife would find out, just as much as I was terrified that there would be a scandal, so he arranged for the baby to be 'kidnapped' from the hospital. He promised that she would be taken somewhere safe and well looked after.'

With this, her confident facade cracked, and tears started to fall. The tears turned to sobs, and her whole body shook. Hugo held her until she calmed down. He had to process all of this. It had been quite a revelation. But his sister had been an innocent abroad, and no doubt these men had taken advantage of her.

Charles had already been through all the emotions of his part in the death of Tom Delaney, and he wasn't going to go through it all again. He needed a drink, and he was past caring about going into the restaurant. He went straight to the bar and ordered a whisky. The barman recognised him immediately.

'Hello again. Good to see you. Hang on a minute; someone left a note for you yesterday.'

With that, he reached under the counter and produced a sealed envelope.

Charles took it to a table in the almost empty restaurant and downed his Scotch in one. He opened the envelope.

Surprise, the letter began.

I am still alive, no thanks to you. But I would probably have done the same if you were drowning.

I have been looking out for you because I have some news. I know where your baby is.

I could just go there and do the story, (and will do anyway) but what I really want is a picture of Daddy and baby together. There would be good money in it for you.

The truth will come out in the end, my old fruit, so why not make some cash out of it?

We're talking five figures.

Please call me on the number on the back of this note as soon as you get this. We could go together, and I want us to be the first to get there.

Tom Delaney

Charles put the note down. He put his head in his hands.

There was a commotion going on outside. The barman and waiter ran to the waterfront to join a group of people who were looking into the harbour.

Within minutes there were sirens. Time for Charles to leave.

* * *

Ria, Mandy and Richard stopped off at a roadside cafe to take stock. Ria and Mandy were fighting to hold back the tears. Richard bought coffee and cakes and placed them on the small table in the corner in front of them.

'We have to look at this calmly and logically,' he said. 'What time did you put Matilda in her cot, Ria?'

'It was just after lunch, at about two. And then we took Roxy for a walk, and Mandy took over.'

Mandy felt guilty and defensive. It was a long way up those stairs, and she hadn't checked enough. In fact, she hadn't checked at all. 'I went in the garden to read my book,' she said, 'but I was right below her window so that I would hear her if she cried.'

'So, what time did you check on her?' asked Richard.

Mandy hesitated. 'It's important,' said Ria.

'Don't you think I know it's important!' Mandy snapped.

'OK, let's look at who knew where Matilda was.' Richard was trying to calm things down.

'Just us and Pierre,' said Ria. 'I suppose he could have told Jack.'

'Anyone could know.' said Richard. 'Mandy, you said the estate agent had given your number to the police. It would be easy for them to trace it.'

'Maybe,' said Mandy, 'but the police wouldn't just sneak in and take the baby.'

Richard had to agree that this was true. 'What about the father, your son, Ria?'

'I don't see how he could possibly know where we are,' she said.

'Unless he also went to the estate agent and got Mandy's number.'

'And then there's that journalist,' said Mandy.

'And the special services,' said Richard. 'But I think we can be pretty sure that whoever has taken her will not harm her. It's not as if it's likely to be some random paedophile.'

Richard immediately knew that was a mistake as Ria started to sob.

Sgt Gill was back in the incident room that had been set up to find the royal baby. He had given Mandy's mobile number to other officers to trace, and they had news. The phone signal had been picked up about 25 miles from Paris, on the road to Normandy, but was now dead.

So they were in France! He passed the news onto MI6 and Interpol. They would check the area, and maybe put out a public alert. They would also be interested to know how they had got there.

Then he was off to interview a certain Tony Ellis. He arranged backup. If this was the man who had kidnapped the baby from the hospital, he could be dangerous.

It was 6am when Tony Ellis awoke to the sound of banging on his front door. He knew this day would come but was still not prepared for it.

He had always been law-abiding, and his thoughts were seldom devious. Now he would have to lie, and he was no good at that. And what would his wife think? He had no choice but to open the door before the whole neighbourhood woke up. He had no doubt that the police would kick the door down if he didn't open up. The shock of being awoken, and then getting out of bed too quickly made him feel faint. He was not as young as he used to be.

Sgt Gill flashed a warrant under Tony's nose, and then eight officers rushed into the house. Tony sat at the kitchen table. He heard his wife screaming as they rushed into the bedroom.

'You know why we're here, don't you, Tony?' Sgt Gill began.

'No,' said a shivering Tony, 'I have no idea.'

'OK, you want to play it the hard way.'

Sgt Gill told Tony how his car had left the vicinity of the maternity hospital just after the royal baby was kidnapped, and travelled to a Hertfordshire village, and then straight back to Tony's home. A baby had then been heard at the home of an elderly woman who had since disappeared. What was his explanation for that?

Tony looked at his feet and said nothing.

The officers gathered together Tony's phone, computer and tablets, and eventually placed him in the back of a police car to be taken away for questioning.

This one is going to be a doddle, thought Sgt Gill. He was wet behind the ears. He would probably even fall for good cop bad cop. He was certain he had his man, but who had put him up to it?

It would look odd if Charles left the boatyard without asking what all the excitement was about. He had to pass the little crowd and the police and ambulance on the way to his car, so he asked a bystander what was up.

'Some poor guy managed to drown himself,' he said. 'He was a drunk. We've already had to fish him out of the drink once this week. Looks like he banged his head when he fell this time, and he didn't make it.'

'Sorry to hear that,' said Charles. 'Some people just can't take their drink, can they? Very sad.'

Charles couldn't believe his luck. He was home and dry, and his enemy had gone forever. He started towards the car, and overheard a policeman saying to the barman, 'Could you take me to get the CCTV tapes, please. It will be useful for the coroner to see what happened, although it seems pretty cut and dried.'

Charles swung around and looked up. He was an intelligent man, why hadn't he looked before? Sure enough, there were two CCTV cameras on the roof of the restaurant, covering the boatyard and the harbour.

* * *

'Tindra, you have a visitor,' called her mother. 'Please come down now.'

Tindra was not expecting a visitor and liked to be prepared. 'Who is it?' she shouted.

'I'm not shouting up and down the stairs,' said her mother. 'Just come down.'

Tindra looked in the mirror. She looked dishevelled, her hair unwashed and her clothes creased. She hadn't worn make up for weeks. She quickly put a brush through her hair and wiped her face.

She slowly walked downstairs, hoping to hear a voice to get some clue as to the identity of her visitor. Her mother appeared in the hallway.

'He's in the library,' she said. 'Someone you knew in Canada apparently.'

She looked hard at her daughter and walked into the sitting room to leave her to it.

William was an impressive looking man. Tall, with blond curls and an easy smile. He looked younger than his 27 years. Tindra was delighted but embarrassed to see him. She looked a mess and had only had a short fling with him. What was he doing here?

'Hello, Tindra,' he said with a smile. 'I hope you don't mind... I mean, me taking the liberty of coming to your home, but I had to know.'

'It's good to see you, William. You're very welcome. But what did you have to know?'

'Well, I'd better come straight to the point. This is difficult... um, I read that you had had a baby.

I know we only, well, we weren't together long, but the dates seemed right, and I wondered if—?'

'If the baby was yours,' interrupted Tindra.

'Well, yes. I couldn't help wondering. And I was mortified that she had been stolen from you. I am so very sorry. Is there any news?'

Tindra was not expecting this. She had no idea what to say. This man made her go weak at the knees. She'd forgotten about that feeling.

'No, no news, I'm afraid,' she stuttered.

'I had to come here and ask you face to face. It's only right that I should know if I have a daughter,' William persevered.

Tindra wanted to hug this lovely man. She thought about her daughter's wispy blonde hair and the dimple on her chin that exactly matched his. They both had blue eyes, but then all babies had blue eyes, didn't they? She didn't want to tell him the truth. She wasn't a good time girl with slutty ways, and she didn't want him to have that opinion of her. She had just been lost and alone in a strange country and in fear of marrying a man she didn't like, let alone love, when she returned home.

William looked at her with kindness and confusion in his eyes. She had to put him out of his misery. She took a deep breath.

'Yes, she is yours,' she whispered.

Ria, Mandy and Richard sat looking into their empty coffee cups.

'Well, we can't stay here much longer,' said Ria.

'No,' agreed Mandy.

'I'll take you to a hotel in Normandy.' Richard was taking charge. 'Then we'll decide what to do tomorrow. We're all tired.'

The women nodded wearily. Even Roxy looked despondent.

As they left the cafe, Richard reached for Ria's hand. She clasped his broad, strong hand with gratitude. How she needed some reassurance.

As they got into the car, Richard's phone rang. It was a short conversation. He said, 'OK, I'll be back soon. Thanks.'

The women looked at him. 'That was my gardener. He said that the place is swarming with gendarmes.'

'Oh, Richard, I'm so sorry.' said Ria. 'What will you tell them?'

Richard took the battery out of his phone and started driving.

'What would you like me to tell them?'

Chapter six

Tony had never been in a police station before, except for that time when he wanted to report that his wallet had been stolen. They didn't bother much about that. But he had respect for the police. He was shocked to have his fingerprints taken, and then his photograph, and then they took swabs of the inside of his mouth for DNA, they said. They even took footprints of his shoes. He then stood in front of a desk, where a sergeant was told by Sgt Gill why Tony had been arrested.

He had to take off his shoes and was placed in a cell, like a common criminal. The door banged shut, and he felt the room spin. There was a concrete bench with a thin plastic covered mattress on top, and a thin blanket. In the corner was a lavatory without a seat.

It seemed like hours before he saw anyone again, although he could hear other prisoners shouting to each other, and ringing the bells that were in each cell. Nobody ever seemed to answer them. Eventually the door opened, and Sgt Gill said that they were ready to interview him. He was led to an interview room where another officer was waiting.

There was just a table with a tape recorder on it, and chairs either side.

Tony had never been more frightened in his life.

Suddenly a pain shot through his chest and down his arm. He clutched his chest and fell to the floor.

'What the fuck? Is he acting?' said Sgt Gill. The other officer hit the alarm bar on the wall, and officers came running. 'Call an ambulance... who can do CPR?' he shouted.

Charles was between the devil and the deep blue sea. If he could be identified from the CCTV, he would be arrested for murder. He would lose everything. If he was identified as the baby's father, he would also lose everything.

So that wretched Tom Delaney knew where the baby was? Could that be true? Damn it. Charles wondered if he had told anyone else. Probably not. Should he get out of the country quick and go back to Canada? Was his mother OK?

He drove down the motorway from the boatyard and slept in his car that night in a services car park. Not the most sensible for a man on the run, but he wasn't thinking straight. Where was that bloody baby? He had to get at it before any DNA tests could be done.

After driving for almost two hours, Richard, Mandy and Ria arrived at the Hotel Barriere in

Normandy. It was very grand, and probably five-star they thought. Richard booked them in, and then they hit a snag. The hotel would not allow dogs.

'I'll take Roxy back with me,' he said. 'She'll be fine with Mufti, and she knows her way around. I'll bring her back when we find somewhere else for you to stay.'

Ria and Mandy were very grateful. He had booked them a room each, and he went with them to help with luggage and check that everything was OK. They settled Mandy into her room, and then Richard went with Ria to hers. She sat on the bed, looking exhausted. Richard's heart went out to her.

'I'd better get back and face the music,' he said. 'Will you be alright?'

'I'll be fine,' said Ria. 'What will you tell the police?'

'Oh, I don't know. I'll think of something.' He smiled. 'I have a very good poker face.'

Then he leaned over and kissed her on the forehead.

She took his hand, and he sat on the bed. He then cupped her face in his hands and kissed her passionately on the lips. Ria felt alive for the first time in years. It was two hours before he left Ria's room and headed home with a very big grin on his face. He had found love again.

Sgt Gill decided to go to France. With the death of Tony Ellis, they couldn't even be sure that they were following the right baby, but it was their only decent lead.

Amanda Anderson's phone had led them to a mill house near Paris before it went dead. The gendarmes had stormed the place, but no one was at home. There were certainly baby clothes and paraphernalia about the place, but that didn't necessarily mean anything, although it was duly noted. Lots of people kept baby things in the house for visiting grandchildren.

The gardener Phillipe had told the police that he hadn't seen any visitors, and that only Monsieur Richard Smythe lived there. He would probably be back soon, but he didn't know where he was. He didn't know about the baby things. He was just the gardener and didn't go into the house. No, he didn't know the registration number of his employer's car. An officer was left at the house to await the return of Monsieur Smythe.

Sgt Gill had to convince his superiors that his trip was not a wild goose chase or a jolly. He had a feeling that he was on the right track.

He flew to Paris and met with a French officer who took him to the Mill House. He arrived just as Richard was pulling into the drive.

William Larson was delighted to discover that he was indeed the father of the royal baby. He was even more delighted that the Princess Tindra genuinely liked him as much as he liked her. But this was a bittersweet new love with their little daughter missing.

Tindra could see a future with William. He was everything she wanted her husband to be. Kind, caring, gentle and sincere. He wasn't interested in status or money. He was just a decent, honest guy.

She decided to confide in him. After all, if he was the baby's father, he had a right to know the truth. Well, a version of it anyway. She told him that she was so ashamed and afraid of the scandal the baby would cause that she arranged to have her 'kidnapped'. The child would be taken to the mother of a friend of hers in Hertfordshire, England, where she would be cared for and possibly adopted.

William was horrified. All this uproar in the press, and Tindra had arranged the kidnapping herself! So where was the baby now, he asked?

Seeing that she might have caused a rift with William, Tindra welled up. 'I don't know,' she said softly, biting back the tears. 'I have had no news.'

'Why don't you contact your friend and ask him, or her, if his mother still has the baby?' he asked gently, seeing how upset she was.

'Because I swore I would not contact him again in case he could be traced and blamed for the kidnapping,' she sobbed.

'Do you know where to find him?'

'No, I never did know his address.'

'Where in Hertfordshire does his mother live?'

'I've no idea.'

'OK, well, give me his name. He will probably have the same name as his mother, and we can look on the English electoral roll.'

'I only know his first name,' said Tindra.

'You said this man was a friend, but you don't know where he lives or even his surname, and you entrusted him with our baby?'

Tindra was distraught. William was obviously upset, but he didn't understand what she had been through. She started to feel angry.

'Now listen to me, William. You were happy to go to bed with me. You were not the one to become pregnant and have to face the wrath of your family, who happen to be pretty high profile. You didn't have to run away and secretly give birth, all the time trying to stop the whole scandal kicking off in the papers. Did you think that a woman has no feelings for her baby and is happy to give her away to strangers just because she isn't married? I was alone. You had returned home without a care in the world, so stop judging me. I did the only thing I could think of at the time.'

William put his arm around her. 'I'm sorry,' he said. 'It's just all been a lot to take in. We'll find her, or the police will, and then we can all be a family if you'll have me.'

Charles decided that he would be better off in France, away from the English police, and with just a chance of tracking down his mother and the baby. That guy Jack seemed to make regular trips across the Channel. And he was the one who took his mother there, to Cherbourg he said.

But by now the whole boatyard would probably know about the CCTV tapes, and there might even be wanted posters up for him. No, that was melodramatic, wasn't it? Did they still do wanted posters? But he would be taking a huge risk going to the boatyard. Unless... unless he went there at night and if he saw Jack's catamaran, he could hide on it until he left for France. Of course, at some point Jack would see him, but he would deal with that when the time came. Yes, that was a plan.

Ria and Mandy were dining in luxury at the hotel, but they didn't have much of an appetite. Ria wanted to tell Mandy about the encounter with Richard the previous night, and how she was besotted with him. But she felt that with her little granddaughter missing, now wasn't the time.

'Who would have thought a few weeks ago,' said Mandy, trying to be cheerful, 'that we would have been living the high life in a five-star hotel in Normandy!'

'And I would have a granddaughter,' said Ria.

'And you would have a granddaughter,' sighed Mandy.

As she spoke a waiter came to their table. 'Excusez-moi, Madame, il y a un appel téléphonique pour vous.' He was addressing Ria.

She leapt up and followed him to the telephone at the reception desk.

'Is that Ria Radcliffe?' came an unfamiliar man's voice. 'Yes, speaking,' replied Ria, and with that the phone went dead. She tried to get back to the caller, but it came up as a private number. He had hung up.

She returned to the dining table. 'Well, that was weird,' she told Mandy.

The call had spooked them both. Someone now knew where they were. Why didn't she ask who it was before saying it was her? Ria was annoyed with herself. She wanted to talk to Richard, but neither she nor Mandy could use their phones, and Richard could only contact them via the hotel. She had thought the call would be from him. She had no idea what had happened to him once he got home. Were the police still there? What did he tell them? Could he have been arrested? Had anyone found the baby yet?

She suddenly felt panicky. 'Let's get out of here,' she hissed at Mandy. And with that she made for the lift to get back to her hotel room to pack. Mandy followed.

Sgt Ellis was feeling quite pleased with himself. Now that he had Richard's car registration number, it didn't take him long to discover that he had made a journey to Normandy. His guess was that he had taken the women and the baby there. Richard had been no help at all. He appeared to be senile and unable to understand his questions. He didn't seem to know what day it was. Poor old chap. The women had probably taken advantage of him. No point taking him in. By the time they got to the police station, he wouldn't remember his own name.

A few phone calls to the major hotels confirmed the sergeant's theory. Ria Radcliffe was at the Barriere Hotel. He needed to get there quickly. He notified the Normandy police and set off.

Richard pulled up in the hotel car park just in time to see Sgt Gill and his French host leaving. There was no sign of the women. When they were out of sight, he went to the hotel receptionist and asked her to contact Ria. She said that Ria was popular today! But unfortunately, she and her friend had checked out. 'Did she leave a message?' asked Richard.

Another receptionist, overhearing the conversation said, 'Are you Monsieur Smythe?'

'Yes, I am,' he replied anxiously.

'There is a letter for you.'

He sat in the reception area and read the letter.

Dear Richard

We had a phone call via the hotel from an unknown man who asked if I was Ria Radcliffe and then hung up. We decided to leave quick. We called Pierre for advice. He said go to a place called La Cochere which is less than half an hour away, and we would be able to get a gite there. He couldn't help us as he is in England, but he will be back tomorrow.

Hoping you will find us! It's only a small place apparently.

Love Ria xx

Richard was relieved. They had missed the police and he would surely be able to find them.

When Charles got to the boatyard at 11.30pm, he couldn't believe his luck. There at the end of the jetty was a catamaran! He parked in a nearby layby and quietly made his way past dozens of moored boats to the very end of the boardwalk. There was a light on inside the boat, but it seemed many of them left a light on for security. Did Jack stay on the boat overnight? Maybe not as he was English. He no doubt had a place nearby. This was not a fishing harbour. These were pleasure boats, hobby boats for the wealthy.

Charles carefully stepped on to the craft and waited to see if there was any sound or movement. Nothing. So he gingerly tried the door handle. To his amazement the door opened. He stepped inside into a luxurious sitting room. He crept along the plush carpet to another door which was slightly ajar. He peeped inside, and there was a man in bed, gently snoring.

There were two old ladies who didn't speak French, trying to hitch a lift to La Cochere in the dark. Taxis were too traceable. And they had no idea how to get there by public transport, if there was any.

'This is dangerous,' said a nervous Mandy.

'Why, they're not going to rape us are they!' Ria said, grinning.

'And why the devil not? I'll have you know that back in the day the men were queuing up.'

They both laughed, and a mixture of nervousness and fatigue gave them the giggles.

They trudged on, dragging their suitcases on wheels and sticking their thumbs in the air. Nobody stopped. After they had walked a very long mile, they sat on their cases to rest. And just then a car carrying an elderly couple pulled over.

'Salut. Ou est-ce que tu vas?' said the man.

'What did he say?' asked Mandy.

'Not sure,' Ria replied, and to the man, 'Um, sorry, nous sommes angles, comprenons pas.'

'Thank gawd for that,' he laughed. 'I'm fed up with trying to speak French! Where are you trying to get to?'

To La Cochere they explained, and he said he was happy to take them there. It was not much out of his way. The couple were from north London but had a holiday home nearby. The man introduced himself as Colin, and his wife was Janice.

It wasn't long before they were in La Cochere. But the kindly couple were worried about leaving the two ladies to try and find accommodation in the dark. Colin stopped the car, and in very acceptable French asked a man on a bicycle if he knew where there were gites to rent. They were just a hundred yards down the road, the cyclist said, on the left.

Colin found the place and even went to find the owner and asked what they had available. A round woman in a pinny came out to the car, followed by two dogs. She led them down a track to a gite that was in darkness.

She let them in, put on the lights and said she would bring some bread and milk over a bit later. Colin and Janice wished the women luck, and Colin gave them his card in case they needed a contact, or just to meet up for a drink. Colin Jenkins, it said, Plumbing and Heating Engineer.

Mandy plonked herself down on the sofa while Ria went off to explore the rest of the gite. There were two bedrooms, a bathroom, a kitchen and a sitting room/diner. It was small and basic, but clean. There was fresh linen and towels on the beds.

Once the pinny lady had brought the bread, milk and homemade jam, they fell exhausted into bed.

Sgt Gill had booked into an Airbnb. The force would not run to a five-star hotel. He was less than amused. He knew he had missed his targets by a whisker, and they seemed to have vanished into thin air. Taxis had been checked, along with buses and hire car companies. Zilch. The strange thing was that the hotel said that the two women had stayed there, but there was no baby. Definitely no baby.

Could he have been on the wrong track all along? No, the baby must have been dropped off somewhere. There was a cot at the Mill House, but surely they wouldn't leave a baby with that senile old man? No. He felt he was so near and yet so far. He would ring the incident room and see if anyone else had come up with something. He was now wishing that he hadn't been so bullish about being the big hero who would come to France and find the baby almost single-handed. He may have only missed the women by minutes; but were they even the right women? And the truth was that they could be anywhere by now.

Charles decided to leave Jack to sleep, and he would try to sleep on the sofa. If Jack discovered him before he woke that could get tricky, but he would have to take that chance. Jack would almost certainly have been in the bar at the restaurant and would know that Charles was wanted for murdering Tom Delaney. He wondered if Jack would remember him from the brief meeting they had had on the quayside when Charles had asked him about the whereabouts of his mother.

Before he knew it, it was light, and he heard stirrings from Jack's bedroom. He didn't want to appear threatening, so he stayed seated on the sofa, his heart pounding. He heard a shower running. A few minutes later, a totally naked man stepped into the room with a towel slung over his shoulder. Difficult to know who was the more shocked. The man was not Jack.

He was a total stranger.

'What the fuck you doing on my boat?' he said with a French accent.

'I'm so sorry,' said Charles. 'I thought this was my friend's boat.'

'Who is your friend?' asked Pierre as he wrapped the towel around his hips.

'Jack, do you know Jack?' Charles replied. 'He said I could come on board anytime... I'm so sorry, I thought this was his...'

'It's OK, I know Jack, that sounds like him. He likes company. His boat is almost the same as mine. Easy mistake.'

'You want coffee?'

'Ooh, yes please. Are you sailing today?'

'Oui. Back to France.'

'I was going to hitch a lift with Jack. I don't suppose I could come with you, could I?'

'Any friend of Jack's is a friend of mine. We might see him over there. Where are you headed? I'm sorry, I don't know your name.'

'Charles.'

'I'm Pierre.'

'Oh, I'm just being a tourist. Got itchy feet, you know how it is.'

'So, no definite plans then?'

'No. I'm just a happy wanderer.' Charles smiled, pleased with the way things were going.

Chapter seven

Richard had decided to leave it until the morning to go to La Cochere. It would be easier to find Ria and Mandy in daylight. He had borrowed Phillipe's car just in case.

The police had come and gone and didn't have the benefit of knowing that the women were heading for La Cochere, and not one of the main towns. He found the gite quite easily. The site was the first one he saw, and maybe the only one in this area.

Ria and Mandy were delighted to see him. He had become their rock.

They sat down to a late breakfast of homemade bread and jam from Mrs Pinny, and several cups of coffee. Richard told them how they had missed the police by seconds, and the women told him all about Colin and Janice and Mrs Pinny, as Ria now called her. Richard became quiet and serious.

'I have something important to tell you,' he began.

'Oh dear, that sounds ominous,' said Ria.

Richard looked hard at her. 'You are not going to like this but hear me out because it is actually very good news. I hope you won't be angry with me.'

The women looked at each other, not sure whether to be afraid or happy.

Richard continued, 'The good news is that Matilda is safe and well.'

'Oh, thank God!' cried Ria. Mandy burst into tears.

'Where is she?' sniffled Mandy.

'I need to explain what happened,' Richard continued. 'While you were at my place the police put out an appeal, and a reward via the French press for anyone who had knowledge of the baby. You didn't see the papers, but I did. I have lived here for many years and people know me. You remember, Ria, that we went into a baby store and practically bought out the shop?' Ria nodded. 'Well the woman recognised me and thought it was odd that I had arrived with an English woman of my age and bought so much baby stuff. She called the newspaper, who told the police. Luckily, they happened to speak to Officer Antoine Bisset, the brother of my gardener Phillipe.

'Of course, Phillipe, who is the most loyal friend, tipped me off that the police could arrive at any moment. I was in a flat spin. It would take more than a minute to get you two, the baby and Roxy away from the house to safety. The most important thing was to make sure that Matilda was safe.'

'What are you saying?' said Ria, her hackles rising.

'If you'll let me finish,' said Richard. 'I had to get Matilda out of the house pronto without us all panicking. I asked Phillipe to take her to my son Pierre's place, where I knew she would be safe.'

'But we have been to hell and back worrying about her!' said a furious Mandy. 'Why didn't you tell us?'

'Because, dear lady, if the police had questioned you, and put pressure on you, you couldn't say what you didn't know.'

'You had no right to do that!' said Ria.

'Maybe not,' said Richard, 'but Matilda is safe, and at least for the moment, so are you.'

'But Pierre is in England.' said Ria. 'We spoke to him last night.'

'Stop worrying,' said Richard. 'His wife is looking after Matilda.'

'I need to go to the bank so I can withdraw some money so we can go and get her,' sniffed Mandy.

'No,' Ria retorted, 'if you withdraw money we can be traced.'

Richard stepped in. 'Look, I know this has been a shock, but please calm down. Everything is fine. We need to talk about the best way forward.'

The Channel crossing took a few hours in the catamaran, and Charles and Pierre had plenty of time to chat. It occurred to Charles that he might be stopped at whichever port they were going to if the police had asked them to look out for him. In fact, as the murder had happened at a harbour, they may well expect him to escape by boat. He couldn't risk it. But what to do?

'I'm an idiot,' he said to Pierre, 'I left my passport in my car. So sorry to mess you about.'

'Can't turn back now,' said Pierre, looking worried. 'You'll have to stay on board for a couple of days until I come back.'

'Oh dear. Is there no way I can get into France?'

'Well, I know Jack managed to drop off a couple of passengers on a sandbank a while back, but you're not supposed to do it.'

'Do you know where the sandbank is?' Charles asked.

'I should do. I was the one who had to pick up his stranded passengers!' laughed Pierre. 'Tell you what,' Pierre continued, 'the sandbank is only 15 minutes from the harbour where I dock. I'll drop you off, get my car and fetch you. Come and have a bite to eat with my wife and I.'

Sgt Gill had a video call with the incident room team, which was now quite small.

'To recap,' explained the inspector, 'one of the minor Scandinavian royals had a baby secretly in London. The baby is stolen by a man we believe to be Tony Ellis, who inconsiderately died before we had a chance to speak to him. The baby's mother, Princess Tindra, would not name the father, and refused to speak to us any more. Ellis's car was tracked to a village in Hertfordshire, where we believe he left the baby. Two women pensioners vanished at the same time, and both put their houses on the market. They are Ria

Radcliffe and Amanda Anderson. We got their phone numbers from the estate agent. Radcliffe's phone was dead, but we traced Anderson's to a house in France. The house is owned by an Englishman, Richard Smythe. A local shopkeeper reported that he and an English woman had bought numerous baby items.

'The house was searched, but the women were not there, and neither was the baby. Smyth was questioned but was apparently suffering from dementia and made no sense. However, his car made a journey to Normandy. We discovered that the women, but not the baby, had stayed overnight in a hotel there. We missed them by minutes. So that is where the trail runs cold. By now they could be anywhere.

'Any suggestions?'

'Have they withdrawn any money?' asked a young DC.

'No.'

'Have they been in touch with the estate agent?' asked another.

'No, the agent has been trying to contact them to progress the house sales, but nothing.'

'Sir, if this guy Smythe took them to Normandy, he can't be that dopey. Maybe he's still in touch with them?'

'Yes, the French police have put a tracking device on his car, but it hasn't moved in days.'

***

William and Princess Tindra had become an item. Her parents liked him, although he was not an aristocrat or a royal. His parents were university lecturers, and William, by contrast, was a restorer of old paintings, so that could come in useful they supposed. A perfectly good profession, but not, they thought, worthy of their daughter. The man hardly earned enough to keep himself, let alone a girl who had been brought up in a country estate. But Tindra was adamant that this was the man for her, and she was a grown woman, so there was not much they could do about it. She would learn, they thought, when she was living in a poky flat somewhere on the wrong side of the tracks. She would come crying back to them.

Tindra and William were putting a lot of pressure on the secret services to find their baby. Tindra's parents were adamant that until the baby was recovered, and DNA tests done, they would not allow it to be public that William was the father. At least if they did get married, they mused, it would make their indiscretion a little more palatable.

Pierre duly dropped Charles off at the sandbank, and then went back for him as promised. He had called ahead to his wife, who had made onion soup, with a delicious coq au vin and chocolate soufflé to follow, all to be washed down with their favourite French wine. Pierre's wife, Giselle, did not speak much English, but Charles had schoolboy

French, so they managed. They all chatted happily through the best meal Charles had had in a long while.

Matilda was asleep in the next room. As Giselle served cheese and biscuits, the baby started to cry.

'Oh,' said Charles, 'I didn't know you had a baby.'

'No, no,' started Pierre, 'we're just—'

'Giselle interrupted. 'Au, nous ne sommes que nouveaux parents, donc nous ne savons pas vraiment ce que nous faisons.' She laughed.

'Sorry, what did she say?' asked Charles.

Pierre looked at his wife. 'Yes, she said we are just new parents, so we don't really know what we're doing!'

'Oh,' laughed Charles. 'They don't come with instructions, do they!'

'Do you have any children, Charles?' asked Pierre as Giselle brought the crying baby into the room.

'No, they're too noisy for me,' he shouted above the racket.

Taking the hint, Giselle took Matilda back into the next room.

'I was thinking,' said Charles to Pierre. 'You kindly helped Jack's passengers to find somewhere to stay, I was wondering if you had any ideas for me?'

'Well no, they went to stay with my father just outside Paris. But actually, he might be up for taking in a paying guest.' He stressed the word paying. Charles nodded, of course he would pay.

'I'll give him a ring.'

Richard was sitting in the gite garden with the girls when his phone rang. It was his new phone. He had left the old one at home. Only Pierre had the number so far.

'Bonjour, Pierre,'

'Bonjour, Papa. I have come across an English tourist who would like to find somewhere to stay near Paris. Wondered if you would like a paying guest? He seems like a decent chap.' He smiled at Charles.

Charles smiled and looked down.

'I'm not there at the moment, son, I'm with Ria and Mandy. But if he wants to come in the morning, that would be fine. Be good to have some male company for a change.' He gave Ria a big grin. 'Baby OK?'

'Yes fine, Papa. I'll give him your address then. He says he'll be hiring a car. Shall I give him your new phone number too?'

'Yes, I suppose it won't hurt, in case he gets lost.'

When Richard finished the call, he and the women had to have a serious talk. What were they to do next? They were so relieved that Matilda was safe, that they had to forgive Richard for his actions, but were not happy that he had caused them so much distress.

'Right,' said Richard, once again taking charge. 'You can't spend the rest of your lives running about trying to hide a baby. She won't be a baby for long, and she needs a proper life.'

'Well, the plan had been to sell our houses and move into the beach house,' said Mandy, wondering if the beach house was still theirs to move into. They should have kept in touch with the agent. That snake Tom Delaney might have snatched it from them by now. And they had no idea where they were with their house sales.

'You need to contact the agents,' said Richard. 'You need to get a burner phone. I saw that on telly. They are phones that you can use a couple of times and throw away so they can't be traced.'

Ria smiled. Richard seemed to be enjoying the drama of it all.

'We'll do that,' she said.

'But the beach house, or wherever you go, will be traceable.'

'Unless we change our identities,' said Mandy, who had even surprised herself by saying that.

'Yes, I'll wear a moustache,' said Ria, who was relaxing now she knew that her grandchild was safe.

'You already do,' quipped Mandy. 'But seriously,' she said, warming to her theme, we could change our names and dye our hair. If we buy the beach house under new names, who would know?'

'We've already given the agent our names,' said Ria.

'There is that,' said a crestfallen Mandy.

'I could buy it,' said Richard.

Both women looked stunned.

'All you'd need to do is tell the agent that you've changed your minds. Then I ring soon afterwards and offer the asking price, cash.'

'But she might offer it first to Tom Delaney,' reasoned Ria. 'She knew he was keen to buy it.'

'But did he have cash?' Richard replied.

'No, I heard him talking about selling another property and getting a mortgage,' said Ria, who had a very useful nosy streak.

'Well there you are then,' said Richard. 'You can pay me back when your houses are sold. But I'll only do it on the condition that I can visit.'

Ria hoped he would do more than visit.

MI6 had discovered that Ria had a son called Charles. He had been working in the embassy in Canada at the same time as Princess Tindra had been there. Well, there was a turn up for the books! He had come to England recently. How interesting!

It didn't take them long to discover that he had been a friend of Tony Ellis, the suspected kidnapper. This was a big breakthrough. But they could not find Charles. They felt sure that he would lead them to his mother, and to the baby.

They must pull out all the stops to find him.

Charles wanted to hire a car but would be putting himself at risk. Would Pierre hire one for him?

After all, he didn't have his passport, did he? Pierre was a little reluctant but agreed as he could see that Charles was in a bind, and also that his father was expecting him. Charles said his goodbyes and thanks to Pierre and Giselle and went off to buy a burner phone. He had discarded his old one. He tried again to phone Ria, but the phone was still dead.

As he drove towards Paris, he thought things through. He knew now that Ria and her friend and the baby had crossed the Channel with Jack and that Pierre had picked them up and taken them to his dad's place. Could they still be there? If not, the old man would surely know where they were. The gap was closing. He was getting close. But supposing they *were* there? What would he actually do? Even if he could get his hands on the brat that was causing him all this trouble, where would he take it? When the baby was first born, it could have been taken to the social services as a foundling, no questions asked. But now there was so much publicity it would be impossible for the connection not to be made. And then they would probably do DNA tests. But then again, they didn't have his DNA to compare it to. Yet.

Ria and Mandy were enjoying the peaceful gite and beautiful surrounding countryside. But they needed to get a burner phone... something they had never heard of before. Maybe Mrs Pinny would know where to get one from. They must call the estate agents and get things moving. Mrs Pinny was sitting outside her bungalow in the sunshine shelling peas into a colander. She smiled as Ria approached.

'Is everything alright?' she asked in a strong French accent.

'Yes, thank you... lovely,' said Ria 'Um, I was just wondering if you know where I could buy a burner phone?'

Mrs Pinny looked puzzled. 'Burner phone? I don't know what is this. Wait.'

With that, she put down her bowl of peas and went indoors. She came out a few minutes later, followed by two scruffy dogs and a burly man wearing a vest and shorts.

'You want to buy a phone?' he asked in good English.

'Yes, I don't know where to go to buy one,' said Ria.

'I have an old phone you can have if it's any good to you,' he said.

'Oh, that's very kind of you. Is it a burner phone?' Ria asked, feeling stupid.

The man laughed. 'I think maybe you have been watching too much television,' he said. 'You are not bank robbers, are you?' Then he laughed until he coughed, and went indoors to get his phone.

It was a pay as you go phone, he said. So no contract. He gave Ria directions to a place where she could pay in advance with cash. She didn't want to use her credit card. Richard had left her with 200 euros to help her out. The shop was not far, so Ria and Mandy took a walk to get a few supplies and top up the phone. Ria bought some dog food. It occurred to her that Mrs Pinny might allow Roxy to come to the gite as she had two dogs herself. That would be good. It was useful to know that there were a few shops nearby. A small supermarket, a boulangerie (hoorah fresh bread), a post office and a pharmacy.

Later they sat in the gite garden with cups of tea and plucked up courage to phone the estate agents. Mandy was feeling brave. Ria had found a way to withhold the number of the phone, and she had handed it to Mandy to call the beach house estate agent. But then she looked at Ria. 'Are you sure we're doing the right thing, letting Richard buy it? And anyway, how are we going to contact him to tell him he needs to ring them today?'

Ria trusted Richard, despite his deception with Matilda. After all, he did that for everyone's good, bless him.

'It's OK, he gave me his burner phone number,' said Ria. 'We'll call him after you've spoken to the agent.'

Mandy found the number in her diary and dialled it.

The woman they usually dealt with answered it. She had almost given up on them, she said. She had been trying to contact them for ages. What was happening?

Mandy said they were terribly sorry, but their circumstances had changed, and they could no longer buy the beach house. It was so hard for her to say, as she longed to be there, but it had to be done. The woman at the other end was obviously disappointed and a bit cross but stayed professional and polite. This was the second time the sale had been cancelled. What were they playing at? But this time she knew at least it was Mandy she was speaking to. Oh, well, she had that other journalist guy interested.

Now it was Ria's turn. She rang the estate agent who was selling Lavender Cottage and The Gables. The man had been just as frustrated with them but knew that something was up because he had had a call from the police as he had previously told them.

He now had buyers for both houses, he was pleased to report, both at the asking price as it was currently a sellers' market, and they had priced both houses realistically. Ria congratulated him and told him to go ahead. They were on holiday at the moment she told him, but they could instruct solicitors and do most of the business online or on the phone. He was happy with that for the moment and asked her to keep in touch.

Mandy was unfazed about the sale of Lavender Cottage. She had only been there for five minutes, so had no great attachment to it. But Ria felt a nervous pang of the loss of her home and felt adrift. In the moments when she felt she wanted to 'go home', she no longer had a home to go to. There were a lot of memories in that house. But she had to admit that not all of them were happy, and she had been lonely for much of the time.

She would cheer herself up by phoning Richard to tell him that they had pulled out of the beach house and to give him the estate agent's number. It was good to have a phone to use again.

Chapter eight

Tindra had a call from the royal lawyer. MI6 in England wanted to talk to her. Was she willing to speak to them? Did they have news of her baby, she asked eagerly. He didn't know; they just said they wanted to speak to Princess Tindra privately. The lawyer insisted that he should be there if they had a meeting, whether it was in person or online. Tindra agreed and subsequently an online meeting was planned for 4pm that day. Tindra wanted William to be there too, so that had to be agreed.

On the dot of 4pm, the call came through. 'Do you have news for me?' said the impatient princess.

'Well, we have something we want to ask you,' he said. 'When you were in Canada did you know a man by the name of Charles Radcliffe?'

Oh no. This was a bag of worms that Tindra did not want to open. She looked at William. He assumed this was the friend Tindra had mentioned. What should she do?

William stepped in. 'Is this relevant to finding the baby?' he asked.

'We don't know yet. I'd be grateful if you would let the princess answer the question, sir.'

It was no use denying that she knew him. But had he been talking to the police? Had he been linked with the kidnapping? She was floundering.

'Has he said we knew each other?' she asked.

'With the greatest of respect, ma'am, I'll ask the questions. Do you know Charles Radcliffe?'

'Yes, just as an acquaintance. We both worked at the same place for a while.'

'Did you have a relationship with him?'

At this point the lawyer stepped in, feeling he should justify his existence and large pay packet, and not just be a spectator. 'I'm sorry, but I don't think the princess should answer that, or be questioned about her private life,' he said haughtily.

'OK,' said the MI6 investigator, 'let's move on. Did you know that Charles Radcliffe recently left Canada and came to England?'

'No, I didn't,' said Tindra.

'Do you know where he is now?'

'No, I have no idea.'

'We have established that he was friends with a man called Tony Ellis. We believe Ellis took your baby from the hospital to the home of Charles Radcliffe's mother. Do you know anything about that?'

The lawyer again. 'What are you insinuating?'

'I'm not insinuating anything. Just asking the question.'

'Of course she doesn't know anything about that,' the lawyer spat. 'She had her baby stolen and is desperate to get her back. That is your job.'

'OK, to continue. Princess Tindra, is Charles Radcliffe the father of your baby?'

'No!' said Tindra.

At this point the lawyer called a halt to the meeting.

William was uneasy. He tried to bat away doubts. Why would this man who was just an acquaintance, or even a friend of Tindra's, not only arrange for the child to be taken by someone else to his mother's house, but then also go to England himself from Canada? Could he indeed be the father of the baby?

Charles finally found his way to the Mill House. He stopped on the road outside to gather his thoughts. He wished he had had the presence of mind to change his name. But now Pierre knew it, and he had no doubt told his father. If his father had been in the company of Ria and Mandy, no doubt his name would have come up. But there were lots of men called Charles. He was being ridiculous. He would just give another surname if asked. Richard stood at the front door, once more resplendent in his red smoking jacket and yellow cravat. This was the outfit he liked to use when greeting people. It gave an impression of sophistication, he thought.

He had phoned the estate agent to put the wheels in motion to buy the beach house. He said he wanted a holiday home and it looked perfect. He would go ahead sight unseen and get over there when he could. He would pay in cash. He then referred her to his solicitor, who he had then briefed. He was quite excited about it.

Richard held out his hand, and Charles shook it with a good firm grip. Good man.

'Good to have another chap about the place,' said Richard as he led him into the sitting room. 'No luggage, old boy?'

'No, I like to travel light,' said Charles, 'and it was a bit of a last-minute decision to come.'

They chatted over a few drinks, about good old blighty, football and cars. Charles wondered how to bring up the subject of his last visitors. Obviously, they had moved on, but where to? It would have to wait until tomorrow. He had to play this very cool indeed.

'We need to go and see Matilda,' said Ria as they cleared up after dinner.

'Yes,' Mandy agreed. 'I'm sure she's fine, but she should be with us.'

'Shall I ring Pierre and ask him if we can sort something out?' Ria asked.

'The trouble is, if we're honest, she's safer there than with us,' countered Mandy.

'But we don't even know where she is. We don't know where Pierre lives!'

'Like Richard said, maybe it's better that we don't,' Mandy continued. 'That way we can't let it slip, even if they put the thumbscrews on us.'

'But are they prepared to look after her until we go back to England, to the beach house? It could be months?'

'And how are we going to get her back to England?'

'I'm sure Pierre would sort that out,' said Ria.

In bed at night, Mandy started to get an uneasy feeling about all of this. They had no idea where Matilda was, and a comparative stranger was buying their beach house. They were losing control of everything that was important to them. And nobody knew where they were. But everyday things often took on a sinister side at night. It would all make sense in the morning.

Giselle was in her element. She adored babies and was thoroughly enjoying being a 'mum' again. Pierre was not so keen. All that squawking and smelly nappies. And neither of them was getting much sleep. He'd be glad when he was out at sea again. That would suit Giselle fine. She could have the baby to herself without anyone complaining.

She knew that Matilda was hot property. She had heard the story from her husband and seen the papers. It was a problem. At first, she didn't know what to tell her friends and neighbours. Some had even joked that maybe this was the missing princess! But the story they told was that a cousin was going to a wedding in Nice and had asked them to look after the baby while they made a bit of a holiday out of it.

Everyone knew Giselle to be a straightforward and honest woman and accepted her story without question.

Richard and Charles were taking a stroll around the Mill House grounds in the hot sunshine. Roxy and Mufti were bounding about at their feet. Charles recognised Roxy as his mother's dog, especially once he knew her name. Maybe this was his opportunity.

'Lovely dogs,' he said, which didn't fool Richard who had noticed that Charles was not a fan. Still, each to his own.

'Yes, thank you,' said Richard. 'Only Mufti is mine. Roxy was left for me to mind for a while by the last visitors I had. I'm happy to do it as it's company for Mufti, and Roxy's a little character.'

'Yes,' said Charles, and choosing his words carefully. 'Pierre said you had a couple of English ladies here.'

'I did, and charming they are too.' Richard smiled as he thought of the lovely Ria.

'So, you're still in touch with them then...? I mean, I suppose you have to be for the dog.'

'Yes, in fact I'm sure we'll stay friends. This is the wonderful part of having guests, you make a lot of new friends from all over the world.'

Richard's phone rang. 'Oh, speak of the devil.' He grinned. 'Please excuse me.' And he strode off back to the house to take the call.

Mandy's car had been parked at the boatyard for some weeks now and was drawing attention. The restaurant staff remembered that it had been parked there by two women, but it now appeared to have been abandoned. There was some concern, so the bar manager mentioned it to a policeman who liked a regular pint or three.

He checked it out. It was registered to one Amanda Anderson, of 23 Herne Lane. She had not changed the address to Lavender Cottage, so the car did not raise any interest, especially as there were hundreds of Amanda Andersons throughout the UK. This was not the one they were looking for. This was a harbour, and the women had probably gone off on holiday in a boat. Case closed.

Ria and Mandy wanted to know when Richard would be coming to see them. There were things they wanted to talk about, and could he please bring Roxy, as Mrs Pinny had said that it was fine to bring a dog into the gite. Richard explained that he had a house guest but said that by tomorrow he would feel comfortable about leaving him on his own. He would see if he could borrow the gardener's car again, just in case.

As he came off the call with Ria, which he had taken in the kitchen, Charles wandered in from the garden.

'Everything alright?' he said, smiling.

Richard put the kettle on. 'Yes, fine, thank you. I hope you won't mind being left to your own devices tomorrow. I'll be out for most of the day, but you know your way around now, don't you?'

'Yes, of course,' said Charles. 'Don't worry about me. Going somewhere nice?'

That question always irritated Richard. He wanted to say, no, I'm going somewhere horrible, and it was always just somebody being nosy.

But he said, 'Just going to visit some friends. I'm making tea, would you like some?'

There was something about Charles that Richard did not like. He was charming enough and polite, but Richard wasn't sure that he could trust him. Also, Charles didn't like dogs, and that was not a good sign as far as he was concerned.

Charles was convinced that Richard was planning to visit his mother and her friend the next day. Fantastic. He would follow at a distance. The old codger wouldn't notice. Charles could see Richard's car from his bedroom window, so he could keep an eye on it.

The next morning Charles overslept, and jumped out of bed in a panic in case he had missed Richard leaving. But no, all was fine. The car was still there. He quickly dressed and went down for breakfast. There was no sign of Richard. He was probably taking his morning constitutional around the grounds. The gardener was already hard at work trimming the hedges.

The girls were delighted to see Richard, and Roxy was delighted to see them. She jumped about like a puppy until Ria finally settled her down with a bone that she had bought on her little shopping trip. Richard wanted to take them out for lunch, but Ria didn't want to leave Roxy so soon after arriving at her temporary home, so she made a salad and opened a bottle of wine. They sat in the sunshine to eat.

Mandy was beginning to feel a bit like a gooseberry. Ria and Richard exchanged loving glances, and at one point, Richard held Ria's hand under the table. Ria had not said much, but their relationship was becoming obvious.

'So, my dear beautiful ladies, what did you want to talk to me about?'

'Well,' said Mandy, 'if we change our identities and you buy the beach house, then we pay you for it when our houses are sold, whose name will be on the deeds?'

'Good point,' said Richard. 'Well, if you have your names on it, even with new identities, it would defeat the object.'

'How so?' asked Ria.

'As I understand it,' Richard continued, 'if you change your name by deed poll, your previous identities are still on the record. Look, what I suggest is that the house stays in my name, Richard Smythe, and one of you could register yourself as Mrs Smythe,' he smiled at Ria, 'and the other could be my sister. All would be Smythe.'

'Well you certainly seem to have worked it all out,' said Mandy.

'And what about Matilda?' asked Ria.

'I think Matilda Smythe has a nice ring to it.' He beamed.

'But whose child is she?' Ria persisted.

'She's the granddaughter of the Smythes.'

'So where are her parents?' asked Mandy.

'They sadly died in a car crash just after she was born,' said Richard.

'And is that what we tell Matilda?' asked Ria.

'There's plenty of time to worry about that,' Richard continued. 'Let's not get too far ahead of ourselves.'

But Mandy was worried. 'If we give you the money for the beach house, but you still own it, what happens if we want to sell, or God forbid, you die?'

'If you want to sell it, that's what we do.' Richard was getting a bit miffed. He thought he was doing them a favour and now he felt that he was on the defensive. 'If I die the house will come to you in my will.'

The atmosphere had become a bit tense.

They were all quiet while they finished eating.

'Richard,' ventured Ria, 'as the beach house is being paid for in cash, and is currently empty, the sale should go through quickly, right?'

'Yes, I see no reason why not.'

'And if it does, would you have any objection to us moving in before our house sales complete?'

'Ooh, I'm not sure if I can trust you!' Richard teased.

'Yes, of course you could. But I'm hoping you won't leave France too soon.'

Richard's phone rang.

It was Charles. 'Are you OK?' he asked, 'Only I couldn't find you anywhere, and your car is still on the drive.'

Richard was beginning to get irritated with the man. 'Yes, as I said, I'm visiting friends today, Charles.'

'But your car...'

'I got a lift. I'll see you later.' And with that he hung up.

The girls stared at him.

Ria was first to speak. 'Did you say Charles?'

'Yes, he's my house guest, but he's beginning to get on my nerves. Why?'

'I suppose there are a lot of Englishmen called Charles travelling around France, but one of them is my son, so I hope it's not him!'

'How did you find him?' asked Mandy.

'I didn't. Pierre did. He brought him over in his catamaran.'

'What does he look like?' asked Ria.

Once again, Richard was wrong-footed. He wasn't the most observant man.

'Oh, I don't know. About 50-something, fair hair. Doesn't like dogs.'

Surely he hadn't been harbouring Ria's son, the one that had told her he wanted to take the baby and somehow get rid of it to save his own reputation and marriage?

He suddenly remembered something.

'He went to Pierre's place when he first arrived. He would have been in the same house as Matilda!'

Both women looked alarmed. 'It's OK, it's OK,' he assured them. 'He would have had no way of knowing who she was. And we know Matilda is still fine with Pierre and Giselle.'

'Dear God, where are my blood pressure pills?' said Ria.

Richard drove back home feeling that he had failed. He hadn't twigged that Charles could be the Charles that Ria had talked about. Why hadn't he even thought of that? He surely was getting old. And the girls seemed reluctant to trust him about the beach house. Or maybe they were just being careful. Understandable really.

Perhaps he had gone too far with his talk of Mrs Smythe. It was his fantasy that he would marry Ria and move to the beach house, not hers. He had become nervous about Matilda and stopped to call Pierre, who explained that they had told their visitor that the child was theirs and he had accepted that without question. But Pierre was shocked to know the man's identity, if indeed it was Ria's son.

The officers in the much-depleted incident room in London had discovered that Charles arrived from

Canada via Heathrow some weeks ago. From there he had hired a car. They tracked this by ANPR and saw that he had made several visits to the boatyard. But that was where the trail stopped. They sent local officers to the boatyard, but the hire car was not in the car park. Then a sharp-eyed PC noticed it in a nearby layby.

Sgt Gill was still very much on the case, but he had been called back to London once the trail had gone cold in Normandy. He rang the local police station to the boatyard. What did they know about the place?

They told him that a body had been fished out of the harbour. It was a journalist who had had one too many and fallen in, banging his head. He had fallen in a few days before and been rescued.

'Any CCTV or witnesses?' asked the sergeant.

'No, sir,' said the PC. 'There are cameras, but they had no tapes in them. The coroner said it was death by misadventure.'

'Anything else?'

'Not to my knowledge, sir.'

'Can you make some enquiries at the boatyard? We're looking for a guy called Charles Radcliffe. You guys found his hire car near the boatyard. I'll send you his details.'

'I'm sure that can be arranged, sir. I'll talk to my guv'nor.'

***

Charles was getting impatient and angry. He had wasted quite enough time trying to get a lead from this old git. He paced about, wondering if his mother and the baby were within walking distance of the Mill House. How else did Richard get to visit them when his car was still in the drive? There had certainly been no taxi.

Then he got his answer. The gardener's car pulled into the drive and out stepped Richard! Maybe his own car had broken down.

Richard was feeling a mixture of trepidation and anger. If this was *the* Charles, he needed to get rid of him quickly. Charles had made himself at home in the sitting room when Richard entered. As they glanced at each other, they both knew that the game was up. It was written all over their faces.

'I think you'd better go,' said Richard.

'Don't worry, I'm going. But not before you tell me where my mother and the baby are.'

'I have absolutely no idea what you are talking about, old chap.'

Charles pulled a gun from his pocket. It was a lucky find behind a sofa cushion on Pierre's boat. Maybe he was afraid of pirates. 'Look, don't 'old chap' me. You are going to take me to them,' he said, pointing the gun at Richard.

'That would be difficult, dear boy, as I don't know where they are.'

Charles put his finger on the trigger. 'I have killed once so one more will not make the slightest difference to me,' said Charles.

'Don't be a fool, man. You are worried about losing your marriage and your job, I know all about it. But if you have already killed someone, you've lost them anyway. Why are you so keen to find the baby?'

'Take me to that baby or I will blow your brains out right now.' He cocked the gun. The red mist had descended.

'I can't help you,' said Richard.

The gun went off. The old man fell to the ground.

Charles grabbed Richard's phone and his car keys and went to the car. He found Ria's burner phone number and sent her a text.

Coming to see you, but last time I got a bit lost. Please text me your address so I can put it in my satnav. Love Richard.

Chapter nine

'Sergeant Gill, we've had a call from France to say that the old man's car is on the move,' said a young DC. 'He's heading toward Normandy again. We've got the local gendarmes on it.'

'Great. Keep me posted.'

Ria had not hesitated to send her address to Richard. She was glad he was coming back, and desperate to know what had happened with Charles, and was it her Charles? She started to prepare a meal for him.

Meanwhile, Charles was heading towards them at breakneck speed. Finally, he had found them, no thanks to the old man. It was not long before he saw a police car in the rear-view mirror. He looked at his speedo. Damn, he was going too fast. The car pulled him over.

'Pourquoi êtes-vous si presse, monsieur?' enquired the lone policeman.

'Sorry, don't speak French,' replied Charles.

'You are Monsieur Richard Smythe, yes?'

Well why not, better than being Charles Radcliffe right now. This way he might only get a speeding ticket which he wouldn't have to pay anyway.

'Yes, that's me,' he said.

'I would like you to come to the police station for questioning. Please get in the police car.'

'Questioning about what?' said a flabbergasted Charles.

'The inspector will explain when you get to the station.'

A bit of quick thinking was needed here. He was driving away from a murder scene, in the victim's car, with a gun in his jacket pocket. Once he was at the police station, it surely wouldn't take them long to establish his real identity, and find that he was wanted for another murder and that he was possibly connected to the kidnap of a royal baby. Even if they continued to believe he was Richard Smythe... well, Richard Smythe was obviously in some sort of trouble. Well, he *was* in some kind of trouble. So, it was not a good idea to go with the nice policeman to the police station. It would not end well. So, he took the gun out of his pocket and shot him.

Thank goodness for these endless country roads he thought as he looked around. Not a soul about, and no cars had passed in the last five minutes. He dragged the policeman into his patrol car, and drove the car onto a farm track, behind some hedges. He needed to buy some time.

People would keep getting in his way. This was becoming tedious. Hopefully, his mother would have more sense. He got back in Richard's car and continued his journey.

* * *

Ria was getting dolled up. She was falling in love with Richard. Maybe she was already in love. She started to worry about her roots. Since the grey hairs had appeared, she had died her hair auburn, which was her natural colour. But since she had been away from home, she had not visited a hairdresser, so her roots were growing through grey, well almost white.

So what, said Mandy. Richard knew how old she was.

But Ria wanted to look nice for him. She had made her signature lasagne and was waiting eagerly for him to arrive. Mandy wondered if she should make herself scarce, but dammit, why should she sit in her room alone? She felt as if she was losing her friend.

She was beginning to resent Richard. It was just going to be Mandy, Ria, Matilda and Roxy at the beautiful beach house. And now it looked as though she was just going to be in the way. And it was her idea to go away in the first place! So, she was selling Lavender Cottage just to play gooseberry to 'Mr and Mrs Smythe', and she was going to be the spinster sister!

She had also become besotted with the baby on her doorstep before anyone else knew about her and had wanted a baby since she was a child herself. But no, she had to be Ria's granddaughter. Ria was getting the baby and the man, and already had a son of her own. She, Mandy, had nothing.

As her mood darkened, Mandy saw a car coming up the track. It was Richard's. She would let them get on with it. She would stay in her room. She settled down with a book.

Ria went out to meet the car and got the shock of her life.

Out of the driver's seat stepped her son Charles. Despite everything, she loved him, but was worried that he had seemed a bit threatening when they last spoke.

'Darling, what a surprise. How lovely to see you,' she said, with her stomach churning, and threw her arms open to him.

Charles was surprised to find that he felt an overwhelming love for his mum and hadn't realised how much he had missed her. He was that little boy again, needing that big hug that only mums knew how to do. They embraced for several minutes, while Mandy looked on from her bedroom window in horror. Where was Richard?

Ria led him into the gite. Roxy ran and hid under the table.

'How are you, darling? What are you doing here? Where's Richard?'

'I'm OK, Mother. And come on, you know why I'm here. Have you got the baby?'

'First things first, where's Richard? We had a text to say he was coming.'

Mandy crept downstairs and was listening in.

Charles smiled. 'Richard said, go and surprise your mum. He even lent me his car. He says he'll give you a ring, but he can't make it today.'

Mandy felt alarm bells ringing. Richard knew that they were trying to avoid Charles at all costs, she thought, so why would he send him to us?

Then she heard Charles's tone change.

'Answer me, Mother, where is the baby? Is it here?'

Mandy stepped in from the shadows.

'She's dead,' she said.

Charles looked to Ria in disbelief.

'I'm so sorry,' said Ria, equally shocked but quick on the uptake. 'We were trying to contact you to tell you.'

'What do you mean it's dead?'

'Cot death,' said Mandy. 'It's very sad, but not uncommon.'

'I don't believe you. Where's the body?'

Ria took charge. 'Now listen, Charles, it's over. Stop obsessing. The baby has gone. You need to get yourself back to Canada before you lose your job and your lovely wife. It's been a hard lesson for you, but you're not a teenager anymore. Now let's eat. I have your favourite, lasagne!'

'That would be lovely, Mother. But first I need to get something from the car.' He kissed her forehead, gave Mandy a nod, and left.

The car was still there when the gendarmes arrived minutes later with sirens blaring. But there was no sign of Charles.

***

131

Richard was a little miffed. It's not every day that people take potshots at you, well not since he left the army anyway. He knew as soon as he saw that pistol that an untrained person couldn't hit a barn door with it at five paces, but it made a good bang, and throwing oneself to the floor at that moment was usually enough to make the perpetrator run for the hills. It was a slight gamble, of course, because they might decide to make doubly sure by firing another round or two.

But throwing oneself to the floor when one was no longer young had its consequences. Richard couldn't get up. He had to crawl to something that he could hold on to. His pride would not let him call the gardener, and there was no one else around. Eventually he got to his feet but felt decidedly shaky. He sat on the sofa and noticed a bullet hole in a wooden panel on the wall. Miles out!

The idiot had taken his phone and his car. But Charles didn't know where the girls or Matilda were, so there was no rush to call the police. He needed to rest first and have a dram or two. He actually had a dram or three and fell asleep.

Sgt Gill was following the events from London. He wished he had stayed in France. Now it was all happening without him. Richard Smythe's car had been tracked on the road towards Normandy. A gendarme radioed in to say he was about to pull the car over. Then the radio went quiet and they couldn't contact him. Other officers were sent out to find him. It was only when a farmer called in to say that there was an abandoned police car on his field that they found the officer, unconscious, but alive in the back seat. He had a bang on the head, but no other visible injuries. There was, however, a dead cat on the grass verge opposite.

Surely that old dodderer Richard Smythe had not been responsible for this? But then maybe he had totally lost the plot. His car had been tracked to the vicinity of La Cochere. There was a huge effort to find him. It was not long before the car was tracked to a gite site. Sgt Gill waited for news with bated breath.

Officers knocked on Ria's door.

'Ou est le conducteur de cette voiture?'

Ria looked to Mandy for a translation, but she just shrugged.

'Ou est Richard Smythe?'

They both just shrugged.

'Where is the driver of this car?' said the officer.

Mandy stepped forward, in full acting mode. 'We didn't see who got out of it. They didn't come here. What's the problem?'

The officers pushed past them and searched the gite. Nothing. They didn't notice that the table was set for three. *Great detective work* thought Ria.

They walked away, muttering that these two old dears were no help, so they went to have a word with Mrs Pinny, who was also useless.

Charles had to rest. He had run through the fields for about three miles, and he wasn't in great shape. He sat under a tree in a copse to get his breath. He reached into his pockets and felt secure in the knowledge that he still had his gun and Richard's burner phone. He had a close look at the phone. There were only two numbers on it. Ria's and Pierre's.

Pierre. Maybe he could help him get out of the country. But then again, he might not be too impressed that he had killed his dad. Charles wondered if he knew yet. Hardly anyone actually went inside the Mill House, so maybe his body wouldn't be discovered for days. Was it worth a try? What was the worst that could happen? He'd get an earful, and they would try to trace the burner phone. But he would take the battery out if that happened.

And what if Pierre received the news about his father when he was with Pierre? Well, actually, who was to say it was he who had killed him? Could have been a burglar. He would act shocked.

'Hello, is that Pierre?'

'Yes, Hi Papa.'

Oh shit. He hadn't thought of that. Of course, Richard's name would come up on Pierre's phone. Still, at least he hadn't heard the news yet.

'No, Pierre, it's Charles. Just borrowing your dad's phone as mine is on the blink.'

In fact, he didn't want to use his own burner, just in case. He had used it for some time now. He needed a new one.

A helicopter circled above. Charles crept right under the bushes.

'Pierre, sorry to ask, but I need another favour. Can you get me back to England?'

'When?'

'As soon as possible. I have to get home. My wife's ill.'

'Your wife's in Canada.'

'No, she came over to stay with her sister in Bournemouth,' he lied.

'OK, well, I'll be going across tomorrow.'

'I really need to go today.'

'I'll ask Jack; I think he might be going later.'

'No, don't worry Jack. Tomorrow will be fine.'

'If you can get here by 9am, that will be great.'

It *would* be great if he had a car, and if Pierre was still in the dark about his father. But by then surely the cat would be out of the bag. And even if Charles was not suspected, Pierre would hardly be toddling off to England after hearing such dreadful news.

No, he needed another plan.

The helicopter had moved on. It would soon be dark. He could disappear into the woods until the search was called off. Then he had another idea. If the police hadn't taken Richard's car from outside the gite yet, he could drive it back to the Mill House and get his hire car. He was sure Richard's car was being tracked, but who would be watching in the middle of the night? Especially as they believed that Richard had run from the gite. He was hardly likely to return to it was he?

And if the car had been taken by the police, at least his mother would shelter him for the night. He would wait a little longer until everyone was in bed and start his journey back to the gite.

Mandy and Ria were in a flat spin. What the hell was going on? The police were very keen to find Richard. Was it because he had been harbouring them and Matilda? It must be. And it was odd that he had loaned Charles his car to come and surprise them. He knew they didn't want to see him while he was hunting for Matilda.

Ria tried to phone Richard, but the phone was switched off.

And where had Charles disappeared to? He just went to get something from the car.

The police had told Mrs Pinny that they would send a tow truck to collect Richard's car in the morning.

'Something is very wrong. We need to do something,' said Ria.

'*Your* son. *Your* lover,' said Mandy, a little more sharply than she meant to. 'I mean you need to decide what you think we should do.'

'OK, I think I should take Richard's car back to him. Charles left the keys on the table. Then I could check that everything's OK.'

'And what do I do?' asked Mandy.

'Stay here in case Charles comes back.'

'Oh thanks.'

'Well, I can't be in two places at once.'

The unconscious gendarme was no longer unconscious. He was sitting up in his hospital bed with a bandage around his head, enjoying all the attention. He was a hero. He had tackled a fugitive. Sgt Gill had been on the first plane over and was now by his bedside. Luckily, the gendarme had spent some time in the UK and had good English.

'Tell me exactly what happened,' said Sgt Gill.

'Well,' said the gendarme in a dramatic manner, as nothing remotely exciting had ever happened to him before. 'I had a radio call to look out for Monsieur Smythe's car. And a few minutes later it was right there in front of me, so I decided to stop it.'

'On your own? Didn't you call for backup?'

'No. I called in to say I was going to stop the car.'

'OK, carry on.'

'The car pulled over, and a man got out. I asked him if he was Monsieur Smythe, and he said yes. He was English, as I expected. Didn't seem to speak much French.'

'And?' Sgt Gill was getting impatient.

'I asked him to come with me to the police station.'

'And then?'

'He took out a gun and pointed it at me.'

'A gun!?'

'Yes. Great big thing it was. Then he fired it.'

'At you?'

'I think so, sir, but I fainted, and that's when I must have hit my head on the kerb. The next thing I knew I was in here.'

'But you did not receive any gunshot wounds?'

'No, sir. But I could have been killed!'

'Yes, indeed,' said the sergeant.

'Can you describe the man?'

Mr Bean would probably have given a more accurate description than this hapless gendarme.

'Well, he was a big fella. Really mean face.'

'What sort of age?'

'Um well, it's hard to say.'

'Guess.'

'Well, he wasn't young but was very fit for his age.'

'Mr Smythe is a pensioner in his seventies.'

The gendarme looked shocked.

'Well, he looked bloody good then.'

Richard was a little surprised to read in the local paper the next day that he had tried to shoot a gendarme. His memory wasn't good, but he was pretty sure that wasn't him.

He had lost a day to drink and was now recalling his brush with death at Charles's hand, and thinking about reporting the incident and his stolen car and phone to the police. But he was reluctant to engage with the police about anything at the moment. What good would it do? He had other things on his mind.

He wanted to call Ria, but her number was on his burner phone which had gone. In fact, he realised he didn't have a phone he could use at all. He would go to see her. Charles's hire car was still in the drive. But where were the keys? No doubt still with Charles. But he hadn't been in the army for nothing, and soon got it started with the help of a screwdriver and a few expletives.

Ria and Richard passed each other on the Normandy road going in opposite directions, neither noticing the other. Soon Richard arrived at the gîte. It was in darkness. He knocked, and a sleepy Mandy put her head out of the bedroom window. Her heart was pounding. She expected to see Charles on the doorstep.

'Oh, Richard. Just a minute.' She threw on a T-shirt and jeans and made her way to the door.

'Where's Ria?' he asked.

'She's gone to your place!' said Mandy, thinking what a bloody mess everything was becoming.

'What? Why?'

'Because Charles turned up here in your car, and then the police arrived looking for you!'

'Charles came here? But how did he know where to find you?'

Mandy explained about the text request from Richard's phone, asking for the address for the satnav.

Richard sat heavily at the kitchen table. 'That man is dangerous. Where is he now?'

Mandy sat wearily opposite him. 'No idea. He said he was going to the car, your car, to get something. Then he disappeared just before the police arrived.'

'So now what?' Mandy asked.

'When Ria gets to my place, she will realise that I'm not there and come back here, so there's no point in me rushing back home. We would no doubt miss each other again. OK with you if I hang on here? I know it's late.'

'Of course, I'm glad you're here. I was worried about Charles coming back.'

Chapter ten

Charles had stealthily made his way back through the woodland and fields to the gite site. Richard's car had gone, but he was shocked to see his hire car parked outside the gite. His mind was doing somersaults. How did that get there? But who cares, he thought, it was a car. He took the keys from his jacket pocket, gingerly opened the door, climbed in and drove away.

Richard, Mandy and Roxy heard the car start up and flew to the door. Too late.

'Shouldn't we report it?' asked a flummoxed Mandy.

'We couldn't if we wanted to,' said Richard. 'I have no idea of the registration number. It's a hire car. It will turn up. They will sort it out. My guess is it was Charles.'

Mandy put the kettle on. It's what you do when there is any sort of a crisis.

Richard sat back down. He realised that he hadn't really noticed Mandy before. He had been too busy looking at Ria. Even with her dyed blonde hair, tousled from sleep, and her blue T-shirt revealing that she was not wearing a bra, she looked pretty good for her age.

'Did you never marry?' he asked gently, noticing her naked ring finger.

Mandy brought two cups of tea to the table. She hated this question. It seemed to imply that there must be something wrong with her. Married people didn't have to explain why they were married, so why should single people have to explain?

But he was just making conversation. She didn't want to seem rude.

'No. I guess I was too busy globetrotting.' It was her stock answer.

'Oh, how interesting,' said a surprised Richard, somehow always assuming that ladies of a certain age had been housewives and WI jam makers.

He was fascinated as she recalled her career, working with stars of the stage and screen. Her eyes started to sparkle, and she seemed to come alive when thinking about it. This lady had much more about her than he had thought. Truth was he hadn't really thought about her at all until now.

They were both enjoying the conversation when Ria burst in. 'Oh, there you are! I've been to the Mill House looking for you!'

'I know,' said Richard kindly. 'Sit down, have a cup of tea. I came here looking for you.'

'Thank goodness you're alright. I was so worried when the police came looking for you. Should I hide your car?'

That was a good idea, so Richard moved it a good 15 minutes' walk away, behind an old derelict barn. Then he returned, and he brought the girls up to date with his shocking news, and they did the same.

Charles was on his way to Cherbourg, to Pierre's place. Fingers crossed he hadn't heard about the demise of his father yet. On the two-hour drive, he had time to think about his dear wife, Anna. He had emailed her from libraries here and there to tell her that his work in Europe was ongoing, and he was missing her terribly. He worried that the emails might be intercepted, but there was nothing incriminating in them.

She had replied that all was well at home and she couldn't wait to see him again.

He truly loved Anna and would do anything for her.

He remembered when he first saw her. She had walked into a lecture hall at uni wearing a white silk blouse and blue jeans. Her long brown hair was glossy, and she had a beautiful heart-shaped face. He smiled at the memory.

He had been too shy to approach her then, but two weeks later he saw her sitting in the canteen alone and sat at the same table. Everything about her was adorable, and as soon as they left uni two years later, they married.

He was offered a job in Canada, and so off they went, and loved it. There was no doubt it had been a blissfully happy marriage. It was true to say that he had strayed once or twice, but they were meaningless drunken one-nighters, of which he was not proud.

His mood darkened as he thought of the future. He just wanted to be with Anna and live happily ever after. But now he had drowned a journalist, killed the old man and even shot a policeman. And that was all without fathering an illegitimate royal baby and having it kidnapped. Dear God, every policeman in the world must be looking out for him.

Hopefully, Pierre would get him back across the Channel, but then what? He would surely be stopped if he tried to fly to Canada, or anywhere else for that matter. But once in England maybe he could lie low until he was forgotten about. Maybe he could get Anna to come to England? Shouldn't be a problem, unless they were watching her. He would have to take that chance. They would have to be careful.

Sgt Gill was up at the crack of dawn to follow the progress of the search for Richard Smythe. He might have evaded the police last night, but he was an old man and couldn't have gone far. The areas around the gite site were thoroughly searched. Nothing. But his car had gone missing. Why didn't the idiots take it last night instead of giving Smythe the opportunity to make a getaway? Pointless search. He could be anywhere by now.

In fact, Richard and the girls had decided that they didn't want to wait around for the police to return and had left in Richard's car in the early hours. Richard didn't dare drive for too long in a car that he suspected was being tracked, so he decided, with the girls' approval, to leave the car at a railway station, and then walk half a mile to a car hire place in an attempt to throw the police off their trails.

This worked well, and soon they were all travelling in a very small, but inconspicuous hire car. The only plan was to get away from La Cochere. Beyond that, they would have to stop and have a brainstorming session.

Giselle carefully lifted Matilda out of her cot. She was such a good baby. She was awake and gurgling happily. Giselle felt a rush of love for this poor tot, who was being pushed from pillar to post. She sat on her bed and cuddled Matilda as she gave her her morning bottle.

Pierre had said that Charles would be coming at 9am to have breakfast before going to England. She liked Charles. Best of all she liked pretending that Matilda was hers. It felt good. Like a real family again. Giselle, Pierre and Matilda. Perhaps she wouldn't keep the name Matilda. Leonie was a nice name. Yes, Leonie would suit her. As she hugged the infant tightly, she glanced at a photograph on the dresser of her younger self holding a little girl. A tear dripped onto Matilda's blonde hair.

Richard pulled into a roadside cafe in the middle of nowhere, and the trio and Roxy settled at an outside table. When coffee and croissants had been ordered, and a bowl of water for Roxy, the geriatric fugitives set about planning what to do next.

Ria was first to speak. 'We can't expect Giselle to look after Matilda for much longer. It's not fair.'

'She's happy enough,' said Richard. 'Loving every minute of it, I'm sure.'

Mandy turned to Ria. 'What would happen to us if the police caught us?'

'Well, let's see. Charges could include kidnapping a child, not sure if there is a special category for a royal baby.'

'Definitely treason,' quipped Richard. 'Off with your heads!'

Ria continued, after giving Richard a look that said, not funny. 'Maybe they could throw in a conspiracy charge, or even harbouring a fugitive... Well, two actually, you Richard, and Charles.'

'Now stop this!' said Richard. 'My dear girls, none of this will happen, so stop torturing yourselves. What would happen if an army sat around thinking about being defeated? Life is like any other war. Lots of little battles and some big ones. You take them on one at a time and win them.'

'OK, Colonel,' said Mandy. 'How do we win this one?'

'I have an idea,' he said, passing a bit of croissant under the table to Roxy.

'If you agree, I will ring the agent and find out if we can rent the beach house until the sale goes through. Then we can pick up Matilda and go straight there.'

'Just one problem,' said Mandy. 'The idea of buying it in your name was fine before you started shooting gendarmes.'

Richard smiled. 'You know very well, dear girl, that that was not me.'

'We know that, but the police do not.'

'They will in time. The truth will out.'

'So, we continue as the Smythe family?' asked Ria.

'Maybe we'll change it to Smith,' said Richard. 'If the agent questions the change, I'll say we pronounce it Smythe. But Smith will then be on the legal documents.'

'Might that not cause problems further down the line...' started Ria.

'Probably, but we'll all be long dead by then. I'll get more coffee. You need to think of changing your Christian names. I'm going to be Rupert. This is such fun!'

Charles arrived at Pierre's house on the dot of 9am, after killing some time looking around the harbour.

It was such a beautiful sight on a sunny day. But he still didn't know if Pierre had heard the tragic news about his father, so his nerves were jangling.

Pierre opened the door. 'Come on in. We have time for breakfast before we go.' Charles was hugely relieved but wanted to get going as soon as possible, in case the news arrived at any minute and the trip was cancelled.

Giselle held Matilda in one arm, while she served breakfast of buttered baguettes with jam or honey, and a pot of coffee in the other. The men ate hungrily.

'I think it's grown, the baby, I think it's grown since I was last here,' said Charles awkwardly.

Pierre translated. Giselle looked pleased 'Au, ma petite fille se porte a merveille.'

'She's doing fine,' said Pierre with a mouthful of bread. 'Allez allons-y, come on, let's get going.'

'Oh, yes, Pierre,' said Charles. 'Many thanks for hiring the car for me. Is it OK to leave it here?'

'Oui. I'll get it back to them no problem. When they tell me how much it is, I'll get them to call you for the payment.'

'Great, thanks,' said Charles.

They walked in the morning sunshine to the harbour, and along the jetty towards the catamaran, which was larger than most of the other crafts.

Suddenly Pierre looked alarmed. 'There are flics looking at my cat.'

'What?' Charles's heart started racing.

'Flics, police! Looking at my catamaran.'

Charles tried to appear cool. 'They're probably admiring it,' he said.

Were they looking for him? Had they come to tell Pierre about his father? Was Pierre up to no good?

Pierre turned to Charles and took him by the arm. 'Turn back. Just keep walking,' he said. Charles remembered the gun that he had purloined from the catamaran, and that was still in his pocket. He was going to throw it away after the murders, but he felt safer having it with him. He did as Pierre said, and as soon as they rounded a corner, they went into a cafe. They could see the cat out of the window. They watched as the two officers looked around the boat, made a few notes, and then spoke to the people working on the yacht that was alongside.

They waited until the police left and then returned to the boat. They were now both in a hurry to get away.

'You left the door unlocked,' said Charles as he went on board. 'You did that last time.'

'I know,' answered Pierre. 'Just habit. None of us used to lock up. It was never necessary, but these days…'

'You get unsavoury stowaways like me creeping about.'

Pierre laughed.

Charles went to the window to check that the police had not reappeared and noticed that Pierre was looking behind the cushions on the sofa. When Pierre went to the window, Charles took the gun from his pocket, wiped it, and placed it back behind the cushion where he found it.

Tindra and William had started to make wedding plans. They had to. She was pregnant again. Her parents were mortified. There would be more scandal as the dates became known. Tindra said they were being old fashioned. Lots of people had babies nowadays without being married.

'Not in our bloody family,' said her father.

'Didn't you have sex with Mother before you were married?' asked a wide-eyed Tindra.

Her father's face was always florid, but now it was positively puce.

Her mother stepped in. 'Darling, you are a grown-up now. That is not the sort of question you ask people.'

'I'll take that as a yes then,' Tindra said. 'Bloody hypocrites.'

And with that, she flounced off to her room.

William was still none too sure about the parentage of the missing princess, but he wanted to believe she was his, and was certain the new baby was. He loved Tindra, and although the couple still wanted to find the child, they had stopped pressuring the authorities after the special services began to suspect that Tindra had something to do with her disappearance. They now had a lot to think about with the new baby and the wedding, so the missing child had taken a back seat. Tindra knew that she was in good hands, that's what mattered.

Richard, Ria and Mandy had moved on to another small town and had booked into a campsite that hired out caravans. Easier, and probably safer than finding a hotel that would take dogs.

They were enjoying each other's company, and as both women now fancied Richard, and he fancied both of them, it was an interesting threesome. Not that it was a threesome in any modern sense. They were all far too correct for that.

They felt safe at this place. It was off the beaten track and nobody bothered them.

Mandy was making ham sandwiches. 'I think I'll call myself Lucy,' she said. 'I've always liked that name. Who are you going to be, Ria?'

The mood was light and playful. 'Maybe I'll be Arabella or something else upmarket like Octavia,' she said as she posed in front of the small mirror. 'What do you think, Rupert?'

Richard was amused and loved the banter that he had missed so much since leaving the army, although of course, squaddie banter was a little different!

'Now let me see, I think Maria suits you, and it's got Ria in it.'

'Ooh, how clever!' said Mandy. 'That's perfect.'

Ria looked at her. Was she flirting with him? She'd noticed in the last few days that Mandy was laughing more at his jokes, and touching his arm, or picking fluff off his jacket.

'Yes, Maria is fine,' she said.

After lunch, Richard rang the estate agent on the new phone he had bought on the way to the campsite. He asked about renting the beach house and had a call back soon after. The vendor had said that although his solicitor would warn against it, he was happy to rent it. He wanted to leave all the furniture and fittings as he was now living abroad. Was that OK?

The girls remembered the furniture being beautiful. It was the perfect solution. So now Mr Rupert Smith, Mrs Maria Smith and Lucy Smith could get their granddaughter Matilda Smith and move into a glorious seaside villa.

'What shall we call Roxy?' asked Mandy, as Roxy chewed at Richard's shoelaces.

'A pain in the arse!' he laughed.

'What's going on over there?' said the inspector in the incident room to Sgt Gill.

'We have found Richard Smythe's car at a railway station,' he said. 'Trains go all over the place from there, but we're checking if anyone has seen him.'

'For crying out loud,' puffed the inspector, 'we can't have a demented pensioner running around with a gun.'

'France is a big place, sir. And really, this is no longer our concern. The gendarmes are taking care of it.'

'What about the other chap, Charles Radcliffe?'

'Nothing new, sir, I'm afraid.'

'And the two women with the baby?'

'We lost the women after Normandy, sir, but they didn't have the baby with them then. We have no leads on the baby.'

When Pierre was at the helm of the catamaran, Charles sat down to have a think. He had spent so long obsessing about the baby being a danger to him that he had not really given a thought to this child as a human being. His child. His baby. His daughter.

And now she was dead. At first, he had, God forgive him, felt relief. The threat was over. But now he felt a sadness deep inside him. His one and only offspring and all he had wanted to do was get rid of it.

With a sudden pang, he thought of Tindra. She parted with her baby because she had no choice, but she must have been heartbroken. She needed to know about the child's death, or she would pine forever.

He still had her number in his wallet. He would call her. It would not be easy, but she was entitled to know. He dialled her number.

'Hej. Tindra taler.'

'Tindra, it's me Charles. From Canada.'

'Charles! It is not a good idea for you to call me, but I am glad you did. Your friend moved my baby. Where is she?'

'I'm so sorry, Tindra, but I have bad news. I'm afraid the baby died. Cot death. She was well cared for, but it is not uncommon.'

'No, you are lying to me!'

'I'm afraid not, Tindra. It's not the sort of thing you lie about. I am also very upset. I went to England to make sure she was OK, but I was too late.'

There was a long pause.

Tindra voice was breaking, 'We will have to organise a burial.'

'It's all been taken care of,' said Charles, not wanting to get involved any further in this conversation. 'I just thought you should know. I won't call again. Please do not allow my name to be mentioned in connection with this.'

'The police were asking after you.'

'What did you tell them?'

'Nothing. Just that you were a friend that I knew in Canada.'

'Nothing else?'

'No.'

'OK, thanks. I think it best we don't contact each other again.'

'OK. Thanks for telling me, Charles.'

Word of the baby's death soon filtered through to the police and the press. It had a certain amount of credence as the news had come from the man the police believed to be the father, and the one behind the kidnapping. But they were sceptical.

Newspapers screamed 'Royal Princess Dead?' or 'Kidnapped royal baby in cot death mystery'.

Grannies cried into their knitting, and flowers and toys were tied to the gates of Tindra's country home. There was a lot of grieving for the infant that nobody knew.

Sgt Gill was inclined to believe it. There had been no ransom demand for the baby, and it would account for the fact that the two women were believed to have the baby with them at the Mill House, and then went without her to Normandy. A cot death was possible, but could there have been foul play?

They would continue their search for the two women, and for Charles, who must surely know the answers. If anything, since the interest of the public had been piqued again, the investigation had to be ramped up.

Chapter eleven

Ria, Mandy and Richard decided that they needed Pierre to get them to England. It would be the only safe way to avoid the authorities. They wanted to go as soon as possible, within the next few days. Richard would need to make a brief visit home to get Mufti, who was being cared for by Phillipe the gardener, and a few belongings.

They were all quite excited at the thought of their new lives by the sea, with their very own beach.

Pierre received the call from his dad as he was sailing back to England with Charles. They were both laughing and chatting at the helm. Pierre ducked inside to take the call in private.

'Papa, how are you?'

'I am very well, son, and you?'

'Yes, Papa, thank you. I am fine.'

'I would like to go to England with my two lady friends within the next few days. Is there any chance that you could take us?' he asked.

'Of course, Papa. I am crossing to England right now with Charles, but I will be back tomorrow, so I could do it the next day if that suits you.'

'You have Charles with you?'

'Yes, is anything wrong?'

'That absolute arse took a potshot at me. Useless aim, missed by a mile, but left me for dead and stole my car and my phone.'

'What! Why didn't you tell me?'

'I didn't have a phone for a while, and then things got a bit hectic.'

'Are you alright?'

'Fit as a flea, dear boy, don't you worry about me.'

'Papa, I will call you later.'

Charles was lounging on the deck. Pierre reached behind the sofa cushions for the gun. He had never felt so angry. A man that he had befriended and helped had attacked an old defenceless man and left him for dead. He noted that the gun was loaded, put it in his pocket and walked slowly up onto the deck.

Charles saw Pierre's face and thought he must have been told of his father's death. He must keep his wits about him.

'I have just been speaking to my papa,' said Pierre.

'Your papa?' said Charles stupidly. How could he have done, he's dead.

'Yes, Charles, my papa.'

Charles started to feel faint, seriously faint. The man was dead. He had shot him. He had seen him lying on the floor. What was Pierre trying to do? He tried to get up, but staggered.

'You thought you had killed my father and then you came and ate breakfast with me and asked for my help.' Pierre was quivering with rage. He took the gun out of his pocket and pointed it at Charles. 'You are a dead man, tu es un tas de merde!'

Giselle wanted to have a special talk with Pierre when he returned from England. So, she prepared his favourite supper of boeuf bourguignon, with frangipane tart to follow. But he was late. It happened sometimes, that's why she made food that wouldn't spoil. But when he was later than usual, she put Matilda in her buggy.

'Let's go to the harbour and see what's keeping Daddy,' she said. 'We might have to drag him out of the bar!'

But the cat was not in the harbour, so Pierre would not be in the bar.

She tried again to call him, but he was not answering.

He was probably sleeping off a drinking session at the boatyard.

Richard was kicking himself for telling Pierre about how Charles had attacked him. He had placed his son in danger if he repeated it to Charles. This was a dangerous man. He tried to phone Pierre. No answer.

The girls noticed that Richard was quiet.

'You OK?' asked Ria. 'Yes, fine, just thinking. Pierre was going to ring me back to confirm our trip, but hasn't, so I think I'll take a drive up there to see him.'

'It's a long drive. Will you stay over?'

'Maybe. Don't wait up.' And with that, he was gone.

When he arrived at Pierre's house, Giselle was cuddling Matilda and looking worried. Pierre was not home.

Giselle reheated the boeuf bourguignon for them both, leaving enough for Pierre. They both tried to reassure the other that Pierre was fine. He had probably stayed over in England and not charged his phone. It had been known. Richard did not tell her what had happened between him and Charles. Instead, he made a fuss of Matilda who was smiling and gurgling at him.

'She is a beautiful baby,' he said. 'You are doing a great job with her.'

'Thank you, Richard. I am in love with her. I wanted to ask Pierre tonight if we could adopt her. She doesn't have parents, does she? Just an old granny. We're still quite young and could give her a good home. She's very happy here.'

Richard was nonplussed. He didn't expect this.

'Giselle,' he said kindly, 'her grandmother loves her very much, and is looking forward to bringing her up, and she really isn't that old, and very fit for her age.'

This seemed to go over Giselle's head. 'Leonie is a nice name, isn't it? That's what I call her.' And turning to Matilda, she said, 'What has happened to that naughty daddy of yours, eh?'

Richard needed to tell her that he would be taking the baby away from her the day after tomorrow, but he would have to wait until she had news of Pierre. It was ironic, he thought, that this baby that nobody wanted was now in high demand.

Pierre was looking into the terrified eyes of Charles. That is what his father must have felt like when Charles pointed a gun at him. He wanted so much to pull the trigger. Nobody would know. He could toss the body and the gun into the sea, and that would be that. The bastard deserved it. But Pierre knew that he could never pull the trigger. He was angry enough, but he could never kill another human being in cold blood. He only had the gun in the hope that it would save his life if he was attacked, or to frighten off an intruder.

Charles was lightheaded. The absolute shock of hearing that Richard was alive, and therefore able to testify against him, and then having a gun pointed at him seemed to make the blood drain from his head. He tried to stand but was unsteady, and as the boat lurched, he fell heavily against Pierre, knocking the gun from his hands. As they both scrabbled for the gun, it slipped off the deck into the sea.

They stared at each other, each waiting for the other to throw the first punch, but neither were fighters and at 50-something, it would be ridiculous.

Pierre went to the galley and poured himself a large drink. He would need to navigate into the harbour soon. Charles went into the spare bedroom to lie down.

Half an hour after docking, Pierre was asleep in a drunken stupor, and Charles had disappeared into the night.

Ria and Mandy were in good form. Although it was with some trepidation that they were looking forward to returning to England, and especially the beach house.

But Ria had something she needed to say, and there would need to be some ground rules. They were not clear if Richard was coming to live with them or just for a visit to see the place and settle them in. What about the Mill House?

Ria had plans for her future with Richard, especially after their night at the Normandy Hotel. Unfortunately, she was starting to notice that Mandy and Richard were flirting with each other.

Mandy was making the tea, while Ria was buttering toast for breakfast.

'Mandy,' Ria began, 'we've known each other for a long time, haven't we?'

'We certainly have.'

'So, you won't mind if I am straight with you?'

'Oh dear, that sounds ominous,' said Mandy as she placed two mugs of tea on the table.

'It's about Richard.'

'Oh, you mean Rupert Smith.'

Ria smiled. She wanted to keep this light if possible. 'You remember how we both fancied the same boy at school?'

'Yes, and you ended up having his baby.'

'Yes, well, moving on. I started having a relationship with Richard, but, well, I've noticed that you two have been flirting lately.'

Mandy put a dollop of jam on her toast. 'And your point is?'

'My point is that I'm hoping to have a future with Richard.'

'We'll both be having a future with Richard if he comes to live with us.'

'Mandy, stop being obtuse. You know what I mean.'

'You're telling me to back off. What if I like him too?'

'Do you?'

'Yes, as it happens. And I think he likes me.'

'Mandy, you do know that I slept with him at the hotel?'

'Yes. And you do know that I slept with him at the gite?'

'No you didn't.'

'No, I didn't,' laughed Mandy as she peeled the top off a yoghurt pot. 'Oh, come on, Ria. I have a laugh and a joke with him, and yes, I do like him, although I had my doubts at first. At the end of the day, he will decide which of us he likes the best. There is nothing we can do about it.'

At that moment, the lothario in question stepped into the caravan. There was an awkward silence. Had he heard any of their conversation?

'Right,' he said, oblivious to any atmosphere, 'we're all set to go tomorrow. Pierre is back, and sleeping off a hangover, but he'll be fine by tomorrow.'

'Great,' said Ria. 'We're looking forward to it.'

But Richard had not found the right moment or plucked up the courage to tell Giselle that they were taking the baby so soon, and he was concerned about her state of mind. She had started to believe that the child was hers. When Phillipe rushed Matilda to her on the day that the police were descending at the Mill House, he didn't have time to think about the effect it might have on a mother who had lost her own little girl years ago.

It even occurred to him while he was making the journey back to the caravan that maybe it would not be such a bad idea for Giselle and Pierre to adopt the child. As Giselle said, they were younger, if not actually young. Matilda would certainly be better off without contact with her father, Charles. But dear Ria so wanted her grandbaby, and that was a blood tie after all.

Of course, it was not his decision to make. It was really none of his business. So, he would keep his mouth shut.

Charles had caught the train to London, without a plan. He had nowhere to stay in England and couldn't risk getting a flight to Canada. He needed to reassess his situation. The search for the baby was over, although the police would still want to talk to him about the kidnapping. There was apparently CCTV of him drowning Tom Delaney. He hadn't actually murdered Richard, but no doubt Richard had reported his attempt to the police and could now testify. The policeman he shot was so far being blamed on Richard as he was in his car. And all this because he had an affair with the princess. Bloody women.

The only thing he could think of was to go to his mother's house in Hertfordshire. Ria was in France, so he would have the place to himself for a while. He would get in somehow.

Ria had been careful to avoid telling him about her move to the beach house. As she would have Matilda with her, it would only be asking for trouble.

A short train ride and a taxi into the countryside took him to the pretty sleepy village that was familiar to him. The old house was easy to get into with an insecure window into the utility room. He wandered around. It was homely, with a country kitchen and a brick fireplace. Mother had made a comfortable home for herself. But how lonely it must be for her, in the middle of nowhere on her own. So different from his hectic life in Canada. He was emotionally and physically exhausted and fell asleep on the sofa.

Pierre finally emerged from his hangover looking dreadful. Giselle, still clutching Matilda, made him more coffee and they both sat at the kitchen table.

He gave her a weak smile. 'Don't you ever put that kid down?'

'Leonie loves a cuddle, don't you, sweetheart?' she said as she kissed the baby's head.

'Giselle, I have told you, the baby is called Matilda. You can't just rename her.'

'Leonie suits her better.'

Pierre sighed. He knew the baby would be leaving the next day.

'You have become too attached,' he said.

'How can I be too attached to my little girl.' It was a rhetorical question.

'Giselle, listen to me. She is not your little girl. She is going home tomorrow with her grandma.'

'No! Not tomorrow. She isn't ready. She wants to be here with her mummy, don't you, darling.'

Pierre was worried. He knew what was happening here. Giselle was reverting to the mum she had been 16 years ago when their little girl had been lost to meningitis at the age of three. She had never been able to accept the loss and had had a breakdown. She had recovered well over the years but had not wanted to try for another baby.

Pierre had had his doubts about looking after Matilda, but Giselle seemed keen, and it was all so sudden that he hardly had a chance to refuse. It had affected him too, having another baby about the house, but he was hardly ever at home, so he had other distractions. He was a good man, but not the most patient.

'Giselle, enough of this. You don't want to make yourself ill again. Our daughter has gone, many years ago, and is not coming back. This baby does not belong to you, and you can't keep her. Papa is coming for her tomorrow. You need to get her things together.'

Charles awoke to the sound of a key in the lock. He leapt to his feet and looked out the window. A removal van was outside, and three people were walking down the path. A man suddenly appeared in front of him.

'What the fuck are you doing in my house!' said Charles.

'I think you will find this is *my* house!' came the angry reply.

'This is my mother's house. She's been here for years.'

A little crowd of family and removal men had gathered behind the intruder.

A woman spoke, 'Is her name Ria Radcliffe? She sold the house to us.'

She pointed to the sold board in the garden that Charles had failed to notice.

'She would have told me,' said Charles. 'Well, I'm not going anywhere.'

The little group looked from one to the other.

'Look, mate, this house belongs to us now. The sale completed this morning. We are moving in.' He signalled for the removal men to continue with their job.

'If you don't go, I will have to call the police.'

Not the police again. He couldn't risk that. Why did people keep getting in his way!

The wedding of Princess Tindra and William had been announced. It would take place at the Royal Chapel at the Royal Palace of Stockholm on June 19th, a favoured day for royal weddings. There was speculation about the haste of the preparations, especially so soon after the loss of her baby, but people were generally happy for her, except the ever miserable and spiteful trolls.

Her pregnancy was progressing well, except for the morning sickness, but she was not yet showing. Her wedding dress was being designed to disguise her bump.

Her brother Hugo was a little jealous of her devotion to William, having been Tindra's best friend and confidante for so many years. But he was looking forward to being an uncle, for real this time.

Tindra's parents wanted to crawl under a bush in shame. They had old fashioned values and had never wanted to be part of the permissive new world. They had started their family late in life and were shocked by the views of the younger generation.

They were well aware that their peers would be gossiping behind closed doors and in aristocratic circles about them. Their daughter, a royal princess (just about), has one child secretly to an unknown father, and it is smuggled away and then dies. And then, before you know it, she is pregnant again to a new man that she is yet to marry. The shame!

However, the show must go on. Arrangements must be made, and hopefully her pregnancy will not be apparent at the wedding. Then, when the baby arrives, they will have to say it was premature. For God's sake, she was making liars of them!

Richard had been back to the Mill House for his dog and a few belongings. Now they were all ready to leave and start a new adventure back in the UK. There had been no sign of the police, so they had relaxed a bit and were all hoping that they would now be getting away from any chance of detection. They could hardly move in their tiny hire car as they made their way to Pierre's place.

When they arrived, Pierre invited them in for coffee and croissants. He even invited Roxy and Mufti in, which was not one of his better ideas as Roxy pinched a croissant, and then the dogs fought over it. Ria and Richard put them both back in the car. There was a lot of small talk around the table as Richard and Pierre did not want to discuss the Charles incidents in front of the women, although they were both impatient to.

There was no sign of Giselle.

'She's upstairs getting the baby's bits together,' said Pierre.

'I'll go and help her,' Ria volunteered.

'Don't worry, she'll be down in a minute,' said Pierre. 'Have another coffee.'

There was a long pause.

'Come on, darling,' shouted Pierre. 'People are waiting, and we need to catch the tide.'

He turned to his guests. 'Giselle is finding it hard to part with the baby. She is probably having a last cuddle and saying her goodbyes.'

'She can always come and visit her. You'd both be most welcome anytime,' said Mandy.

Richard and Ria nodded in agreement.

There was not a sound from upstairs.

Finally, Pierre got to his feet, obviously embarrassed and angry, and marched off upstairs. He came back down slowly, sat at the table and put his head in his hands.

'What is it, son?' asked Richard.

'She's gone. They've both gone. Her suitcase and all the baby stuff, all gone.'

'Not this again,' spat Ria. 'Is this another one of your antics?' She glared at Richard, who was gobsmacked.

'No, of course not,' he managed. 'Don't be ridiculous.'

'Well, you brought her here without our permission and had us worried out of our minds, and now she disappears again!' Mandy chimed in.

That poor baby, thought Richard, first taken from her mother, then whisked away by two new 'grannies' who should have known better. Then he had no choice but to whisk her off to his son's for safety, and now she has been taken again! You couldn't make it up. And he worried for her safety, and that of Giselle's, as he knew how Giselle was relapsing back to a dark time in her life. He should never have sent Matilda here.

Ria and Mandy couldn't bear the thought of going through all this worry for a second time. Giselle did not have a car, so they decided to split up and go and look for her. The men to cover the harbour area and the women to cover the side roads and shopping areas by car.

Chapter twelve

The red mist was descending on Charles again. People were getting in his way. Why did people always get in his way? Why couldn't they just leave him alone? This was his mother's house. They had no right to be here. He picked up a poker from the fireplace and walked towards the intruders, his face contorted in anger. The removal men decided that they were not paid enough to get into a fight, and the couple and their teenaged son backed off in terror. It was quite obvious that he meant business.

Charles slammed the front door behind them. *How dare they!*

He stood by the door and listened. He could hear the husband calling the police, and after a short conversation, the man saying to his wife, 'Would you believe it? They say it's not a police matter. We have to get a solicitor and take him to court to evict him.'

'But how long is that going to take?' asked his distraught wife. 'And he threatened us, what about that?' she continued.

'They just said that no threat was actually made. He just held a poker, and there is no law against that.'

'Lazy buggers,' said the teenage son.

Charles no longer had a number for his mother but felt sure she would not sell his inheritance from under him without so much as a by-your-leave. In any case, the police weren't interested, and he now had some time before a solicitor could take any action.

The sobbing wife and her family left not knowing where to go as their previous home was now occupied by a new family. The removal men would have to put their furniture into storage. In any case, Ria's furniture needed to be removed first.

But for now, Charles was glad that the house was furnished and comfortable.

What was his mother playing at? Had she gone mad? There was food in the freezer, but no fresh food, so he would have to go out, which would be a risk. Those damned squatters might come back again. Ah, of course, online shopping! The next morning everything he needed was delivered to his door.

He would have a lazy day watching TV.

Except that when he used his credit card for the shopping, it pinged up on somebody's screen in the incident room.

Richard and Pierre were scouring the harbour area when the English skipper of an old crock of a boat called out to Pierre.

'You looking for your Mrs, mate?'

'Hi, John, yes I am.'

'She's on board your cat. Saw her hours ago with the little 'un.'

'Thank God for that. Thanks, John.'

The two men hurried along the jetty to the catamaran. And there she sat, cradling Matilda on the sofa.

'Qu'est-ce que tu crois que tu fais?' shouted Pierre angrily.

'No,' said Richard. 'Don't shout at her.' He sat down beside Giselle.

'We were worried about you. We've been looking everywhere.'

'If Leonie is going to England, then I am going too,' she answered in French.

'Jesus, I haven't got time for this,' said Pierre. 'We need to catch the tide.'

'Go and find the women,' said Richard. 'Phone Ria. Here's her number.'

Richard turned to Giselle and gave her a hug, which prompted floods of tears.

Then he said in French, 'You were a wonderful mother to your little girl, and you have looked after Matilda well. We shouldn't have asked you to babysit. It wasn't fair. But Giselle, you are still young. It is not too late for you to have another baby of your own. Or you could adopt.'

'I want to adopt Leonie,' Giselle wailed.

'Sweetheart, she is Matilda not Leonie. You know that.'

John put his head round the door. 'Is everything alright, mate?'

'Yes, everything's fine. Maybe you would be kind enough to walk Giselle home and make her a cup of tea.'

'Yeah, no problem.'

'Now, Giselle, pass the baby to me.'

Giselle hugged Matilda, who was asleep, and passed her gently to Richard.

'Good girl. Thank you. She will be well looked after.'

Richard nodded to John to take Giselle and took Matilda into the bedroom along with her buggy to settle her down.

'Sarge, Charles Radcliffe has used his credit card,' said the DC to Sgt Gill.

'All that tells us is that he's still alive, unless it was at a cashpoint,' scoffed the defeated policeman, now back at his desk in London.

'No, sir. He ordered food from Sainsbury's to be delivered to this address.'

'Isn't that his mother's place?' said Sgt Gill as he inspected the piece of paper that had been handed to him.

'I don't know, sir, but Hertfordshire had a call yesterday about a disturbance at that address.'

'Did they indeed. Did they attend?'

'No, it was a civil dispute by all accounts.'

'Get Herts HQ on the phone.'

The upper echelons of the police force and secret services regarded the shire's police as carrot crunchers and plods. But it was worth a try.

Sgt Gill introduced himself to Sgt Fothergill and explained that they were interested in Charles Radcliffe. What was the SP on what had happened yesterday? Sgt Fothergill said that a family had tried to move into a house they had bought, but there was a man living there, who claimed to be the son of the previous owner. He appeared to be unaware of the sale and had an aggressive manner, and the family were advised to see a solicitor to take action to evict him.

Sgt Gill thanked him and hung up. Bloody woodentops. If the man was being aggressive it was a police matter.

Here was his chance at last. He would go there himself. It was only a 40-minute drive. He grabbed a DC and took off.

Ria and Mandy were exhausted when they finally climbed aboard the cat. They were not getting any younger, and the strain of the last hour had taken its toll.

Pierre was very quiet and took to the helm.

Richard made coffee for them all, as Ria and Mandy peeked at the sleeping child.

At last they were on their way to their new life.

Richard was first to speak. 'Now you know you must remember your new names,' he said as if talking to children. He had rather taken a paternal role.

'Yes, Rupert,' said a weary Ria.

'I've forgotten mine,' said Mandy.

'It's Lucy,' chorused Ria and Richard.

They laughed, as much with relief as anything. They could all relax now, at least for a few hours.

Suddenly Mandy had an idea. 'I've got an idea,' she said. 'What's the point of having our own beach if we can't land on it!'

They all thought about it for a moment. 'That would be great,' said Ria. 'I'll go and ask Pierre if it's possible.'

Pierre was still looking solemn as he sat at the helm. He was thinking about what he had to go back to. Ria explained what they would like to do.

Pierre looked pensive. 'Well, we're going to have to avoid the authorities as you have dogs and a baby, so I was going to beach somewhere anyway. But I don't know where this place is, or what the water depth is like. How will you recognise it from the Channel?'

'The house is very distinctive. I'm sure we'll know it when we see it,' Ria enthused.

'I'll do my best,' he said. 'But if it's rocky, I won't be able to drop anchor.'

Charles was watching the news, just in case he was starring on it, when he got a text.

'Surprise! I'm in London. Can't wait to see you. Where are you? Can you meet me?

Love and hugs, Anna xx'

He leapt off the sofa. His Anna, his adorable wife, was here in London. He couldn't be more thrilled.

He texted back, '*Can you be at King's Cross in two hours?'*

'*Here already,*' she replied. '*Will be in upstairs coffee shop.xx'*

He was there in an hour and fifteen minutes.

The nightmare of the last few weeks dissolved as he set eyes on the love of his life. She looked more beautiful than ever with her long brown hair and big brown eyes. She threw herself into his arms, and it seemed, in that moment, that everything would be alright.

But he couldn't let his guard down, so he took her hand and led her away from King's Cross station to the bus stop. He hadn't thought about what he was going to tell her. He so wanted to be able to just tell her the truth. She was his soulmate after all. But it was not possible. How do you tell your wife that you had an affair with a princess, who had your baby, which then died, and that you drowned a journalist, shot at an old man and a cop?

The funny thing is she would laugh and not believe him. But she knew something was up because she had to come to England as he couldn't return to Canada.

They went to Covent Garden and sat down at a pavement cafe for a bite to eat.

'So what's up, sweetheart?' Anna asked with her usual good humour and innocent charm.

Charles had to think on his feet. 'I had a row with my boss, and I've left my job,' he said. 'As you know, I had to come over here for work, but it was not as described to me, and I decided I'd had enough.'

She was quiet.

'But I love England,' he continued. 'It's my home, and I want you to come and live here. You'd love it.'

'But what about *my* job?' asked Anna.

'Darling, you can teach anywhere.'

'I suppose I could…'

'Of course you could.'

'But where would we live?'

'We could rent something. And we could rent out the house in Canada and see how things go.'

'And what about your job? What will you do?'

'Oh, I'll find something. Let's book into a hotel tonight and go flat hunting tomorrow.'

It occurred to Charles that they could go back to his mother's house, but he was going to get chucked out anyway, so it wasn't worth the hassle.

When Sgt Gill and the DC from Special Branch arrived at The Gables, there was no sign of life. A SOLD board was in the front garden.

Sgt Gill knocked at the front door while the DC went around the back. Nothing. Sgt Gill looked through the sitting room window. The TV was on. Ah, so there was someone around. He banged on the door again and again. Nothing. He *could* push the door in. If he could be sure that Radcliffe was in there, he would be within his rights. Or he could always say that he smelled gas...

But he decided that they would be better to watch the house from a distance as he had left the TV on, so he had probably only popped out for a few minutes.

They parked at the end of the road, and Sgt Gill rang the estate agent whose name was on the board, to check that the new owners had not moved in. No, said the agent, it was all very unfortunate. They were waiting for the courts to sort it out. The agent said he had tried to ring Ria, but with no joy.

Sgt Gill and DC Wentworth sat in the cold all night, while Charles and Anna had a warm and passionate reunion in a comfy London hotel bed, just 10 minutes from the incident room.

Ria sat at the helm of the catamaran with Pierre to try to cheer him up.

'It's great being out at sea,' she said. 'No wonder you love it so much.'

Pierre just gave a weak smile.

Ria tried again. 'How often do you make this crossing?'

'As and when,' he said.

He obviously wanted to be left to his thoughts, so Ria went back to the main cabin, where she walked in on Richard and Mandy kissing. They sprung apart. There was an uncomfortable silence, and Ria walked away into the bedroom.

Mandy followed her. 'It was just a kiss, Ria.'

'Have I complained?' said Ria, her eyes glistening. 'We are all free agents.'

Richard appeared in the doorway. Always one to try to lighten the mood, he said, 'It is very difficult for a man surrounded by gorgeous ladies, who he has come to adore, not to show his affection. But I accept that it is very naughty of me, and if we are going to be sharing a house, we need some ground rules.'

'Damn right,' said Ria.

He took Ria in his arms and started singing, 'Maria, I just met a girl called Maria.'

She pulled away. 'You're doing it again!' she snapped.

Mandy had left the room. She would back off. She knew that Richard's feelings were stronger for Ria, and that Ria was in love with him. She was Ria's best friend. She would have to keep herself in check. But it was nice to feel attractive and wanted again, even for a few minutes.

Pierre called to his passengers, 'I think we're nearly there. Can you come up on deck and show me the house please.'

They were passing some beautiful houses with gardens that reached down to the beach. Some children waved, and dogs barked, which set off Roxy and Mufti, and then woke Matilda. Ria picked her up, and they all watched as their new home came into view.

'Hang on,' said Pierre. 'It could get a bit bumpy.'

It was quite a palaver getting three pensioners, two dogs and a baby onto dry land. Nobody got away without getting their feet wet. But here they were, on a beautiful day in early summer, on their very own beach.

Pierre seemed to have cheered up, and joined the girls at a patio table, while Richard made the short walk to the estate agents to get the keys. He came back clutching a bottle of bubbly to celebrate.

They all went into the house to explore. It seemed a long time since they'd seen it, and they were keen to show Richard and Pierre. It had gathered a little dust but was just as beautiful as they remembered. The dogs scampered around sniffing everything, and everyone's mood lifted. They had all been through a lot. This would be a fresh start. Hopefully, a chance to put all their troubles behind them.

Ria opened her arms to them, and they had a group hug.

'Pierre, why don't you stay the night?' suggested Ria.

'Yes, son, that's a good idea,' Richard agreed.

* * *

Sgt Gill had been nicknamed Dreyfus by his underlings as he had started to twitch at the mere mention of Charles Radcliffe, or any of his 'gang'. On the one hand, he was obsessed with catching him and the women. On the other, he could hardly bear any further humiliation.

Once again, Radcliffe had slipped from his clutches with minutes to spare. And now he was back to square one.

His Inspector was losing interest. He had bigger fish to fry, he said. And in any case, the baby was probably dead, and it was really Sweden's problem, not theirs. OK, she was kidnapped on British soil, but they had caught the guy and he had promptly popped his clogs, so what was the point of all this? Waste of manpower.

The French police, however, begged to differ.

They had discovered that Charles's fingerprints were on the steering wheel of Richard's car, which they had recovered from the railway station. They had assumed that Richard was responsible for trying to shoot their gendarme but had also been a bit puzzled that the policeman involved had described a younger man.

They now thought it more likely that it was the work of Charles Radcliffe, and not a senile old man. They wanted to find him. They contacted the English policeman who had been involved in the investigation in France, Sgt Gill.

In between twitches, Sgt Gill explained that their target had been at his mother's old house until yesterday but had now disappeared again. Luckily, the local taxi company was helpful, and CCTV showed Charles boarding the train for King's Cross.

King's Cross Station probably has more cameras than some small countries, and he was seen meeting a woman. Cameras then spotted them catching a bus. It would be a big job to check every camera at every bus stop on the route, but it wouldn't have helped them anyway because the pair jumped off the bus when it was stationary in a traffic jam.

This morning, after a full English breakfast, and browsing online, Charles and Anna had decided that London was too expensive, so they would look for a flat further north, and caught a train to Bedford to have a look around.

The little Smith family could not be happier as they ate a breakfast of scrambled eggs, bacon and toast on the sunny patio. The dogs ran around exploring the garden and the beach, and Matilda gurgled happily in her buggy.

Pierre had stayed over and was in good spirits. 'That was a lovely room I stayed in,' he said. 'How many bedrooms do you have?'

'Four,' Ria replied.

'Well five, if you count the box room,' corrected Mandy. 'Why do you ask.'

'Does that mean that you have a spare room?' Pierre continued.

'Why, are you thinking of joining us?' laughed Ria.

'No, but I might have a proposition for you.'

Richard looked at him. 'I don't think so, Pierre.'

The girls were intrigued.

'Pourquoi pas, Papa, ils pourraient gagner beaucoup d'argent?'

'In English please, son. Well, it's up to the girls.'

Pierre was keen to explain. 'You will have noticed that Jack and I make regular crossings across the Channel. Well, there is a reason for that.'

Richard chimed in, 'Years ago, I met a French girl and we wanted to get married. But the French authorities would not let me in to stay permanently. During the sixties, I had been caught smoking dope, my one and only time!' He was still smarting at the injustice of it. 'And so I had a conviction.'

Pierre took up the story. 'Papa had a friend who had a yacht, and they decided to have a go at getting Papa across the Channel without anybody knowing.'

Richard said, 'It was illegal, of course, and still is, but love can overcome anything.' He laughed. 'And we eventually managed to get married by sneaking her back here for the ceremony and then going back to France.'

Pierre smiled. 'When I grew up and had a boat of my own, Papa told me the story, and how his friend with the yacht was retiring. At about that time our neighbour, Jack, needed to get to a funeral in the UK, but he didn't have time to get a passport. So I took him in my little boat, and then someone else asked me to do the same. I started to charge them for fuel as it was not cheap, and then realised that there was a business to be had.'

'Hang on,' said Ria, 'I'm not sure you should be telling us this. People-smuggling is a terrible business, and you can go to prison for a long time for it.'

'We're not talking about dozens of Africans in a rowing boat,' said Richard. 'This is just a service for wealthy individuals on a one to one basis. Decent people who get tied up in red tape. Very often they just visit for a day or two.'

'But if they are decent and just visiting for a day or two,' asked Mandy, 'surely they would be allowed in anyway?'

'Maybe they would,' Pierre continued, 'but they might want to bring extra cigarettes or drink with them.'

'So, smuggling as well!' Ria gasped.

'Oh, stop being a bloody policewoman,' said Mandy. 'What harm are they doing, bringing in a few fags and a drink or two? We let thousands of dodgy people from all over the world into our country every year, murderers, rapists the lot. Who cares if a few decent people pop back and forth from France? And if Pierre can make a living out of it, good for him.'

'But what about the coastguard and customs and excise?' Ria continued.

'They were interested in us at first,' said Pierre, 'but we managed to persuade them that we were just hobby boat enthusiasts, and now they are used to seeing us. They used to search us in the early days, but when they found nothing, they left us alone. And every now and then they appreciate a bottle of French wine!'

Ria shook her head and smiled.

'You said you had a proposition for us,' said Mandy.

'Yes,' said Pierre. 'This would be an ideal place to drop people off. Often they are businessmen, who used to fly over in private light aircraft, but that is getting harder nowadays. Sometimes we have to come in after dark, so it would be great if they had somewhere to stay for the night. They pay a lot of money for this service, and a percentage of it could come to you.'

'Absolutely not,' said Ria.

'How much?' said Mandy.

'About 600 euros a night,' said Pierre.

'That's over 500 pounds!' said Mandy.

'And you could do that on average twice a week,' Pierre said.

'Can't spend it in jail,' said Ria.

Surprisingly, Richard chimed in, 'Pierre and Jack have been doing this for over 20 years. How do you think they could afford to buy these cats? They cost hundreds of thousands of pounds... I think it would be a good income for you girls. What else have you got apart from your state pensions? And you will need money to bring up little Matilda. Pierre and Jack would look after you. And if ever anything did happen you could just plead ignorance. You were just asked to put a friend up for the night.'

'But what would the neighbours think about the cat landing on our beach every other day?' asked Ria, who was thinking what they could do with over a thousand pounds a week.

Pierre said, 'All these people have boats, that's why they have houses here. They will be coming and going all the time, just like us.'

Ria was thinking about Richard's words. It didn't sound as if he intended to stay for good. He had never said he would, but ever since he had looked at her and called her 'Mrs Smith' she had hoped.

Chapter thirteen

Soon it was June, and the Swedish Royal Wedding was just around the corner. Tindra and her family wanted a quiet affair, in the circumstances, but it seemed the whole world would be offended if they were not invited, so the guest list grew by the day.

William was spending most of his time at Tindra's family's country estate. Today he was sitting in the library, stewing. Tindra was going through the guest list.

'Don't you want to invite the father of your baby to the wedding?' he sulked.

'What? What did you just say?' fumed Tindra.

'Your first baby. Don't you want to invite the father?'

'He will be there at the altar with me, you idiot. What's the matter with you?'

'Sorry, sorry…'

'I should damn well think you are sorry,' she said. 'You want to bring up my dead baby when I am pregnant and about to get married?'

'I was just jealous,' he said. 'I was never really sure whether I was the father or not.'

'What does that matter now?' she snapped.

'It matters to me!'

'Why, because you wanted your wife to be unsullied by anyone else?'

'If you like.'

'And what about you? Was I your first?'

'I think we've had this conversation before.'

'Then we've no need to have it again.'

'Maybe you would like to call off the wedding and go and find a virgin.'

'Maybe I would.'

Truth be told, William had cold feet. He was not ready to be a father, and his wife to be had a bad reputation, which the press had exploited to the full. He was afraid he would become a laughing-stock. She may be a low ranking royal, but she still hit the headlines. He had also become a target for the press, who had speculated about whether he was indeed the father of the missing baby. And when they knew about this one, would they wonder about its parentage too?

Yes, he loved Tindra, but he hated the limelight and wondered if he would have to live in the spotlight for the rest of his life. His parents were worried about him and not too keen on the liaison. Maybe it would be easier for him to go and find himself an uncomplicated girl that he could settle down with somewhere quietly and have a family when the time was right. He was still very young.

Tindra ran to her room. She had known somewhere deep down that this was coming. The signs had been there, but she had chosen to ignore them and get on with the wedding plans. Now she had to face it. He didn't want to marry her. He could probably be pressured into it, but that's no kind of start for a marriage.

Once again, she would face having a baby on her own. It was too late for a termination, even if she had wanted one. OK, her parents would be around, but again the baby would have to be kept a secret. Unwed mum again! And she had the added humiliation of having to call off the wedding.

No, she couldn't face it. She had to get away.

Charles and Anna had found a charming flat, overlooking the river at Bedford.

Within days they had interviews for local jobs. Anna as a teacher at a comprehensive school, and Charles, as a salesman in a car dealership. He had little interest in cars, or sales for that matter, but it was a job, for the time being.

They were sitting having lunch, admiring their view of the river and people out enjoying the sunshine, when Charles's phone rang. He was horrified to see it was Tindra, especially with Anna sitting beside him. He suddenly had an unwelcome picture in his head of himself and Tindra making love in her bedroom in Canada. He clicked the phone off.

'Who was that?' asked Anna as she wrestled with her spaghetti.

'No idea,' said Charles. 'It just cut off.'

'They'll ring back,' said Anna, smiling.

Yes, she probably bloody well would ring back! He had specifically asked her not to, but if she was ringing, there must be a reason. He probably ought to find out what it was, and when Anna was out of earshot.

When Anna was clearing away the lunch, Charles nipped outside and sat on a bench by the river. He phoned Tindra.

'I thought we agreed not to speak again,' he said tersely.

'I'm sorry, Charles, but I didn't know who to turn to. You helped me out last time.'

'What's happened?'

'I have to get away.'

'Why, I thought you were getting married?'

'I was, but he left me.'

'Oh... well, I'm sorry to hear that.'

'Charles, I'm pregnant.'

'Oh, Tindra, not this again for fuck's sake! Well, it isn't mine this time!'

'No, of course not, but I can't go all through that scandal a second time. My parents want me to go to the clinic in London again, but I hated it there, and it has so many bad memories.' She burst into tears.

'Tindra, I have my wife here with me. I can't get involved.'

'Do you have to tell her anything?'

'There is nothing to tell her.'

There was a pause, and Tindra's tone changed. 'Well actually, Charles, there is quite a lot to tell her.'

Another pause.

'OK, look, if your parents can get you to London, I'll meet you there. We'll try and think of something. Text me when you are going to be there and give me at least a day's notice.'

'Thank you so much, Charles, I knew you wouldn't let me down.'

Ria and Mandy had settled into the beach house, and Richard was spending most of his time there. Every now and again he would pop back to France with Pierre or Jack, just to check on the Mill House, or spend time with Pierre and Giselle, who had now calmed down.

There had been long discussions about whether or not to go along with Pierre's idea to use their beach and guest bedroom for his 'business'. There was a time when Ria wouldn't have entertained the conversation, but as she got older, she began to see things differently. Laws were catch-all, black and white, and didn't allow for the nuances of life. How would it hurt anyone for a boat to park on their beach for an hour or so a couple of times a week? And if a visitor came from France or the UK and spent a night as a paying guest, where was the harm? OK, she could see the laws of immigration were there for a good reason, but this was not hordes of economic migrants from the third world, it was just a visitor or two who just didn't happen to have a passport on the day he or she wanted to come. Or they needed to keep their visit quiet. She and Mandy had certainly learned about that in the past few months.

And if you can't do what you like when you are in your golden years, when could you?

Golden years, that was a joke. The fear years more like. The years when the ticker starts to play tricks, the bones start to ache, the senses dim, and the stomach will only accept gentle foods that the teeth have managed to chew. And the medicine cabinet is full of beta blockers, blood thinners, stomach pills, statins and Gaviscon.

The house sales had finalised, and the money was now in the girls' accounts. There certainly wasn't going to be much left over when Richard had been paid.

Mandy and Ria were sitting in a cafe in the small seaside town near the beach house. Mandy was worried. 'We have to pay Richard, of course,' she said, 'but the house will still be in his name, so if we fell out with him, he could just sell it from under us.'

'He wouldn't do that,' said Ria, a little affronted.

'I'm sure he wouldn't, but we need to cover ourselves legally.'

So, Ria, Mandy and Richard had a meeting with a lawyer, and they put a charge on the house so that if it was sold in the future, the girls would get the money. And if Richard died first, the same would apply.

They were all happy with that, and it eased the atmosphere in the house. Richard had his money, and the girls had the small amount that was left to live on. They all knew where they stood.

Richard was friendly with both women, but there was no hanky-panky. Ria longed to get closer to him but could see that it would change the dynamic in the house and make Mandy uncomfortable. But life was short. She would reconsider when they had been there for a few more months.

Matilda was sleeping in Ria's room, and Mandy and Richard had a room each, so that left a spare room which was a good size, and they transformed it into a guest room that wouldn't have looked out of place in a hotel. There was also a box room, which Matilda could have as she got older.

She was growing into a happy, placid child, with blonde curls and a magnetic smile.

She could almost sit up on her own now and loved to watch the dogs running about in the garden.

Tindra was waiting in a cocktail bar in Great Portland Street when Charles arrived.

He was nervous about being spotted in London. 'I can't stay long,' he said, without so much as a greeting. He sat down and could see that she had been crying.

She didn't speak.

'What do you want to do?' he asked.

'I want to go somewhere where I won't be recognised. Maybe start a new life, I don't know.'

'You and me both,' he muttered under his breath.

'But how are you going to do it on your own with a baby on the way?'

'I won't be the first and I won't be the last,' she said tearfully. 'Trouble is people in the UK recognise me.'

'What about France?' Charles asked.

'Why France?'

'Oh, I don't know, maybe because I've just been there.'

'I went to the Sorbonne,' Tindra brightened. 'I do know one or two people in Paris, and my French is good.'

'There you are then,' said a relieved Charles.

'But how do I get there?'

'Tindra, you are a grown woman. You get there in the same way as we all get there. You can fly or go across in a ferry or through the tunnel.'

'You seem to forget that I don't want people to know where I am. The press would have a field day again. With any of those routes, it would flag up my name. Unless I could get a fake passport.'

'Jesus, who do you think I am? I don't do fake passports.'

There was a pause, as the cogs turned. 'But I do have an idea.'

The French police had decided to send two gendarmes to London to try to track down the man who had taken a pot shot at their colleague. They met Sgt Gill at King's Cross, where Charles was last seen on CCTV. They decided to take the No. 17 bus which the couple had taken days before. Sgt Gill could not see the point in this, but the gendarmes seemed keen. He suspected that they just wanted a sightseeing tour of London. Surely, they didn't expect to see Charles Radcliffe just walking down the street?

They might have done if they had stayed a bit longer at King's Cross, as Charles was now on his way to St Pancras station, right next door, to catch his train to Bedford.

He had now secured the job as a car salesman, so would have to wait until his day off to help Tindra. He would borrow a car and take her to the boatyard, where he would tell her to ask for Pierre or Jack. But under no circumstances was she to mention his name. They would take her across the Channel, and she would be on her own after that.

Tindra's father had given up on his errant daughter. She had always been wilful and disobedient, while he believed that duty and discipline were everything. The family name was highly respected and had been for generations. What was the matter with the girl? Had they spoilt her? Her brother Hugo had never been a minute's trouble. They both had the same upbringing. Well, her father had had enough. One pregnancy was bad enough, but two was beyond the pale. He didn't want to hear her name mentioned again.

Her mother was not a tactile or passionate person. She had always done what had been expected of her and was careful never to rock the boat. But her daughter was her firstborn, her child. Tindra had taken the wrong path, but she had been lonely in Canada, and this time she was in love and due to marry. She had been irresponsible and careless, but she was just human. If she wasn't a princess she would have just carried on and managed with her family's help. But now she had to go away again and hide her pregnancy, at a time when a mother should be joyful and looking forward to the future. It was a sad and worrying time. She would be deprived of yet another grandchild. And all because of convention.

Luckily, Charles' day off coincided with a school day, so Anna was at work. He had taken a fancy to a car on the forecourt of his dealership, and so became his own first customer. He drove down to London and picked up Tindra, whom he scarcely recognised. Her long brown hair had gone and had been replaced by a short blonde spiky style. She wore big sunglasses and a baseball cap. The only thing Charles recognised was her knapsack. It was her new look, she said. He agreed that nobody was likely to recognise her now.

They headed south. She seemed happy and relieved that she now had a plan of sorts. They were both in good spirits and reminisced about their time in Canada. After everything that had happened, she couldn't bring herself to admit to Charles that he was (probably) not the father of her first baby. He was also keeping quiet about his efforts to find the baby, and the trouble he had found himself in. As they neared the boatyard, Charles wondered if he was doing the right thing. He liked Tindra, despite everything, and felt sorry for her.

'Have a good look in the marina,' he said. 'If you see a large catamaran it will almost certainly belong to Pierre or Jack. Go to the bar in the restaurant and ask for them. Do not mention my name under any circumstances. The police are still after me because of the 'kidnapping' fiasco. Just say that you need to cross the Channel, but don't have a passport. I'm sure you can think of a convincing story. But you might want to change your name. Tindra is unusual in England, and you have been all over the papers.'

'I'll use my second name; Louise,' Tindra said.

'They might want paying. Have you got any money?'

'Yes, money is not a problem,' she said.

'Good. OK, well, good luck.'

She looked nervous and worried. He needed to make her laugh.

'I suppose a quick bonk is out of the question?'

She laughed in the way that she used to in Canada, and he felt a rush of love for her. She climbed out of the car, grabbed her rucksack, gave him a little wave and walked into the boatyard. She looked such a lonely figure that he almost ran after her. But he didn't.

As Charles drove back to Bedford, he realised that he needed petrol. Wow, this car used a lot of juice! He would stop at the next services. And then it hit him. He couldn't use his credit card. It could be traced. OK, he wouldn't be in this location for long, but they would be able to see his car on CCTV, get the registration, and the ANPR cops could pick him up on the motorway. He had very little cash, less than 20 pounds. And withdrawing money from a cash machine would cause the same problems. Until now he had managed with Anna's money, and some left over from his last visit to England. So, he had no choice but to put £18.97 worth of petrol in the car and hope it would get him home.

A young girl with blonde spiky hair and a baseball cap was standing on the jetty looking at a catamaran. A man was working on the engine. He looked up.

'Hello,' he said. 'Are you lost?'

'No, sorry, I didn't mean to stare. Is this your boat?'

'Yes, for my sins. Not a bad craft is she.'

'She's gorgeous.'

'You can have a look around if you like.'

Tindra hesitated.

'It's OK,' he laughed, wiping engine grease from his hands. 'I don't bite. My name's Jack.' He smiled as he leaned over to help her onto the cat.

'I'm T... Louise.'

Jack gave her a guided tour of the boat and offered her a coffee.

'So where are you off to with your rucksack? Gap year backpacking around the world?'

'No, no, nothing so exciting. I just want to get to Paris to see some friends. My passport has just run out, and it's such a bother to get a new one. I was wondering if someone here could get me across the Channel?'

'You naughty girl. You do know that that's illegal?' said Jack, who had to cover himself.

She nodded.

'I couldn't take you to the usual ports. I would have to drop you off along the beach somewhere.'

'That would be fine, really.'

'OK, but I can't do it for a couple of days. Engine trouble. I'm waiting for a part.'

Jack wondered about letting her stay on the cat for a couple of nights, but it might not be a good idea for a young woman on her own.

Tindra's face fell. What would she do for two days?

'Look,' said Jack, 'about a mile along the seafront there is a beach house where they take paying guests. I could pick you up from their private beach in two days if you like.'

'That sounds great,' said a grateful Tindra.

'Give me a couple of minutes to clean up and I'll take you down there. They will only take you with an introduction from me. My car's the silver 4x4 in the car park. I'll see you there.'

Tindra wandered over to the car park, admiring the other boats along the way.

Jack made a call to Ria.

'You OK to take a young girl backpacker for a couple of days? She's en route to Paris, but I've got engine trouble and I'm waiting for a part.'

Our first guest, thought Ria, and a young girl would be less scary than an unknown man.

'Yes, that's fine. When will she be coming?'

'I'll bring her over now if that's OK.'

'Oh... OK, yes, we'll manage.'

The English police were having a meeting with the gendarmes at New Scotland Yard.

'So what's the SP on Radcliffe and the two women?' asked an inspector, who was rifling through papers and seemed unfamiliar with the case.

Sgt Gill started to twitch. 'Radcliffe was definitely in this country within the last few days,' he said, dropping his pen on the floor. 'He was seen at King's Cross with a woman.'

'Do we know who the woman is?'

'Not yet, sir. She was not his mother or the other woman. She was younger, and they were all over each other.'

'Is he married?'

'Yes, sir, but his wife is in Canada as far as we know.'

'Well check, man! Has she come into the country recently? We need to know who this woman is.'

'Yes, sir.' He picked up his pen and dropped it again.

'Are you alright, Gill?'

'Yes, I'm just, it's…'

'So where are we with the two women?'

'Nous les avons perdus en France, monsieur,' said the gendarme.

'In English please.'

'Pardon, I said we lost them in France, sir.'

Chapter fourteen

Charles got home by the skin of his teeth with an empty petrol tank. Anna was still at work, so he sat and poured himself a drink. He had advised Tindra to use another name, but he was still using his. He and Anna had rented the flat in their name. He had given his name to his employers and bought the car in his name. He had begun to have a false sense of security as life seemed to feel more normal. But he had been an idiot. It was too late now. He could hardly go to his employers and say he was now called Tarquin De Vere.

He so wanted to be able to talk his problems over with Anna, but if she left, it would kill him. He couldn't take the risk. He was only in all this trouble because he was trying to keep his adultery from her.

The silver 4x4 arrived at the front of the beach house. Jack climbed out and knocked on the door. Richard opened it wearing a red smoking jacket and yellow cravat.

'Hello, Jack. Having some engine troubles, I hear?'

'Yes, damned thing packed up yesterday. Luckily, I had just docked.'

'And you have a visitor for us?'

Jack turned to the car and signalled for Tindra to come in. She grabbed her rucksack and joined them.

'Hello, young lady,' said Richard. 'I'm Richard.' Damn, he should have said Rupert. This was going to get very confusing.

'I'm Louise,' said Tindra, who was quicker witted.

Jack said he would be back in a couple of days and left.

'Come on in,' said Richard. 'I'll introduce you to the ladies.'

Ria had put Matilda down to sleep and was coming down the stairs.

'This is, er,'

'Maria,' said Ria.

'Yes, yes, Maria,' said Richard. Or Rupert.

They went into the kitchen where Mandy was preparing lunch. She wiped her hands and smiled at the newcomer.

'I'm ...'

'Lucy,' said Richard. 'And this is Louise.'

Mandy, aka Lucy, took Tindra, aka Louise to her room, and left her to settle in. Lunch would be in half an hour if she would like to join them on the patio. She would, and she did in exactly half an hour.

There was an amazing spread on the patio table. Salad, salmon, wholemeal and white bread, prawns, coleslaw, cherry tomatoes, cucumber, celery and various dips and pâtés. Mandy brought out a jug of orange juice and another jug of water. Ria followed with a pot of tea and a jug of milk. Richard then appeared carrying a plate of fairy cakes.

It was a perfect day, and from the patio they had an enviable view of the neat garden, the sandy beach and the blue sea. Tindra felt a bit overwhelmed, but loved the place, even if the oldies seemed a bit dithery. They were all keen to find out about 'Louise'.

She told them that she was off to see some friends in Paris. How interesting, said Richard, who had lived near Paris for so many years. Where did her friends live?

Luckily, her Sorbonne days were recent history, and she still remembered some place names.

'Do you have somewhere to stay?' he asked.

'Not yet.' She smiled.

They all dug into the food. Ria asked her about her accent, having first said that she spoke very good English. Danish, said Tindra, hoping that nobody spoke Danish or would recognise the difference between Danish and Swedish.

And so the deception continued.

They all helped to clear away, and then Matilda woke and started crying.

'You have a baby!' cried Tindra.

'Yes, my little granddaughter,' said Ria proudly. 'Would you like to meet her?'

'I'd love to,' Tindra said, smiling.

Matilda was duly brought down and into the garden where they were all now relaxing. She sat on Ria's lap, reaching out to Roxy, who had come to greet her. Tindra stroked Roxy and then knelt down to be at Matilda's height. She took her tiny hand, and with the other hand, stroked her cheek.

'What a gorgeous baby,' she said, her voice cracking. A tear dripped down her cheek.

'Oh dear, are you alright, Louise?' asked a concerned Ria.

'Yes, yes, I'm sorry,' she said, standing and wiping her eyes. 'You might as well know, I'm pregnant and a bit emotional.'

'Oh, my dear,' said Richard. 'You should have said. Come and sit down over here.'

She sat down, feeling foolish. Now they would all make a fuss and ask difficult questions. And they did. But it turned out that the fuss was what she needed, and she simply said that her boyfriend had left her. It was the truth, after all.

Sgt Gill was elated, which hadn't happened for a while.

He had discovered that one Anna Jane Radcliffe had arrived at Gatwick from Canada a few weeks ago. There were no other Radcliffes. It had to be her. Now he was getting somewhere. She would surely lead them to Charles.

The gendarmes had been recalled to France as nothing much had been happening.

Gill would keep them posted. All he had to do now was find out if Anna had been using a credit card, and if so which one and where and when. Did she have a mobile phone? He started to twitch again. This would take time, and they could be on the move again.

Was she met at the airport? Did she hire a car? Where did she go from there?

CCTV must be checked.

And people thought that police work was glamorous!

Charles felt a bit panicky. He was a murderer, not once but twice. And one victim was a police officer! He had also organised the kidnapping of a royal baby, albeit his own. He'd been stupid in using his own name. He and Anna would have to move on, and not take any more silly chances. If he was caught, he would be dragged back to France. Did they still have the death penalty? No, of course not, he must stop panicking. But he would not see the light of day for many years, if at all.

He started to pack.

Anna breezed in from work. She had had a good day. She put the kettle on and put her head round the bedroom door to see what Charles was doing.

'What's up?' she asked when she saw his face, and the pants being thrown into a suitcase.

'We need to move on,' he said.

'What do you mean, move on? Why?'

He turned to her and then slumped on the bed.

'Whatever's the matter? Did you have trouble at work?'

'Listen, Anna. You will need to know this. The police are after me.'

'Whatever for?' said a shocked Anna as she sat beside him.

'You remember that Swedish royal baby that went missing?'

'Yes, but what—'

'Let me finish. Do you remember in Canada I worked with a girl called Tindra?'

'I think so...'

'Well, some guy she met got her pregnant. She was a princess in the Swedish royal family. Anyway, she had to go to England to have her baby in secret, and because I am English, she asked me if I knew anyone in England who might help her to get the baby adopted.

'I suggested my friend Tony. He was a good mate, and he could keep a secret. So, Tony went to the hospital and took the baby to my mum's place to be looked after until a family could be found. But the papers got hold of it, and Tindra had to say the baby was kidnapped. The police found out that it was Tony and that I was his friend, and that the baby had gone to my mum's.'

'So, you just get your mum to give the baby back.'

'That's what I wanted to do, but my mother had taken off with the baby and her neighbour. I tracked them down to France, but the poor baby had died of cot death.'

'Yes, I saw that in the papers,' said Anna.

'So you didn't actually *do* anything,' she continued. 'Just asked Tony to get the baby. Would Tony tell on you?'

'The police arrested him, it was in the papers, but he died in police custody.'

'Oh my God! Did they kill him?'

'Who knows. They said it was a heart attack. But you see why we need to move on. We've been using our real names, credit cards etc., and I don't want to spend the rest of my life in jail.'

'Now hang on, honey, slow down. What you did was try to help a girl who was in trouble. That's not a hanging offence. Why don't you go to the police and explain? I suppose the baby's father just ran for the hills?'

'Probably, I don't know.'

'Let's go to the police together.'

Oh no, this was not what he wanted to hear. Dear sweet Anna. She was so honest and naive. But then again, he had neglected to mention the murders.

* * *

Tindra was thoroughly enjoying herself at the 'Smith' household. She loved playing with the dogs, and especially liked cuddling Matilda. 'Maria' and 'Lucy' had encouraged her to look after the child as it would be good practice for her.

Ria was pleased to have a break from the exhausting job of looking after a baby, but she had mixed feelings when she saw 'Louise' with Matilda. She was jealous of their obvious bond, and the natural way Louise had with her. Ria was her grandmother after all, and she wanted Matilda to know that she was family. Mandy had not exactly lost interest, but couldn't really get a look in.

After two days there was a phone call. The engine part that Jack needed had not arrived. He was so sorry but couldn't take Louise across the Channel today as expected. If he couldn't get the repair done by next week, Pierre would be coming over, and maybe he would take her across. Tindra was secretly delighted. She had nowhere to go in France, and she was happier than she had been for years.

Richard decided that if Pierre came over, he would also go back with him, to make sure Louise was alright, and to catch up with a bit of business at the Mill House.

Tindra had taken Matilda out in her buggy to the local shop. Ria and Mandy were having a chat in the kitchen over a cup of coffee.

'Louise is brilliant with Matilda, isn't she?' said Mandy.

'Yes, she's a natural. And Matilda adores her,' Ria agreed. 'In fact, sometimes I feel a bit envious if I'm honest.'

'But you have a great bond with Matilda. We both do.'

'Yes, but maybe it's because Louise is young and more energetic than us.'

'Well, in a few months she'll have a baby of her own to care for, so this will be a great experience for her.'

'She fits in well here, doesn't she? Always willing to help.'

'Yes, she's a lovely girl. But where are her family?'

'I asked her about that. She said that she was not close to her parents, and her father was a bully. She has a brother that she keeps in touch with.'

'Well, that's something I suppose,' said Mandy. 'Poor kid. This is not the time for her to be going backpacking on her own. She doesn't appear to have any definite plans for when she gets to Paris. She had friends there a few years ago, but she isn't even sure if they still live there.'

'Richard would probably put her up at the Mill House, but she would be alone most of the time, and I know he's good with Matilda, but I don't think he'd want to feel responsible for another newborn.'

'I suppose it's not really our problem.' said Mandy. 'She's a grown woman, and it's up to her what she does.'

'She's our first guest. I hope we don't start to worry about all of them!' laughed Ria.

'Speaking of which,' said Mandy, 'is Louise paying us or do we get paid by Jack?'

'I can't imagine that a young pregnant backpacker has the sort of money they usually charge. And to be honest, I wouldn't really want to charge Louise anything,' said Ria.

'You old softie!' laughed Mandy. 'Neither would I!'

Once again, the wheels were coming off for Charles. He felt sure the police were about to pounce, but Anna insisted that he should go and explain his side of the story to them. Tell them the truth. He sat on the bench, looking at the river and thought about that. In his head, he had a sarcastic conversation with Anna.

'Yes, right, officer, here is my side of the story. I wanted to get rid of my own baby because I didn't want my affair to be made public. I bashed a reporter over the head with a brick and drowned him because he was going to expose me. I shot at an old man because he wouldn't tell me where the baby was, and I shot a policeman because he was going to arrest me. And so now I expect you to sympathise and let me get on with my life. Ha!'

Anna came and sat beside him. He just looked down.

'Come on, let's go to the police station and get this over with,' she said. 'You can't spend the rest of your life running away.'

The red mist started to gather. Running away? That made him sound like a coward! Now *she* was getting in his way. What did she know? In her easy perfect life, what did she know! She didn't know she was born. She wanted to turn him in to the police? What sort of wife is that? She wanted to get rid of him, that's what it was. Maybe she had another man, yes, a teacher at that stupid school of hers. Well, he could have the stupid bitch. And he only did all the things he did for her. It was all her fault that he was in this mess.

He had an overwhelming urge to grab her and push her into the river. But instead, he took off his wedding ring and threw that. Then he went back to the flat, finished packing and left.

Half an hour later a tearful Anna opened the door to a man with a twitch. When he discovered that he had missed Charles by minutes, Sgt Gill sat on the bench by the river and twitched some more.

Thinking she was being helpful, Anna told the officer how her husband had only tried to help a girl who was in distress. He was a good man, and certainly wasn't a criminal she said. She told him how she had tried to persuade Charles to talk to the police, but that he had flown into a rage and left. She said she was worried about him.

In a way it was true that everything Charles had done since his affair with Tindra was to protect his marriage. Now he had nothing. His wife had betrayed him and even his mother was uncontactable. Anna had meant everything to him. Now nothing mattered any more. He didn't care what he did. But first he needed to find a way to avoid the police. He needed money. He needed to ditch his car and get another. He needed somewhere to stay. He needed a new burner phone.

He parked in a layby, his heart pounding. Where to go?

He no longer had friends in this country and couldn't get back to Canada. He thought about the lovely Tindra and wondered how she had got on after he left her at the boatyard. She would be in France now.

Richard came in from the garden to find Ria and Mandy deep in conversation in the kitchen. 'Can anyone join in?' he asked, smiling.

'We were just saying what a joy Louise is,' said Ria.

'Indeed she is,' said Richard. 'Poor little girl.'

'She must be in her twenties,' laughed Mandy.

'Well, she's still a little girl to me.' said Richard. 'She shouldn't be backpacking in her condition.'

'That's what we said,' Ria agreed.

'Still, she's a grown woman and has a few months before she's due. She won't get much chance to travel once the baby's born,' said Mandy.

The others nodded in agreement. Richard's phone rang. It was Jack.

'The boat's up and running again, Richard. I can take your guest across tomorrow if she can be on your beach at 10am.'

'That's good news, Jack, thanks,' said Richard, sounding more as if he had had bad news.

'Well, that's that then.' he said to the girls and wandered back out into the garden.

Tindra's mother was beside herself. She had tried to phone Tindra, but the phone was dead. She phoned the maternity hospital where she had expected Tindra to register, but they had no news of her. Her husband would not discuss it. She was furious with William and so would not speak to him. So she turned to her son, Hugo.

He had seldom seen his mother close to tears.

'What can we do, Hugo? Did she tell you where she was going?'

'No, I don't think she knew herself.'

'This is a nightmare. All the wedding guests have had to be told and are all asking questions.'

'It's none of their business, Mother,' said Hugo. 'Couples break up all the time. It's no big deal.'

'Well it's a very big deal when my daughter loses her first baby and takes off to God knows where when she is pregnant with her second! Hugo, you know her better than anyone. I want you to find her.'

'Where on earth would I start?' asked Hugo.

'London, that's where we took her. She was going to register at the clinic and stay at the nearby hotel that we paid for. But she left the same day apparently.'

'So, I wander around London, hoping to see her, do I? Look, Mum, she's very sensible, and I'm sure she'll be fine.'

His mother dabbed her eyes with her silk handkerchief, gave Hugo a disdainful look, and left the room. Hugo then rang Tindra and told her to send their mother a note to say she was OK.

Charles was still sitting stewing in the layby when Sgt Gill drove past, totally oblivious to anything except the fact that he had missed his target *again*! He wasn't looking forward to going back to the office.

Charles didn't notice Sgt Gill either.

He was too busy planning his next move. First, he would go to a car dealership and trade in his car for something inconspicuous. Hopefully, if he was trading down, he would also get some cash. He would buy it under another name.

Then he would go and buy a burner phone, although he was running out of people to ring. After that, he would drive to a town, any town, and book into a hotel and have some dinner. By the morning maybe he would think of something more long term.

The catamaran chugged on to the beach at 10 on the dot. Tindra was waiting, with her baseball cap on her head and her knapsack on her back. Ria and Mandy, who was holding Matilda, came to wave her and Richard off. He had decided to take the trip with her. Jack called out to the girls that they could expect another guest tonight. A gentleman who wanted to come for two days. Was that OK? They gave him the thumbs up over the noise of the engines. And off went their first guest, her new plan being to go to a backpackers' hostel in Paris.

Ria and Mandy went back into the house to change the bed for the new visitor and make sure they had enough food, so that could at least offer him dinner tonight.

Ria was wishing Richard hadn't gone to France. He would no doubt be back within the week, but she didn't fancy having a stranger in the house while he was away.

Maybe she and Mandy should put locks on their bedroom doors, but Mandy laughed at the suggestion and said that no one would be in a hurry to seduce two old biddies!

She hoped the stranger wouldn't mind being woken in the night by Matilda crying, or the dogs barking, which they did, annoyingly, every time Matilda cried.

Ria cleaned the guest room and the en suite, and Mandy made a casserole and a cheesecake. By the time they had settled Matilda in her cot, they were both exhausted and flopped onto the loungers on the patio.

'Blow this for a game of soldiers,' said Mandy, 'I'm too old to be a landlady.'

'Me too,' said Ria. 'And I keep forgetting to call you Lucy.'

'And you never answer to Maria! You kept ignoring me yesterday.'

'I know, I kept wondering who you were calling!' laughed Ria, and they both collapsed into a fit of the giggles.

Anna had very helpfully told Sgt Gill where Charles had been working. So Sgt Gill phoned the car dealership and asked them what car he was driving. They kindly told him and said that he had not come into work today. Was there something wrong?

Sgt Gill said that he didn't expect him to come back, but if he did, they should ring him at once.

He would catch this bloody man if it killed him, and it probably would.

As he walked into the office there was a sarcastic hand clapping, and someone said, here comes poor old Dreyfus! He was so consumed with the twitches that he had to go home. This was no laughing matter. They shouldn't mock the afflicted.

Chapter fifteen

The red mist had lifted, and Charles was back on an even keel, even though he no longer cared about anything much apart from getting caught. He had bought a second-hand car and ordered some false number plates from Ireland. He gave the address of the hotel in Welwyn Garden City where he was staying. He had his burner phone, and some cash, so all was well.

He liked Welwyn Garden City with its tree lined streets and fountains. Maybe he could make a friend or two here and stay for a while. He might even be able to get some casual work, but without any ID or references in his invented name of Sam Lawson, it could be difficult.

Maybe his mother could help him somehow, but where was she? Why had she not contacted him? Why had she changed her number? They were OK together last time they met at the gite.

Ria and Mandy were still sitting on the patio when their new guest arrived on Pierre's cat. They jumped to attention and watched as the man climbed from the craft and gave them a friendly wave. Pierre waved and was off.

'Jeez, he looks like George Clooney!' said Mandy and she fluffed up her hair.

'He. Is. Drop. Dead. Gorgeous!' said Ria, as she grabbed her lipstick from her bag, and applied it quickly as he made his way up the beach and through the garden to meet them.

Mandy leapt up and almost ran down the garden to greet him.

'Thanks for letting me stay at short notice,' he said in a beautiful soft French accent.

'My name is Anton.'

'I'm, er, Lucy,' said Mandy, almost curtsying.

'And this is my friend R... Maria.'

'R Maria?'

'Maria, but we call her Ria sometimes for short.'

'Enchanted.' He smiled, taking both women's hands and air-kissing them.

Ria went all silly and offered him cheesecake before he had had his dinner. Mandy tried to stop the dogs from jumping all over him, but he said it was fine. He loved dogs. Could this man be any more perfect?

They took him into the dining room where the table had been set. 'Are you hungry?' asked Mandy.

'Ravenous,' he said.

'What was I thinking?' said Ria. 'I'll show you to your room first. You probably want to freshen up first.'

He looked her right in the eye and with a cheeky smile said, 'I'm very fresh already, madam. I'm ready to eat if you are.'

Ria blushed to her roots and dashed to the kitchen to heat the casserole and add some rice, or mashed potato or something.

Mandy followed her in. 'I saw him first,' she said, grinning.

'You're old enough to be his mother,' said Ria as she burned something.

'So are you!'

'Maybe he likes mature women,' said Mandy hopefully.

'Like them? I love them!' came a voice from the doorway.

Mandy wet herself, and Ria started choking for no obvious reason.

Then Matilda started to cry, and the dogs started to bark, so Ria ran to the baby and Mandy went to change her trousers.

Anton was going to enjoy his stay here.

Richard had taken Tindra to the hostel for backpackers in Paris. It was better than she expected. It was a bit like halls of residence, but trendier. It was basic but clean, and there were lots of young people about, of all nationalities. She had to share a room with one other girl but had yet to meet her. She put her stuff in the locker provided and went for a walk to acclimatise herself.

She felt as if a weight had been lifted. A new sense of freedom and anonymity. Her parents had felt oppressive, and while she loved being at the beach house, and being looked after by 'grown-ups', she had felt like a child. Now she could truly be herself. She had Richard's phone number if she needed someone to fall back on, and she would keep in touch with Hugo, but she was now on her own.

The hostel was in the 10th arrondissement of Paris, in the Canal St Martin area.

There were bohemian cafes and trendy bars. It was a whole new world.

The trouble with pregnancy was that it made her tired, and soon she went back to her room for a rest. The full-length mirror did not lie. Her bump was beginning to show. But for now, clothes would cover it.

She awoke an hour later to find a girl lying on the next bed reading.

The girl smiled at her. 'Do you speak English?' she asked.

'Yes, hi,' said Tindra, who wasn't quite awake.

'My name is Lizzy. I'm from the Netherlands.'

'Oh, yes, my name's… Louise. From Denmark.' *Netherlands is too near Denmark*, she thought. *I hope she doesn't speak Danish.*

Just to be sure, Tindra added, 'But I never speak Danish while I'm away because I want to practice my English, and French of course.'

'Me too. I understand,' said the other girl in perfect English.

Lizzy was about 21 with a round smiley face and short brown hair. Tindra liked her immediately and hoped they would both be here long enough to become good friends.

Charles sat by the fountain in Welwyn Garden City town centre eating a burger. It was peaceful, and the few people who walked past him were polite and well dressed.

One man was walking past him for a second time, this time with Sainsbury's carrier bags.

'Still here?' he asked, smiling.

Charles was taken aback. What did you say to that? 'Yes, it's such a lovely day,' he said, which he thought sounded a bit lame.

'Mind if I sit for a minute. This shopping's heavy.'

'Of course not, no problem.'

'Thank you.'

They sat quietly for a minute or two, with just the sploshing of the fountain to break the silence.

Then the man said, 'You're Charles Radcliffe aren't you.' It wasn't a question.

Charles froze.

'I remember your mum, Ria. Lovely lady. How is she?'

Was he a policeman or just some guy who knew his mum?

Charles threw his burger wrapper in the bin and stood up. 'Sorry, just remembered something...' and he walked quickly away.

For God's sake. Was there nowhere safe?

*　*　*

Anton, Ria and Mandy eventually sat down to eat dinner, with Matilda in her highchair, and two dogs waiting for scraps under the table.

Anton was well aware of the effect he had on women but was a little surprised that his charms were so appreciated by women of a certain age. The casserole was accompanied by both rice and mashed potato, and the cheesecake had gone a bit gooey in the heat.

Anton didn't talk about himself but wanted to know all about the 'ladeez'. Ria and Mandy had invented new names for themselves but hadn't thought about a backstory. Maybe they could stick to the truth. Or maybe it was an opportunity to reinvent themselves. That could be exciting. They could be anybody they wanted to be.

'I was an actress,' said Mandy. Having been a theatrical agent she had enough knowledge to get away with it she thought.

'Really? That is very interesting,' said Anton. 'What were you in?'

'Oh, lots of things, film, TV, theatre.'

Ria was trying not to laugh. She could see Mandy digging a big hole for herself.

'I was in Hollywood in my twenties, making movies. It was fabulous.'

Mandy was on a roll.

'How wonderful,' said Anton. 'Where did you live? I was in Hollywood for five years myself.'

Cheesecake exploded from Ria's mouth. 'I'm so sorry.' she said, grabbing a napkin, and biting hard on her lip to stop herself having a fit of the giggles.

Anton knew exactly what was going on and continued with the game.

'Oh,' said Mandy, 'I can't remember the name of the street, it was a long time ago.'

'Which studio were you signed to?' asked Anton in a friendly, sincere voice.

'Erm, Paramount,' said Mandy, wishing she'd never started this.

'Oh my goodness, so was I!' said Anton, 'but after your time, of course.'

He winked at Ria. 'But old Joe Whiley would have been there in your day. He had been there for 30 years when I joined. What was he like as a young man?'

Mandy looked stricken. Feeling the need to rescue her Ria said, 'The trouble with getting older is that one's memory fails, isn't that right, Mandy?'

Anton took the hint and changed the subject. This man was mischievous, but not malicious, and they were in for a fun couple of days.

The car that Charles had been driving had been traced to a dealership in Stevenage, where it had been exchanged for a smaller vehicle. Sgt Gill now had the registration number so was on track again. He would check to see if it had been picked up by ANPR.

229

That morning Charles received his false number plates in the post, and stuck them with the sticky pads provided, on top of the original ones. The car with its original number plates had been picked up on ANPR between Stevenage and Welwyn Garden City. Then nothing. He must be in Welwyn Garden City. So, Sgt Gill set off, complete with the bottle of anti-twitch pills that his doctor had prescribed.

Charles had been spooked by the man that recognised him and decided to move on. He drove back through Stevenage and took a left to an old market town called Hitchin. There was a hotel in the town centre with its own car park, so that was perfect. Everything he needed was within walking distance. But he spent most of his time in the bar.

The hotel was old, but without much charm. It was tired and badly managed. The Mediterranean kitchen staff screamed at each other and slammed doors, and the bar was often unattended. Cleaners would sit on the steps and smoke, and the tables in the restaurant were sticky, as was the floor in the bar.

The room was OK and looked out over the narrow street that led into the town square, which was achingly beautiful, with its cobbles and little independent shops with beams and canopies.

Charles liked to sit in the square with a beer and watch the world go by. But at the same time, he was aware that his own life was passing *him* by. He no longer trusted women. His wife had let him down, Tindra had started a whole bucket load of trouble, and his own mother didn't want to know him.

Pity he wasn't gay, he thought.

He would soon be needing some money. Living in hotels was not cheap. He had always been happy to work, but without being able to give an NI number or any work history he was scuppered. He needed something casual with cash in hand.

He wandered back to the hotel bar and had another chat with Dave the barman. Dave and his wife, Jan, ran the hotel.

'I'm looking for some casual work,' he said. 'Just to keep the wolf from the door. Any ideas?'

'They're often looking for labourers on the building site,' said Dave.

'A bit too physical,' said the unfit fifty-something year old.

'Are you any good at organising things?' asked Dave.

'The best.' Charles smiled.

'Well, I need someone to organise events here. I'm too busy. There are companies that do it, but they cost a fortune. If you're here for the long term, and you are any good at it, I could offer you a free room and meals, but no pay I'm afraid.'

Charles felt quite excited about that idea. He would have a free home, food, some company and a job to keep him busy. But what would he do for cash? He'd worry about that later.

'I'd need an office,' he said.

'No problem. We have two empty offices upstairs.'

'And a computer and a phone.'

'We can organise that.'

'OK, tell me more.'

Tindra and Lizzy went to dinner together in the hostel's restaurant. Lizzy was on a gap year before doing her master's degree. She was quite a chatterbox, so it was easy for Tindra not to reveal too much about herself. When she could get a word in, she told Lizzy about her stay at the beach house and the fun she had had with the dogs and the baby.

The restaurant was packed, and two young men came to sit at their table. In this place you didn't ask, you just sat where there was a space. Oh no, they were Swedish! Tindra was sure she'd be recognised. But no, keep calm. With her spiky blonde hair and the tinted specs she had taken to wearing, maybe they wouldn't.

The great thing was she could eavesdrop. Few people outside of Sweden spoke Swedish, so they were speaking openly.

She was amused to hear that they were talking about her, and Lizzy.

'I like the blonde one,' said the tall guy with floppy blond hair. 'The other one's a bit fat.'

The shorter guy with an earring said, 'Yes, but she sounds like a good laugh. And I like a girl who isn't skinny.'

'Shall we ask them if they want a coffee?' said Mr Blond.

'OK, I will,' replied Mr Earring. 'In a minute.'

'Coward.'

'No, they're still eating. Wait 'til they've finished.'

Tindra put her fork down and told Lizzy that she had to go to their room to get something. She'd meet her in the lobby in 10 minutes. With that, she was off.

'Trust you to miss the boat,' said Mr Blond.

Anton continued to tease Ria and Mandy, and they loved every minute of it. How cruel life was to make their bodies old and unattractive when their minds were still the same as they always had been.

Anton was on the beach, sunning himself, when Ria decided to go to his room, just to tidy up and put fresh towels on the bed. Not to snoop. Nothing like that. But she couldn't help noticing a brief case that had been placed behind the desk.

She glanced out of the window to make sure that Anton was still on the beach and opened it. Well, she tried to open it, but it was locked, with a combination. One of the things she had learned from the police was how to open combination locks. That was not something the police advertised in their recruitment brochures, but they should have done because they would have had more recruits.

It took a few minutes, but it pinged open.

She lifted the newspaper that was lying on the top and exposed the biggest stack of banknotes she had ever seen. The case was crammed with euros.

Suddenly she was aware of somebody standing behind her. She would have to change her trousers again. She swung around.

'Thank God it's you,' she said to Mandy. 'Don't do that to me!'

'What are you doing!'

'I was just tidying... but look, I found these!'

Mandy went to the window. Anton was on his way back through the garden and looked up to see her in his room. He waved and smiled. Mandy quickly picked up the towels and shouted, 'Clean towels,' by way of explanation.

To Ria, 'Put that back quick. He's coming.'

By the time he reached the house, the two women were frantically cleaning the sitting room and trying not to make eye contact. Anton went upstairs and checked his room. There were indeed clean towels, and everything else was in its place. His briefcase was locked. That was the most important thing.

The next day he was picked up by a woman driving a large black car with tinted windows. As he left, he thrust a brown envelope into Ria's hand. 'For Matilda's college fund,' he said grinning. Ria tried to protest, but he insisted. He kissed the hands of both women and said he might see them on his return journey.

When he had gone, the women sat at the kitchen table to discuss what had happened. Ria opened the envelope.

'This is ridiculous!' she said. 'There must be 10 grand in here. We can't keep it.'

Mandy was having a silent fight between her conscience and her natural love of money.

'Well, he could obviously afford it,' she said. 'And it's for Matilda, not us.'

'Yes, I suppose we can't deprive her of her college fund,' Ria agreed.

'But Anton's obviously into something dodgy.'

'Not necessarily. He might be needing the cash to buy a car at an auction, or a house for that matter.'

'I suppose so,' said Ria, not believing it for one moment.

Charles, the happily married man who worked at an embassy in Canada and fathered royal babies did not expect to find himself organising bar mitzvahs and tea dances in a scruffy joint in Hitchin. But he found himself enjoying it, and hotel life suited him. His meals were cooked for him, his laundry done, and his bed made.

He had a permanent free parking space, and soon made new friends.

If he was careful, he could eke out the cash he had, but he didn't need much. Just the occasional book or maybe some petrol if he ventured out.

He could get free toiletries and even drinks at the hotel if Dave was at the bar, so his life was pretty comfortable.

He hadn't used his burner phone once. Who would he call? He had moments when he ached to speak to Anna, but there was no going back now. He didn't have a number for his mother. He had a number for Tindra, but there was no way that he was going to get involved in another of her pregnancies.

He found a new friend in Dotty, a rotund lady in her sixties who spent most of her time at the bar. She wasn't a big drinker, but she was a great talker and loved to hold court with anyone and everyone who was passing.

Everybody knew Dotty, and she had many interesting tales to tell, so she was never short of an ear to bend.

She lived in a world of her own, reliving the days of her youth when she had been married to a man who was a household name, a popular game show presenter.

He had long gone, but she was funny, clever and witty, and told tales of other celebrities of the day and wild parties, which had probably been embellished over the years. Nevertheless, it was an entertaining way to pass an hour or two.

All went well until Charles, by now used to his alias of Sam Lawson, was asked to organise a 'retired policeman's ball'. Panic rose, until he thought, what could possibly go wrong? Nobody knew him around here as Charles Radcliffe, in fact he had become quite well known as Sam Lawson. It wasn't as if there were posters all over the place with his mug shot on them. How would anyone know he was wanted? It could even be quite funny, mixing with all these old coppers who didn't have a clue.

Tindra registered at the maternity unit at the local public hospital in Paris. She had decided that after her scan, she would show Lizzy, who would probably have already guessed that she was pregnant.

The nurse seemed happy with the scan and had a big grin on her face. She asked if Tindra would like to know if the baby was a boy or a girl.

Tindra hesitated for a moment and then said, 'Yes, please.'

'Well,' said the nurse, 'you have a boy... *and* a girl!'

Chapter sixteen

Richard was alone at the Mill House. He had some thinking to do. He was falling in love with Ria. The truth was he had fallen in love with her soon after they met.

He liked her better now that she had started to unwind and show the funny, witty side of her character. She was also honest and kind.

He enjoyed Mandy's company too, but he wasn't sure what to do. He would like to ask Ria to marry him, but if she agreed, would they live at the beach house or here at the Mill House? He felt as if he would be coming between Ria and Mandy.

Should he give up the Mill House? It had been in his family for generations, but it was a bit of a money pit these days, and there was only him rattling around in it.

If he moved to the beach house permanently, he could help the girls with the heavier jobs, and be a father figure for Matilda. He suddenly wondered what would happen if Matilda was discovered by the authorities and whisked away. He shuddered. Maybe they had all become a bit blasé lately. They would have to be careful.

His thoughts wandered to Tindra. He felt that he had abandoned her in Paris, but it had been what she wanted. The girl wasn't thinking straight. How would she manage in a foreign country by herself with a baby? He must check on her. He would like to have a strong word with the baby's father!

Then he had a light bulb moment. Giselle was desperate for a baby. Maybe, just maybe, this could work out well.

Tindra was shocked, excited, terrified and had never felt so lonely.

As a mother, the idea of having a boy and a girl was thrilling. As a single mother, it was an horrendous prospect. Twins had never occurred to her, although, thinking about it, her father was a twin.

Her bump seemed to grow very quickly after that, and it was impossible to hide. Some of the longer-term residents at the hostel began to gossip about her; and Lizzy, after her initial fascination, soon lost interest as Tindra was unable to drink or dance the night away any more.

It was time for Tindra to move on.

She phoned Richard, who was still at the Mill House.

'You said I could call you if I needed rescuing,' she said tearfully.

'What's happened?' he asked, feeling alarmed, but not altogether surprised.

'Can I see you?'

'Yes, of course. Where are you?'

'Where you left me,' she said.

'I'll be there in an hour.'

He arrived on the dot, despite heavy traffic, and was amazed to see how much her pregnancy had progressed.

He managed to park on the next street, and they went for a coffee and chocolate eclairs.

'Dear girl, you are blooming!' he said, trying to make her feel better.

'Blooming fat!' she laughed through her tears.

'Yes, that as well.' He smiled. 'Now, what's been happening?'

She told him all about it.

For a moment, she thought he had lost the power of speech. So did he. Twins! For crying out loud, this girl didn't get much luck. But he smiled and said, 'Congratulations! How wonderful! A boy and a girl.'

His head was swimming. He certainly couldn't leave her now. She wouldn't go back to her parents, and why should she if her father was a bully? Her ex-boyfriend had deserted her. Sometimes he was embarrassed to be a man.

'What would you like to do?' he asked her gently.

'Have another chocolate eclair,' she laughed.

'That's better,' he laughed. 'I think I'll have one too!'

* * *

Plans for the Retired Policeman's Ball were coming along nicely. A tribute band had been booked, and the kitchen had their orders to provide a lavish buffet. The only thing bothering Charles was that he didn't have a dinner suit. He didn't want to go cap in hand to Dave again, so he hired one. He put it on and looked at himself in the full-length mirror on his wardrobe. Not half bad. He was really beginning to feel like himself again.

Tickets had been sent out, and nearly two hundred people were expected.

The thought of being in a room with nearly a hundred cops and their spouses was beginning to make him nervous. But they were retired, so his misdemeanours were after their time.

The big night came, and they turned out to be quite a jolly crowd. All dressed up to the nines, and thoroughly enjoying themselves. One or two even came in their old uniforms. An excuse to wear them one more time.

They met up with old friends and colleagues, and stories were told and retold. There were hoots of laughter as they reminisced about raids and arrests that had gone wrong and porkies that had been told in court. In fact, it was quite an eye-opener.

Charles just sat back with a drink and watched happily as the night he had planned was so obviously a success.

Then a voice said, 'Charles! We meet again!'

***

Ria and Mandy were having a heart to heart as they relaxed after preparing the guest room for their next visitor. They had no idea who that would be, or when, but for now they could relax in the sunshine, while Matilda had her afternoon nap.

Richard had not yet returned, so they had the place to themselves.

Mandy kicked it off. 'How are you feeling about Richard, now that he's been around for a while?' she asked.

Ria considered for a moment. 'I think you know the answer to that. I'd marry him tomorrow if he asked me.'

'So, you've gone off George Clooney then?'

'Oh no. I'd keep him for the weekends.'

'Greedy girl. What about me?'

'Nah, don't fancy you.'

'Ria, if you do marry Richard, what happens to me? I'm serious.'

'What do you mean, what happens to you?'

'Well, I wouldn't want to live here as a prize gooseberry.'

'Don't be daft. We're not teenagers. This is *our* house. If anything, he's the outsider.'

'But you would be a married couple. I would feel uncomfortable.'

'It would be no different to what it is now. He'd be around, and so would I. We all get on OK, don't we? Anyway, I need you here to wash the dishes.'

Mandy threw a cushion at her, and the subject was closed.

Just then they heard the familiar chugging of the catamaran approaching. It was Jack. He jumped off into the shallow water and ran towards them.

'Hi. Is Anton still here?'

'No, someone picked him up this morning.'

'Oh, I have something for him. Pierre asked me to drop it off.'

'Anton did say he might see us again on his return journey,' said Ria.

'Well, I'll leave it with you if that's OK. If he doesn't show up again, you can give it back to me or Pierre next time.'

'No problem,' said Mandy as Jack put a parcel about the size of a toaster on the table in front of them.

'Why don't you stay and have some tea with us?' asked Ria.

'Sorry, dashing about as usual. But thanks.'

Richard and Tindra had two more eclairs. Tindra said she had to eat for three now.

Richard was racking his brains. What would he do if he was Tindra's father? A decent father, not a bully.

Take her home of course. But he was not her father.

He thought about the idea he had of Giselle adopting the baby, which Giselle would no doubt jump at, but twins? And in any case, he didn't know if Tindra would consider parting with them. There was one way to find out.

'Please don't mind me asking,' he said kindly, 'but have you thought about having the babies adopted?'

Tears sprang to her eyes. 'Of course I've thought about it, but I've already lost one child.' She had blurted it out without thinking.

'I'm so sorry,' said Richard. 'I didn't know.'

'Of course not.' She forced a smile.

'So, is the plan to keep them then?'

'They are my babies. If there is any way that I can keep them, I will.'

'Don't you think you ought to tell the father that it's twins?'

'No!' snapped Tindra. 'I won't be telling him anything. He gave up the right to be a father when he walked away.'

Richard persevered, 'You said you had some friends in Paris from your days at the Sorbonne. Are you still in touch with them?'

Tindra shook her head.

'Have you made any friends at the hostel?'

'Yes, one, my roommate Lizzy. But she likes to party, and I can't really join in at the moment.'

'No, I can see that could be a problem. But is she a good friend?'

'Yes, I think so.'

'Look, if it's any help to you, I have an apartment in Avenue Montaigne, in the 8th Arrondissement.

You and Lizzy could use it for as long as you like. I'm never there these days. You could stay at my house, but it's in the middle of nowhere, and you will need to be near a hospital and some life.'

Tindra threw her arms around him.

So that would be a yes then, if Lizzy agreed. Tindra said she could not face staying at the hostel with her ever-increasing bump, and no ring on her finger.

Charles tried to stay cool, as he turned to face the voice that was calling him Charles.

'I'm sorry, you have the wrong man. My name is Sam.'

Dave, the manager, was looking on with interest.

'No, Charles, don't you remember,' the man persisted. 'I saw you recently in Welwyn Garden City. I worked briefly with your mum, Ria. Of course we're all retired now. How is she? You had to dash off last time.'

Dave intervened. 'Sorry, you are?'

'James Bassett, I was Charles's mum's sergeant at Bishops Stortford way back when.'

'Sam must have a double!' said Dave. 'I can assure you that this is a man who works for me, Sam Lawson.'

But James Bassett was having none of it.

'Look, chum, I was a copper for 32 years, and I know a face when I see it. His mum used to bring him to our house for tea sometimes. Don't you remember, Charles?'

Charles remembered how he had to sit still for ages while the grown-ups talked. How even when he was 14, they seemed to think he couldn't understand anything they were saying.

Dave took Charles to one side.

'Is there something you want to tell me, Sam?'

'No of course not, he's either batty or he's mistaken me for someone else. I'll go and help out in the kitchen to avoid any further problems. How embarrassing.'

'OK, mate, that's good enough for me,' said Dave, giving Charles a pat on the shoulder.

As James returned to the fray, James Bassett appeared again with another man by his side.

'Where's Charles?' he asked Dave.

'Sam has gone to attend to his other duties,' he said. 'Can I help?'

'This is, well was, Inspector Ed Davis. He knew Charles. He knew his mum Ria, too.'

'That's good. You obviously have some happy memories,' said Dave. 'Are you enjoying the evening?'

Ria and Mandy sat looking at the parcel on the table in front of them. It was a cardboard box, heavily wrapped in brown parcel tape. The dogs sniffed at it, but soon lost interest.

But the girls didn't.

'Shall we open it?' asked Mandy, hopefully.

Ria lifted it. 'It's very heavy,' she said.

'Let's have a peek.'

'How can we have a peek? It's all sealed down.'

'I have a cardboard box about the same size upstairs,' said Mandy, 'and we have Sellotape.'

'That's not the same as parcel tape.'

'Well, Anton won't know what tape was used will he?'

'Maybe not, but we shouldn't.'

'I think we have the right,' said Mandy. 'Bearing in mind what he had in his briefcase. After all, we are handling whatever it is, and it's in our house.'

'True,' said Ria, who didn't need much persuading. 'We'd better take it into one of our bedrooms in case Anton comes back unexpectedly. Get the scissors.'

If they could have run upstairs, they would have done, but wheezy chests and arthritic knees made the climb laborious, especially when carrying a heavy object.

Ria set it down on Mandy's bed. She didn't want to go into her own room and disturb Matilda.

Mandy was soon beside her with the scissors, and they started to rip into the parcel. Once the box was open, they tore away large pieces of bubble wrap and uncovered two handguns and some ammunition.

'Fuck me, we're gun-runners now!' cried Mandy.

'You're such a lady,' said Ria.

'They're guns!'

'I can see that.'

'What are we going to do?'

'Play cowboys and Indians.'

'Ria, why aren't you taking this seriously?'

'There's no point getting excited about it. I am not altogether surprised, are you?'

'Yes, I am surprised. I didn't expect guns.'

'Guns, drugs, cash, people-smuggling, what did you expect? I tried to tell you not to get involved. It was obviously dodgy.'

'Me!'

'OK, I agreed in the end.'

Mandy laughed. 'Well, I did say what good criminals we'd make. Who'd suspect two old ladies! But I thought we were talking about a few bottles of Scotch and some fags.'

'We'd better get them wrapped up again quick. The sooner they leave this house the better,' said Ria, 'and we put a stop to all this from now on. Where's your cardboard box? This one's in shreds.'

Mandy went to her cupboard. 'Oh no,' she said, 'I forgot. I threw it out, didn't I, with the recycling.'

'Well done. They collected it yesterday.'

Richard's apartment was huge and luxurious, and in one of the smartest parts of Paris. Lizzy had jumped at the chance to live there, and after a serious conversation with Richard, agreed to stay with Tindra (Louise) and help her as best she could throughout the pregnancy and with the babies. Just being there, Richard said, was the important thing.

Once they were happily installed, Richard felt free to return to Ria and Mandy. He left 500 euros on the hall table for them and left.

Charles did not go to help in the kitchen. He went to his room and paced about. How stupid he must have been to think that he could organise a do for hundreds of policemen and all would be well. But on the plus side, the guy who recognised him was just reminiscing; he didn't know that Charles was wanted. But how long would it be before he did know? Someone was bound to google him and see press reports.

The red mist started to appear. He had just found a place he liked, with a job he was good at, and some jerk comes along and gets in his way. It always happened. People always got in his way. He had already moved once because of this numbskull. Now where would he go? Dave was bound to be suspicious, however much he appeared OK with it.

His anger rose until he could no longer contain it. He went to the storeroom, picked up a hammer from the toolbox, and waited in a dark doorway for the old git who was ruining his life to walk by to the car park. Trouble was, there would be dozens of them leaving at the same time. How would he get him on his own? If only he knew which was his car. Then he had a flashback. When he had seen the man in Welwyn Garden City, he had watched as he went to an old red Mondeo.

He went to the car park and had a look. There was a red Mondeo... bingo! He took the number and went into the hotel and to the small, unmanned reception desk.

He switched on the PA system and asked for the owner of the red Mondeo to please move his car. He then quickly resumed his place in the dark doorway.

Minutes later an unsuspecting ex Sgt James Bassett walked by jangling his keys, and soon wished he had never heard of Charles Radcliffe. Charles hit him repeatedly, releasing many years' worth of pent up anguish and fury.

He then threw the bloody hammer into the boot of his own car and drove away.

Mandy was panicking. What could they wrap the guns in now? The cardboard box was ripped.

'We must have a box somewhere in the house... What about the garage?' she said.

'I don't think so. We had a clear out. Why don't you go to the corner shop? They're bound to have a box.'

'Good thinking,' said, Mandy. 'Do you want anything?'

'Just some milk please,' said Ria.

Mandy almost ran out of the house, straight into Anton, who was walking down the path.

She stopped dead. 'Anton!' she shouted, loud enough for Ria to hear. 'How lovely to see you. You should have said you were coming.'

He gave his usual George Clooney grin, 'I'm not stopping, beautiful lady. I have just come to collect the parcel that Jack left for me.'

It was a good job that Ria had lots of pairs of trousers.

'Do come in,' she said. 'I'm sure you have time for a cup of tea, or maybe something stronger.'

'Well…'

'Come on now, I'll be offended if you don't just stay for a quick catch up.'

She was praying that Mandy and the box would get back before he left.

'Well, I have a car waiting for me.'

'Bring the driver in,' said Ria. 'I've just opened a very nice bottle of… well, not sure, but something red,' she laughed, as she rushed off to get a bottle from the wine rack.

He loved her laugh. 'OK, just a quick one, thank you, beautiful lady.'

A few minutes later, she heard the front door go, and Mandy creaking her way up the stairs.

'Isn't she going to join us?' asked Anton.

'I expect she's gone to check on the baby,' said Ria.

'Of course, how is the little sweetheart?'

'She's great. She's crawling now!'

Ria jabbered on uncontrollably until Anton was looking at his watch. Then in walked Mandy with a wrapped parcel under one arm and Matilda under the other.

'Can you take this, it's heavy,' she said to anyone.

'The baby or the package?' asked Ria, taking Matilda.

Anton took the package, gave it a cursory inspection, and after a few thank yous and goodbyes, went on his way.

Mandy and Ria were red-faced but relieved. Mandy looked at Ria. 'Another pair of trousers?' she said. 'Yes,' laughed Ria, and they both laughed until they could hardly breathe, and they both needed another pair of trousers.

Chapter seventeen

There was mayhem at the hotel in Hitchin. A hundred ex-coppers trying to solve the murder of one of their own. Dave ran into the kitchen, which was full of detritus from the evenings' buffet. 'Where's Sam?' he shouted to the bewildered staff. 'It's all going mad out there.'

He then ran outside as the ambulance arrived, followed by more police cars than Dave had ever seen at one time. One way or another, the whole of Hertfordshire constabulary must be here, he thought.

The car park was blocked by the emergency vehicles so no one could get out.

An inspector took charge. Once the body had been photographed and removed, he put two officers in charge of the scene, which was taped off. Everybody else had to go back into the hotel to be interviewed. Those who knew the victim were shocked and distraught. Others were secretly excited to be back in the saddle again.

Dave just wanted to find Sam to tell him what had happened to the man who thought he was someone else. He looked in the car park. His car had gone. Where on earth had he sloped off to?

It wasn't like him. He must have gone before the emergency services arrived or he would have been stuck in the car park.

He went back into the bar, where Dotty was in her usual seat, enjoying the pandemonium, and wanting to know all the ins and outs.

'Have you seen Sam this evening?' Dave asked her.

'I did earlier, just for a minute. I think he was going to fix something. He had a hammer.'

'You are so lucky having twins,' said Lizzy. 'I'm quite jealous, especially a boy and a girl.'

Lizzy and Tindra were watching TV. Tindra smiled. She'd swap places any day.

'Have you thought of names for them yet?' Lizzy enthused.

'Well,' said Tindra, 'I'm thinking of naming the boy after my brother Hugo, and the girl, maybe, after a gorgeous little girl I helped look after in England called Matilda.'

'Nice names,' said Lizzy. And after a pause, 'We're so lucky to get this apartment. I hope Richard doesn't want anything in return.'

'No, he's not like that. He's had this place for years, and everybody knows him around here.'

'Why don't we go out and feed our faces?'

'Where to?' asked Tindra.

'Oh, there are lots of places around here. And we have the five hundred euro that Richard gave us.'

'OK, why not!'

Once again, Charles was driving aimlessly while the red mist subsided. It wasn't fair. He tried hard, but people always spoiled things for him. This time he would drive further away, maybe to a seaside town. But first he wanted to call Dave and throw him off the trail. He liked Dave. Maybe, if he could convince Dave that he was Sam and had nothing to do with the murder, he might be able to go back there when the fuss had died down.

He pulled into a layby and called him. Dave answered immediately. 'Where the hell have you been?'

'Sorry, I didn't want to stick around while that nutter was imagining I was his long-lost friend, so I went for a drive. To be honest, I was just very tired and needed to get away for an hour. But when I came back there were police cars blocking the car park. Were they there to pick up the retirees?' he said innocently.

'The nutter you talk about was beaten to death just outside the hotel, that's why the police were here!'

'Oh my God. Poor man. He obviously had a screw loose. He must have upset somebody.'

'I could have done with you here,' Dave snarled. 'Fine time to slope off.'

'I'm sorry, Dave, how was I to know?' There was a pause.

'Dotty saw you leaving the hotel with a hammer.'

'Yes, I caught my jacket on a nail as I came in earlier. I went to knock it in before people left.'

'OK, well where are you now. What are you doing?'

'Look, Dave, I really need a break. I haven't been feeling too well lately. Forgive me, but I'm going away for a few days. Sorry to let you down.'

He threw the burner phone out of the window into a ditch and drove on.

Tindra and Lizzy waddled to the nearest restaurant. The only available seats were in a booth with a fixed table, so it was a tight squeeze, which set them off into silent giggles. The place was very quiet, and everyone was well dressed. They both ordered crab salad with crème brûlée to follow, and a house wine.

'Should you be drinking?' whispered Lizzy.

'Just one won't hurt,' said Tindra guiltily.

From the next booth they could hear the low rumble of men's voices. But it was impossible to see who was sitting either side of them. That was the whole point, they supposed. People came here for privacy. Sometimes they heard snippets of conversation, so they sat quietly while they tried to eavesdrop. The last thing Tindra wanted right now, or expected to find, was a man.

Lizzy was ever hopeful.

Then a man's voice said in English, 'Dear boy, we have the perfect set up. You can't walk away now.' And then something muffled, and then, 'I won't let you. You could blow the whole operation.'

The other man muttered something and then said, 'I don't want to spend the rest of my life in jail.'

To which the first man answered, 'Dead or in jail. Take your pick.'

Tindra's eyes widened. She whispered to Lizzy, 'That was Richard!'

Ria and Mandy were enjoying life now. The weather was beautiful, and they had made the decision not to have any more 'guests' or their packages! They would tell Richard when he returned, and he could pass on the news to Pierre and Jack.

The girls now felt free again, and enjoyed walks with the dogs, and Matilda in her buggy. They occasionally bumped into neighbours, who all seemed friendly, and they never tired of looking at the sea.

This was how Mandy had imagined it would be. As much as she liked Richard, three's a crowd. She liked things just the way they were. Ria was enjoying life, too, although her thoughts were often of Charles, and where she must have gone wrong.

She loved Richard and could see no reason why the three of them could not live happily together.

Maybe they could find a man for Mandy? Perhaps a bit of online dating?

After a walk along the waterfront, they sat down on the patio with a cold drink.

'Have you ever thought of computer dating?' she asked Mandy, casually.

Mandy was offended. 'No, have you?' she snapped.

'No, but everyone's doing it these days.'

'Well, I'm not everyone.'

'Why not have a go. You might meet someone nice.'

'So what's this about? You want to get rid of me so you can be with lover boy? I'm quite happy as I am thanks.'

'Of course not. It would be fun; we could all go out as a foursome. And we all need someone of our own to love.'

'Look, Ria, when we agreed to buy this beach house the plan was for it to be for you, me and Matilda. I have tolerated your relationship with Richard, and he's a nice man, but it is not what I had envisaged. Two old mates sharing their retirement by the sea and bringing up a little girl. That was the idea. Now I have to play gooseberry, and you want to palm me off with someone, so you don't have to feel guilty.'

'I don't feel guilty.'

'Well how would you feel if I moved a man in here and you were on your own?'

'I wouldn't be on my own, would I?'

Matilda started to cry, and the dogs started to bark, so the conversation finished there.

Charles looked at a map. He thought that the best thing to do was drive to a seaside town where he might find live-in seasonal work. He could no longer be Sam. He would have to think of another name. Damn to hell that busybody ex-copper.

He decided to head for Bournemouth. It was an anonymous, busy town. He drove through the night and arrived at 3am. Not a good time to be on the streets. Bored policemen were likely to ask questions if he parked and slept in the car. Then he spotted a hotel car park. That would do nicely. He parked in the furthest corner and dozed off.

At 8am there was a tapping on his window. 'Sorry, sir, this is a hotel car park, for hotel residents only,' came an officious voice.

Charles couldn't think where he was for a minute. 'Um, sorry, no problem. I will be checking in to the hotel. I just arrived too early.'

'No you won't, sir, there are no vacancies.'

Did the man think he was some kind of a vagrant? He *was* crumpled and unshaven.

He looked down and was horrified to see that he was still wearing his dinner suit which was spattered with blood.

He switched on the engine and drove away.

He needed new clothes but had brought nothing with him. He couldn't go into a shop looking like this. It was early, so there were still parking spaces near the beach. Maybe he could strip off, dump the clothes, and go for a swim in his pants to clean himself up. Or wash his shirt and trousers in the sea, but no, they would be stained.

He looked at his trousers. The stains were hardly visible on the black material. If he could find a clothes' shop near to the beach, he might get away with going in there topless.

He drove along the seafront. There was a stall selling, amongst other things, T-shirts. That would do for a start. He picked the first three T-shirts in his size and put one on. And fantastic, they had swimming trunks and shorts. He bought a pair of trunks and two pairs of shorts. And shiny black shoes did not look right, so he bought a pair of flip flops and a baseball cap. Sorted.

Now he would need to dispose of the bloodstained clothes. It would be easy enough to put them in a bin, but someone would soon be asking questions. And then there was the hammer...

He decided to put on the trunks and swim out as far as he could, while there was hardly anyone about, and dump them at sea. The hammer would not wash up, but the clothes might, but if they did, they would have been soaked for so long that they would be no good for forensics.

It was a hot day, but the sea was cold. Nevertheless, this had to be done. He rolled the clothes into a ball around the hammer and stuffed them into his swimming trunks. Good job nobody was near enough to notice his odd shape. He ran into the sea and swam as far as he could before offloading the offending articles. It had been almost impossible to swim with them dragging his trunks down.

When he got back to the car, he was exhausted. He had to find somewhere to stay.

He, and his clothes were now presentable, so he went to the first hotel he came to on the main road. It was not the most salubrious place he had ever been to, but all he wanted was a bed and some food.

Sgt Gill had heard about the brutal killing of an ex-policeman in Hitchin, but had no reason to connect it to Charles, who he still believed to be Welwyn Garden City, some 15 miles away. He heard that the local police were interested in a hotel staff member called Sam Lawson who disappeared on the same night and had been seen with a hammer.

Sgt Gill started doing some foot-slogging around the hotels and B&B's in Welwyn Garden City. He carried a dog-eared picture of Charles, which he thrust in front of anyone who would look. Exhausted and demoralised, he went for a drink in a hotel bar. He had already asked the barmaid about Charles with no luck. Then a waiter came over and looked at the photograph lying on the table.

'That's Sam Lawson,' he said.

Sgt Gill started to twitch. 'Are you sure?'

'Positive. He stayed here for a while.'

Sam bloody Lawson! So that's what he was calling himself now. And now he had actually murdered a policeman, and Sgt Gill knew his real identity. He was the only one who knew. He would make inspector before the year was out! He was so excited that he knocked his drink over as he rushed to his car to call his superiors.

He had added a stutter to his twitch, so his inspector had no idea what he was talking about. But soon he would be a hero. His persistence was paying off.

Tindra and Lizzy would now have to remain seated until Richard and his cohort left the restaurant. They couldn't risk being seen. Three coffees later, the men left, and as they walked past the window, deep in conversation, the girls could see for sure that it was Richard, and the other man was Jack.

Back in the apartment, Tindra was pacing. 'He said dead or in jail... that he couldn't risk the operation, or something like that!'

'Yes, I heard,' said Lizzy quietly. 'I thought he was a really nice man.'

'So did I,' said Tindra, 'but he's obviously doing something illegal.'

'What should we do?'

'I don't suppose we can do anything,' said Tindra. 'For a start, we would lose this apartment.' Tindra was used to the good life, and although she had money in the bank, she didn't have access to it without giving away her whereabouts, so she needed the apartment.

'And if he is doing something terrible, who knows what he would do to us if we told the police. And really there is nothing to tell. We don't know what he's doing.'

'Who was the other man?' asked Lizzy.

'Jack. I met him when I was staying at the beach house. He has a catamaran, and shuttles back and forth across the Channel.'

'So it could be some sort of smuggling?' said Lizzy.

'Could be. I wonder if Maria and Lucy know. The men often bring the catamaran up to their beach.'

'Maybe you should warn them?'

Tindra said she would think about it.

Despite her objections to online dating, Mandy was curious. She wouldn't let Ria know, but she decided to have a look when Ria had gone to the beach with Matilda.

First, she had to put in her own profile. The joining process was all a bit long-winded. What could she say? Well, first she had to knock a few years off her age. What could she get away with? She looked in the mirror. 'You ugly old bag!' she said to herself. She looked at her grey hair, tied up in a ponytail, and her sagging chin and droopy eyelids. 'I was pretty once!'

No good saying she was younger than she was. The man would soon find out when he met her. So, she put her true date of birth.

She went on to say that, like everyone else, she would like to meet her soulmate. She liked jazz, musicals, theatre, travel and good food. She didn't have a recent photo of herself, so that bit would have to wait.

She then looked at the photos of available men in her age group. 'They're all old men!' she cried. 'I couldn't go out with an old grandad like that.'

And then she looked back in the mirror and realised that the old men would look at her and say that there was no way they would be seen with an old granny!

She clicked off the computer. Old age was shit. Crap. Unfair. She felt a tear drip down her cheek, and a soft, gentle little spaniel climbed on her knee to lick her face.

'Roxy, you are better than any man,' she said, giving the pup a cuddle.

Ria came back from the beach with Matilda. 'She loves the water,' she said. 'By the way, I just had a call from Richard. He's on his way back.'

'OK,' said Mandy.

'What's the matter?'

'Nothing.'

'Are you not happy about him coming back?'

'No, I'm fine. Do you want some tea?'

Charles looked out of his Bournemouth hotel window. It was busy with tourists. He had booked in as John Windsor. His funds were now precariously low. He went to reception, where a young woman sat looking bored.

'I'm looking for a live-in job,' he said. 'Any ideas?'

'Best google it,' she said, without looking up from her phone.

Well I would, you ignoramus, he thought, *if I had a bloody phone, or a computer*.

He found his way to the library and had to wait to use a computer. Finally, he checked out the jobs in the local area and made a note of a couple of numbers. Then he went and bought another burner phone.

He sat in the gardens near the beach and rang the first number. The ad was for a live-in gardener in a large country house. He didn't know a weed from a tulip and had no equipment, but it was worth a phone call.

The woman on the phone sounded desperate. The garden had become completely overgrown since Stan died, she said, and she had people coming to stay for the next few months. His was the first call she'd had. Could he come over today?

He most certainly could.

'John Windsor. Pleased to meet you, madam.'

'Please call me Penelope,' she said.

'Now you do know it's live-in, don't you?'

'Yes, that would suit me fine.'

'Good, now tell me about yourself.'

Oh, blimey. Here we go again.

'Yes, well, sadly my dear wife died a few months ago, and I didn't want to stay in the house with so many memories, so I decided to take a short break and then look for a live-in position.'

'You poor man, I'm sorry. Would you like to see the accommodation?'

'Yes please. By the way, I apologise for turning up in shorts and a T-shirt, not to mention the flip flops, but my case was stolen from my car last night, and I haven't had a chance to buy new things.'

'Oh my goodness, you haven't had much luck have you! I think some of Stan's things might fit you. He was the previous gardener, God rest his soul, but he was very smart when he went out, and very modern.'

Charles was not sure about wearing a dead man's clothes, but when he looked in the man's wardrobe he was delighted. Everything was cleaned and pressed, and the clothes were what he would have chosen for himself. Three smart suits, cashmere jumpers, crisp white shirts and several pairs of trousers and jeans.

That'll do nicely, he thought.

His room was large and airy, with a tall ceiling and sash windows with flowing drapes. There was a double bed with piles of cushions, and a desk and chair. Then there was a large wardrobe, and two chests of drawers. The view over the gardens was magnificent, and he could see that he would have his work cut out.

Penelope was delighted to have found someone, and not bothered about the formalities. This John Windsor was a well-spoken and polite Englishman. He would be a pleasure to have about the place. And she was a good judge of character.

He would get a bed and board and £300 per week, cash.

He had asked for cash, explaining that he was still sorting out the finances that his wife used to manage, and needed to set up a new bank account.

Penelope said he could use the mowers and tools that Stan had left. Charles wasn't used to physical labour, but needs must, and he might even enjoy it. It certainly felt safe and out of harm's way here.

Chapter eighteen

Richard was glad to be back at the beach house, where he was spoiled and had the attention of two caring women. He told them all about Tindra (Louise) having twins, and how he had moved her and her friend Lizzy into his apartment. Ria was shocked that she was having twins but said it was just like him to do something so generous, and she fell a little bit more in love with him.

Mandy was concerned about Tindra. That poor girl. She asked if Lizzy would be any good at taking care of her. Richard said that Lizzy was a party girl, but at least there was someone with her. But Lizzy would be due back at uni in October.

Mandy made a decision. She would go and stay with Tindra as soon as she came out of hospital, for maybe a few weeks, until she could cope. After all, she didn't have her mum to turn to. And Mandy now had some experience with babies. It would be a chance for her to see Paris as well.

She suggested it to Richard, and he thought it would be a great idea. There were three bedrooms in the apartment, so plenty of room. Richard would put the idea to Tindra next time he was in Paris.

Ria thought it was a good idea but was concerned that Mandy might be just wanting to get away from the beach house and being with a couple. She felt a rift forming in their friendship and wanted to avoid that at all costs. But she didn't want to give up Richard, the man she loved. She had not expected to find a new love so late in life, and she wasn't going to throw something so precious away.

Mandy went back onto the computer. Lots and lots of old men. Bald ones, wrinkly ones, pot-bellied ones, pictures of men who were so far in the distance that you could hardly see them or sitting on the bonnet of a flash car or a motorbike. Why would she want to see their car or motorbike? And they all ran marathons, did bungee jumping, swam the Channel and had Olympic Gold medals. Most said their interests included football (boring), golf (even more boring), or cricket (yawn).

They were looking for young, attractive, slim women, who were tactile, enjoyed cooking and who would like to share their hobbies with them. And they gave themselves names like Nobby, Thruster and Cockerdoodledo. Irresistible, obviously.

Sgt Gill had caused quite a stir by revealing the true identity of Sam Lawson. But the bloody man had disappeared off the face of the earth once more. Dave at the Hitchin hotel was able to tell the police the type of car he was driving, but didn't have the number plate, and the CCTV wasn't working.

ANPR traced all cars of that type that left Hitchin on the evening of the murder. Most were local, but one went to Northampton, and one went to Bournemouth.

They could rule out the Northampton one because the number plate was genuine, and the car was owned by a Northampton resident. However, the car that went to Bournemouth had a number plate that was registered to a legitimate car in Welwyn Garden City. It was a fake, a copy.

Sgt Gill put Bournemouth in his satnav and took off. His record for actually finding anyone was such that nobody wanted to go with him, even though he was the hero of the hour. But if he managed to find a lead, they would, of course, send backup.

ANPR had clocked the car with false number plates taking a road out of Bournemouth into the countryside. He was getting near, he knew it.

Charles was riding his sit-on mower over the enormous lawns of Waverly Lodge.

It didn't take much brainpower, so he was thinking about things. He had to review his security. He had disposed of the evidence, i.e. his stained clothes and the hammer, and had put false number plates on the car and bought a new burner phone. He suddenly stopped dead. The car number plates! They might have been on CCTV at the Hitchin hotel. The car could then be traced right here!

He leapt from the mower and ran to the car, ripping off the number plates. He needed to get some more fake ones, urgently. But for now, he must hide the car. Luckily, there were unused garages with open padlocks on the outside. He quickly drove the car inside, and closed the padlocks, pocketing the keys.

Now he had to get rid of the fake plates. He had been digging up a flower bed, so he would bury them there. No problem. Then he would order some more plates. He had to keep on top of all this – and remember what his name was today!

Penelope came out of the house to see how he was getting on. She had seen him put his car in the garage.

'I hope you don't mind,' he said, 'but the car has been playing up, so I need to have a look at it. I might even exchange it as it's been nothing but trouble.'

'I don't drive,' she said, 'but if you'd be prepared to drive me about when I need to go into town or for appointments, you could use my car. Well, it was our car, before I lost my husband. That was two years ago, but the car should still be OK. Stan used to take it out every now and again to keep the battery topped up.'

She led him to yet another garage behind the house, where there were other outbuildings. She took a key from a bundle in her pocket and opened the door. There stood a rather dusty, but splendid gold Bentley. He wouldn't be at all conspicuous in that, he thought, although it did have the bonus of tinted windows! He couldn't wait to get behind the wheel.

She'd be giving him a chauffeur's hat and calling him Parker next!

Tindra was on the phone to Hugo. 'Mother is very worried about you,' he said. 'We all are.'

'Well, there's no need to be. I'm fine, honestly. I have a beautiful apartment, and a lovely flatmate called Lizzy, you would love her, Hugo, and the pregnancy is coming along fine. Why don't you come over for a visit? We have an extra bedroom.'

'I'd love to actually,' said Hugo, who was tired of his parents' arguments, and he would like to meet this Lizzy person.

'But what would I tell Mother?'

'You don't tell her anything about me, or coming here...'

'I know that, but...'

'Tell her you're going to see one of your uni friends or something. I can't be your big sister all your life.'

'You'd better be!' he laughed.

And then, more seriously, 'I can't wait to be an uncle. Do you know which sex it is yet?'

Tindra realised she hadn't told him. Maybe she should wait until he arrived.

'Not yet,' she said. 'But if it's a boy, I'll name him after you.'

It would be great to see her brother again, and she was looking forward to hearing all the news from home, although if her father was still angry with her, she knew it would not all be good.

As she looked at her enormous bump, she thought briefly about William, and tears sprung to her eyes. She really had loved him, and here were his babies. He shouldn't be missing all of this. But by now he was probably with someone else, and he didn't love her, so that was just the way the cookie crumbled. She would just have to get on with it.

The evenings were drawing in, and Ria and Richard liked to snuggle up in front of the TV, while the indefatigable Matilda walked around the edges of the furniture.

Mandy was spending more and more time on the computer. She was becoming obsessed. There must be one decent man out there. Then she had a message from the dating site.

Terry wants to meet you. Click here to see his profile.

She clicked.

Terry is a fun-loving man who loves to socialise. He is a retired actor, who lives within 10 miles of your postcode. He is single and looking for a retired woman with a sense of fun. Looks are unimportant.

Mmm. Sounds OK, she thought. I'll agree to meet. Can't do any harm to have a coffee with him.

Click on yes to send him a message. Click.

Then a bloody great screen came up asking for £98 to go ahead!

Click off.

She wandered into the sitting room to play gooseberry with the lovebirds.

'OK?' said Ria, giving her a sad/smug/patronising smile.

'Why wouldn't I be?' said Mandy.

Would Terry be worth 98 quid, she wondered? Did he even exist?

Richard's phone rang. It was Pierre.

'Yes, tomorrow night, no problem,' said Richard. 'See you then.'

He turned to Ria. 'A new guest for you tomorrow night, and a few boxes, but they can go in the garage. It's only for one night.'

'No,' said Ria. Richard looked shocked.

'What do you mean, no?'

Mandy settled down to be entertained.

Ria said, 'I'm sorry, darling, but we don't want to get involved in any more skulduggery.'

'Skulduggery!' he exploded. 'What skulduggery?'

'Well, you don't suppose those boxes will be full of fairy cakes, do you?' said Ria.

'I don't know what they will be full of. Probably the gentleman's clothes and luggage. Where's this all coming from?' he asked.

Ria couldn't admit that they had broken into the briefcase and the box and had seen the money and the guns.

'I just think we've had enough visitors,' she said. 'And it all seems a bit fishy to me.'

'You knew that these crossings were illegal, but harmless, and agreed to them.' He turned to Mandy. 'Both of you did.'

Mandy just shrugged.

'Well, my son is bringing a gentleman here tomorrow night. It's too late to cancel now.' And with that, he went off up to bed.

Sgt Gill had been driving around the country lanes near Bournemouth, twitching, all day. The car he was looking for was very popular, or you might say common, so he got excited every time he saw one. A couple of times he even turned around to follow one if he couldn't catch the number plate. The local police were waiting for it to ping up on the ANPR, but so far nothing. Dreyfus had done it again. More humiliation. He booked into a cheap hotel near the seafront. He might at least make a little bit of a holiday of it. He made straight for the bar. Out of habit, he took the rumpled picture of Charles Radcliffe out of his pocket and showed it to the barmaid.

'Oh him. Yes, he kept interrupting my phone calls. Rude,' she said.

'He was here?'

'Yep. He was asking if there were any live-in jobs around here. I told him to google it. What a wally.'

'Then w-w-what?'

'Nothing. He just left, looking annoyed.'

'Do you know where he went?'

She looked at him as if he was senile. 'How the hell would I know?'

A live-in job. Of course. Sgt Gill went to his room and started to google. There were only two live-in jobs advertised within a ten-mile radius. One was for a chambermaid in a hotel, and the other for a nanny for a German family. He couldn't see Charles in either of those roles.

Penelope had taken down her ad for a gardener, as she was now more than satisfied with her new man. The garden was looking better already, and now he had agreed to be her chauffeur too. He didn't like being asked about his past, but that was understandable as it reminded him of his dear wife.

They took the Bentley out for a drive along the country lanes. Despite being out of action for a while, it drove like a dream. Charles had fallen on his feet again. But the number plate problem was niggling at him. If the police had traced him to this area they could pounce at any moment. He had ordered new fake plates, but he had stopped feeling safe.

Penelope asked if he would take her into town to do some shopping. His heart sank. It was almost impossible to park in the town, especially with a big car. Then he had an idea. He explained about the parking, and asked her if it would be alright if he dropped her off and picked her up again later? That would suit her fine, she said. She could browse for a couple of hours and have coffee.

So, he took her to the town and then drove the Bentley home, did a bit of online research, and made for the nearest car dealership for upmarket cars. This make and model was worth around £100,000. The dealer took a good look at it. 'Isn't this Penelope Barber's car?' he asked.

'Yes,' said Charles. 'She's asked me to sell it for her. Very sad, she lost her husband you know, and she doesn't drive... so...'

'Yes, I heard. It was sad. You won't mind if I ring her, will you?'

'Of course not,' he said, knowing that Penelope never took her phone with her when she went out 'in case she lost it'.

So Penelope's phone rang on her kitchen table while she was looking at knickers in Debenhams.

'OK, well do you have all the documents?' asked the salesman, who was keen to get his hands on the car.

'They're in the glovebox,' said Charles, who had been sure to check.

'We can offer you £60,000,' he said.

'It's worth £100,000,' said Charles.

'I can only go to £75,000,' said the salesman.

'She won't accept anything less than £90,000, and it must be in cash.'

'Cash!'

'Yes, you know Penelope. She doesn't trust any of us. Her husband told her to be careful, so now she doesn't trust banks or dealers of any kind.'

'I can't get that sort of cash today. The banks need notice.'

Charles hadn't thought of that. 'How much can you get today?'

The salesman went into the office. He had a conversation with another suited man who looked out at Charles and the car.

'I can do £25,000 today as we have just sold a car for cash. But if she insists on cash, she will have to wait for a couple of days. We could do a bank transfer for all of it today.'

Bank transfer is no good. He couldn't access his money without it being traceable. But then, the police probably already knew that he was in this area, so if he withdrew money and then disappeared fast that might work. But no, he could only withdraw £300 at a time. No good at all.

'I'd better stick to my instructions,' said Charles. 'I'll take the £25,000 cash.'

'You'll have to leave the car here, of course, sir.'

Damn. 'Yes, of course, but I'd better hold on to the paperwork until the full amount is paid. Could somebody take me back to the house please?'

They were happy to oblige as they knew they would make a healthy profit on this car.

Hoorah! When he got back to the house, his new fake plates had arrived. He went to his car and stuck them on, fetched his things from his room and waved goodbye to Waverly Lodge. He had left the Bentley paperwork on the kitchen table. It was no use to him. He would not risk going back to the garage in two days' time. He was quite satisfied with £25,000 for a morning's work.

Penelope Barber and her knickers would have to catch the bus home.

Pierre's catamaran had chugged onto the beach and he and his passenger unloaded five large boxes. Richard went to help them carry their cargo through the garden and into the garage, which he then locked. Pierre waved goodbye, and Richard brought their new guest into the house.

'This is Gabriel. Gabriel, this is Maria and Lucy.'

The girls had no choice but to be pleasant. He was here now. The men went into the sitting room to talk, while the girls prepared dinner in the kitchen.

'The fairy cakes have arrived,' said Mandy.

'I'd love to know what's in all those boxes,' said Ria.

'Only one way to find out.'

'The garage is locked, and Richard has the key. And in any case, if we tamper with those boxes, we don't have any more big boxes to replace them with.'

'And Gabriel is leaving in the morning.'

'If we opened them very carefully with a Stanley knife, we could seal them again. We have plenty of tape,' said Ria.

'OK, let's do it. Do you think you can get the key when Richard's asleep, and get out without waking Matilda?'

'I can try.'

And so Cagney and Lacey met like excited truants on the front doorstep at 1am.

They cringed as the garage door creaked open. They crept in with a torch and a Stanley knife at the ready. Mandy had the scissors and tape.

They waited to see if all was quiet and then Ria gently pushed the blade into the join on the biggest box, that was sealed with parcel tape. She ran it along the length of the join, and then along the sides. As she pulled open the cardboard, the garage door clanged shut, and the key turned in the lock.

They looked at each other in horror. But Ria was determined to see what was in the box. Mandy held the torch while Ria looked inside. Not a surprise, or fairy cakes. There were thousands of cigarettes.

Ria tugged at the door, and then remembered that there was another door into the double garage, which they had never used. It was at the far end, and it was unlocked, after all their trouble! So, they simply taped the box up again, went out of the door and through the garden to the house.

Richard was waiting for them.

***

Sgt Gill was calling on all the big houses that might employ live-in staff. So, when Penelope huffed and puffed her way up the drive to Waverly Lodge with her two Debenhams carrier bags, she was met by a stranger who was leaning on his car.

'Sorry to bother you, ma'am,' said Sgt Gill, who thought he was Columbo. 'I'm looking for this man.' He thrust the picture at her.

'You and me both!' she said, walking towards the front door, and getting her keys out.

He followed her. 'Have you seen him?'

'He was supposed to pick me up from town two hours ago.'

'This man?' Gill persisted.

'Yes, John bloody Windsor. He took me there in my car but didn't pick me up. He's probably gone to sleep or forgotten.'

He followed her into the kitchen where she took off her shoes and went to the kettle.

So, Charles Radcliffe could be asleep in this very house now. Gill was fit to explode. Should he call for backup? No, why let anyone else get the credit. But then again, Radcliffe was violent. He tried to calm his twitches, took a brown plastic bottle from his pocket and swallowed two of his pills.

'Would you check if he's asleep please, ma'am?'

'Let me see if my car's back yet. Maybe he's gone off somewhere to get some plants or something.'

She looked out of the windows at the back of the house. No sign of the car.

It certainly hadn't been at the front.

'Sorry, I didn't get your name? What do you want to see John about?' asked Penelope.

'My apologies, my name is Sergeant Gill. The man you know as John is using a false name. He is wanted by the police for questioning.'

When they discovered that his car and his clothes had gone and the Bentley was missing, it didn't take a genius to work out that he wasn't coming back. And Sgt Gill had missed him by a whisker once again.

Richard had a smile that didn't reach his eyes.

'What are you doing in the garage at this time of night? I thought I must have left the door open so when I heard it clatter, I went out to lock it,' he said.

Ria decided to face this head on. 'This is my, well our house,' she started, looking at Mandy, 'and we are entitled to know what is being stored here.'

'Did you think to just ask instead of sneaking about in the night?'

'I can sneak about whenever I like in my own home,' she retorted.

'So, did you discover what you wanted to know?'

'Yes, we did.'

'And didn't I tell you at the start that some people would be bringing cigarettes over?'

'Yes, but I thought you meant just a few extra packs, not a van load.'

He put his arm around her. 'Come on, it's no big deal. Go back to bed. You'll be getting a big pay cheque tomorrow, so you two can go out shopping.'

Mandy liked the sound of that bit, but Ria felt patronised and angry.

She felt just a little less angry in the morning when Richard handed her £1,000. Principles were expensive, she decided, but her conscience wouldn't stop niggling at her.

Mandy did not have that problem. Live and let live, she said. And let's go and buy that new bed for Matilda as she will soon be outgrowing her cot. And we could get that red coat that you liked, Ria, and the boots I wanted. So they did.

Chapter nineteen

Charles had a big wad of cash in his pocket, thanks to the Bentley, and in his glove compartment, and in his case. Well, it was Stan's case, but he wasn't going to miss it. That was all very well, but where could he go next?

Being on the run was not really much fun. It might be if this was just a mad holiday, where you just pitched up in a new place every week or so and had new experiences, but when a stranger could possibly grab you and put handcuffs on you at any minute, it sucked all the fun out of it.

Especially when you had no one to talk to.

Still, he had no option but to go on. At least he had money. He didn't need to get a live-in job for a while. He could afford a decent hotel, but maybe hotels were too obvious. A holiday cottage maybe. Yes, that would be good. His own front door. No one coming in to make swans out of the towels or make the ends of the toilet paper pointy.

It was the end of the season, so there were plenty of vacancies along the south coast. He found a little wooden cabin with all mod cons in the middle of nowhere, in Sussex. Perfect. It had a wood burner as well as electric fires, and a fully equipped kitchen and shower room. Plenty of parking space and total seclusion.

It was a fantastic place to wind down for a few days, but after that, Charles became miserable and restless. He would take a risk and go to the nearest pub. No one could possibly know him there, and he needed company.

Tindra was in the boulangerie buying baguettes when her waters broke. She was even more shocked than the shop assistant, and ran from the shop back to the apartment, where Lizzy was making breakfast.

'I have to get to the hospital. My babies are coming!'

Lizzy rang for an ambulance and went to get the bag that had been prepared for Tindra's hospital stay. She was very calm and had been rehearsing for this moment.

She stayed by Tindra's side in the ambulance, and as the babies were born in quick succession in the maternity ward. The little boy first, and the girl three minutes later.

'You lucky Mummy,' said Lizzy, as she squeezed Tindra's hand, above the din of both babies screaming their objections to being pushed out of their comfy home.

'Would you like me to call anyone?' she asked kindly.

'Yes please. Would you call Hugo, and Ria and Mandy?'

The babies were perfect. The little girl with blonde wispy hair and the boy with a shock of brown hair. The nurses always made a special fuss of twins, and they fell in love with these two. No one could deny they were pretty babies, even as newborns.

Lizzy took some pictures on her phone, and sent them to Hugo and Ria, along with a text announcing their birth. In no time excited texts came back congratulating Tindra and saying they would see her soon.

There was great excitement at the beach house. Louise had had her twins! Mandy bucked up immediately. She must find out when she would be leaving hospital so that she could go and help her. She knew there would be sleepless nights, but it would be fun, and a change of scenery. And no doubt Ria and Richard would be glad to have some time on their own.

Richard was being particularly attentive to Ria, and she was kind of hoping that a proposal might be in the offing. She discussed this with Mandy.

'He can't marry you,' she said, beating around the bush as ever.

'And why not?'

'Because to get married you need legal documents and ID in your real names.'

'Well, surely the registrar doesn't go running to the police with the names of everyone who gets married?'

'I don't know, but everything is computerised these days, so it would certainly be a risk. Besides...' Mandy paused. 'If you get married, half of this house will belong to him.'

Ria looked pensive. She would have to look into these laws. She wouldn't care if the love of her life owned half the house, but where would that leave Mandy?

Mandy did not want this marriage, but she felt guilty that she wanted to spoil Ria's chance of happiness. She wanted Ria to be happy, but not this way. She felt threatened and left out. Back to the computer. She was not short of money, so she decided to pay the £98 to meet a man. *What a sad, desperate old bag I am*, she thought as she took her credit card from her purse.

Funnily enough, the gorgeous Terry was no longer available once she had paid her money. Now she could choose from toothless Ted, leering Nobby, Alf with the tattoos and piercings all over his face, enormous Eric, Assan who spoke no English, and Clarence who looked like Father Christmas.

Well that was 98 quid well spent. Wait. There was a message from Paul, with a picture. Not bad. Not bad at all. Nice smile. Message says:

Hi Lucy, I liked your profile. What are you wearing?
Click off.

Charles found his nearest pub and sat at the bar. It was a locals' pub, with a few regulars playing darts or dominoes. There was a TV that no one was watching, and background music that added to the noise of the TV. A woman of about 40 was behind the bar. She gave him a warm smile. 'What can I get you, sir?'

'A beer please.'

'Haven't seen you before?'

'No, I've just arrived on holiday.'

'Ah, lucky you. On your own?'

'Yes, my wife died.'

'Oh, I'm so sorry, I didn't mean to pry.'

'It's OK. You didn't know. I'm just travelling about.'

'I always wanted to get a campervan and travel around the UK.'

'Well, why don't you?'

'Not sure I would enjoy it on my own. But maybe one day.'

She passed Charles his beer. Was he imagining it or was there a bit of chemistry here? She was attractive in a mousy way. Kind green eyes and a ready smile.

There was something about her. And if he wasn't mistaken, she was flirting with him.

'My name's Veronica by the way.'

Charles was stumped. What *was* his name today?

'Ben,' he said.

'You don't seem sure,' she giggled. 'It must be the beer!'

'Haven't touched it yet,' he laughed, and realised that it was the first time he had laughed in months.

'I think it must be old age creeping on,' he said. 'Or maybe it's the effect you have on me.'

She gave him a shy smile and looked down.

'Would you do me the honour of joining me for dinner tonight?' he asked.

'I'm working.' She smiled. 'But I'm off tomorrow night.'

'Excellent. Can you recommend somewhere? I'll book it.'

'My favourite is the Red Lion, about three miles from here. It's just pub grub, but their food is great.'

'The Red Lion it is then.'

As autumn turned to winter there were fewer Channel crossings for Pierre and Jack, but the cargo was bigger. Richard had persuaded the girls to stop prying. What good would it do? So, they just let the men get on with it. The money was more than useful, and so it became easier to turn a blind eye. Their guests were usually respectful, and never stayed long. Mandy made the crossing with Pierre, who also took her on to Paris to stay with 'Louise' and the babies. Hugo said he would come later as there was a houseful.

Tindra was delighted to see Mandy aka 'Lucy'. She had been managing well with the help of Lizzy but was so very tired. Mandy adored the babies and remarked that the little girl looked so much like Matilda. Had she got a name yet?

'I was thinking of calling her Matilda,' said Tindra, 'but that could be confusing. This little chap will be Hugo after my brother, but I suppose that could get confusing too!'

'Maybe make Matilda and Hugo their second names?' offered Mandy.

'Yes, I like that idea. So now we need first names.'

They made a list of names, even checking baby names on the internet.

A decision was finally made. Alice Matilda, and William Hugo.

Sgt Gill was still looking for the same car that Charles had used to drive to Bournemouth. He had no evidence to suggest he had changed cars. But there were thousands of these little silver cars on the roads. He passed one every few minutes.

Absolutely nothing on ANPR. So, something was not right.

Then he got a call from Penelope Barber to say that she had found car number plates in her flowerbeds. So he was looking for the wrong plates! But that was no help as he didn't know the new ones.

Charles was also thinking about the trackability of his car. OK, there were thousands of them, but still.

Veronica had given him a brainwave. He would buy a campervan. And who knows, with a bit of persuasion, she might come along for the ride.

He set off to have a look at a dealership. If he traded in his car and added another £10,000, he reckoned he could get a reasonable one, and he would no longer have to pay for accommodation.

He'd better take his fake plates off first. But hang on, would the car with its real plates come up as wanted when he tried to sell it? He wished he knew how these things worked. Maybe he would dump the car and just buy a cheaper camper van.

Yes, that would be safer. He had cash so didn't have to worry about ID.

So, within an hour, Ben Robson drove out of the dealership with a large 5-berth van, old but in perfect condition, with 65,000 miles on the clock.

He couldn't wait to show it to Veronica.

The dumped car would raise attention, but maybe if he left it in a well-used free car park it wouldn't be noticed for a few days at least.

He met Veronica inside the Red Lion. He had picked a window seat so he could keep an eye on his new purchase. She arrived minutes later. They did a quick hug and air kisses, and Charles bought some drinks. They chatted easily. Then he said, 'Veronica, you gave me an idea for my travels. I don't know why I hadn't thought of it before. Look out of the window.'

'What am I looking for?' she asked.

'The campervan, the big white one. I bought it today!'

'Oh, how wonderful! I'm jealous. I'd love to have a look at it.'

'And you will, when we've eaten.'

Tindra and Mandy had lots to catch up on. Tindra wanted to hear all about Matilda, Ria, and the dogs. She had such lovely memories of her days at the beach house.

Mandy wanted to hear all about Tindra and Lizzy's experiences in Paris. They chatted when they could, in between the endless feeds and nappy changes, and sometimes with a glass of wine, well into the night. They got on well, despite their age differences. Mandy told Tindra how Richard and Ria had become very close. Tindra was quiet and looked at Lizzy, who was on the sofa, reading, but also eavesdropping.

'There's something I probably ought to tell you,' said Tindra.

'Really? What about?' said a puzzled Mandy.

'Lizzy and I went out for a meal one evening and overheard a conversation going on in the next booth. It was two men talking. One of them was saying that he wanted to walk away, and the other was saying that he couldn't because they had a good operation going.'

Lizzy chimed in, 'Yes, and one said, "You can't leave. Or you'll be dead."'

'He actually said,' corrected Tindra, '"I don't want to spend the rest of my life in jail."'

'And the other one said, "dead or in jail,"' said Lizzy.

'Hang on,' said Mandy. 'This is fascinating, but you should be telling the police, not me.'

'No, you see,' said Tindra, 'the men were Richard and Jack.'

'What? Are you sure?'

'Positive. I recognised the voices, but I also had a good look at them when they left. They didn't see us.'

'So, who was saying they wanted to leave?'

'Jack."

'So Richard was threatening him?'

'That's what it sounded like. He was horrible.'

Mandy was shocked. She had never seen that side of Richard. Poor Jack.

Poor Ria. She must let her know, but better to tell her face to face when she got home.

With Mandy being in Paris and Richard away for a few days 'on business', Ria was on her own. Matilda was asleep, and Ria had time to gather her thoughts.   It was good to have some alone time. She thought back to the many years that she had spent on her own and shuddered. Alone time was good sometimes, but not as a way of life. There had been times when she had been excruciatingly lonely.

She never wanted to go back to that again. But now it seemed unlikely that Richard would marry her, for all the reasons that Mandy had so kindly pointed out, and Mandy seemed to resent their relationship. She was probably just jealous, but Ria didn't want to lose her friendship. If only Mandy could find herself a man.

Then there was Matilda. Ria remembered with a jolt that this was a royal child that she had taken. OK, she was the grandma, but could the terrible day come when she was discovered, and Matilda taken away from her? She still loved and worried about her only child, Charles, who ought to be seeing his daughter growing up. But he had done some stupid things and had probably gone back to Canada by now.

She was looking forward to seeing the twins. Maybe they could come back and stay for a few days when Mandy returned. That would be good. Her thoughts were interrupted by the familiar chug of a cat pulling on to the beach. What now?

Charles and his new best friend, barmaid Veronica, chatted happily throughout their meal of steak, chips and salad, followed by apple pie and custard. They didn't bother with coffee as they were both eager to have a good look around the campervan.

It was fairly spacious inside, and in good, clean condition. There was everything you could need, in miniature. Veronica couldn't get the smile off her face. It was what she had always wanted but could never hope to own. Charles was thrilled that she was excited about it.

'Sit down,' he said.

'OK,' she said, sitting at the table.

He sat opposite her.

'Look,' he began, 'I know we've only just met, but I feel we get on really well, and I am just passing through, so I have to say this now. I am going to be travelling around the UK for the foreseeable future, and well, I wondered if you'd like to keep me company?'

Veronica was stunned. 'I'd absolutely love to,' she said. 'But what about my job at the pub?'

'They'll find someone else. It's not a busy pub, is it? And you said you have no other ties. Have an adventure. Live a little!'

She thought for a moment, and then said, 'But I don't know anything about you,' and then laughed as she said, 'You could be a mad axe murderer for all I know.'

'No, a mad hammer murderer maybe.' He laughed as he mimed bashing someone with a hammer.

'OK... yes, thank you. I will!'

'You will! Fantastic!' He gave her a hug and she hugged him back.

This was great because the police would not be looking for a couple in a campervan. And he would have someone to cook and clean and do the shopping. And maybe there would even be some rumpy pumpy. Charles Radcliffe, you have done it again! But he must remember he was now Ben.

* * *

Ria went down the garden and onto the beach to meet the cat. It was Jack.

Before he had a chance to say anything, Ria said, 'I'm sorry, Jack, but I don't want any more of this. I have tried to tell Richard, and so far, I have gone with the flow, but this has to stop right now.'

A look of terror came into Jack's eyes. 'Please, Ria, don't do this. I have to unload this stuff tonight.'

'What stuff?'

He indicated two packages, each the size of a bag of flour.

'They won't be with you for long. They'll be picked up in the morning.'

'No, Jack. I can't afford to have the police asking questions.'

'Why would they? Look, Ria, we've been doing this for years. It's safe.'

'It's illegal, and crime is never safe.' The dormant policewoman was rearing her head.

'Ria, you have to do this, or I will be in a load of trouble, trust me.'

'Who from?'

'Never mind. Look, I'll double your payment, and this time there is no guest, just the packages. Just one night, Ria, one night, please.'

'OK, but you tell whoever you are working for that this is the last time. I mean it, Jack.'

'Thank you, thank you,' he said, handing her the packages. And he was off.

Ria wandered back into the house and put the packages in the hall cupboard next to the front door so that she only had to hand them over to whoever was collecting them.

Just then, Richard called. 'Everything alright, darling?'

'Jack just brought two more packages. I've told him, no more. Will you please tell them both, no more!'

'You worry too much, dear lady. Jack is Pierre's best friend, and Pierre is my son, I can't stop them earning a crust. It's not hurting you, is it, sweetheart? I'll be home soon, and we can talk about it then.'

There was now a huge police search going on for Charles Radcliffe, but he hadn't been named in the press for legal reasons. Sgt Gill was now a small cog in the wheel, but being a maverick, and obsessed with this man, he went his own way as much as he could. The hunt was on for Radcliffe's car, which was soon found dumped in Sussex. Local people said it had been there for days. There was no CCTV. No one had seen him parking it there. Had he got a lift from there? Was he staying somewhere local? Did he have another vehicle?

All local car dealers were questioned. Nobody of that name or his aliases had bought a car. He hadn't hired a car. Nobody thought to check the campervan dealer.

Had he caught a train or a bus? Hours of CCTV were scanned. Nothing.

Sgt Gill went on a pub crawl in the area that the car was found. He showed his tatty photo to everyone he saw. At the third pub/restaurant the waiter said he had seen Radcliffe with a woman. He thought she was a barmaid at a pub a couple of miles down the road. Game on!

At the pub where people were still playing darts and dominoes, a man was behind the bar. Out came the photo again. No, he had not seen that man. Were there any other bar staff? No, he was on his own. Surely, he didn't do all the shifts. Yes, until they found a new bar person. Had they had a female bar person recently? Yes, but she had left. Did he know where she'd gone? No. What was her name? Sod off and mind your own business.

He went and sat with the domino players. They were more than a little surprised as hardly any strangers ever came into the pub, and if they did, they never sat down at the same table when the rest of the pub was almost empty.

'Sorry to interrupt your game,' said Sgt Gill, 'but the lady who used to work here lent me some money, and I came to give it back. It was so kind of her. But she's not here. Do you know where I can find her?'

'No idea, mate,' said the short, thin man. 'But that was typical of Veronica. She was very generous.'

'Was it much money?' asked the old man with the comb-over. 'Only I could give it to her if I see her.'

'That's very kind of you. What's her surname? I could look her up on the electoral roll.'

'No idea. That Tom at the bar was sweet on her, ask him.'

Chapter twenty

Richard and Ria were cuddled up on the sofa watching Downton Abbey.

'Richard.'

'Yes, my lovely lady.'

'I'm worried about Jack.'

'Worried about Jack? Whyever would you be worried about Jack?'

'He seems to be afraid of someone. When I said I didn't want to take any more parcels or guests, he said that he would get into an awful lot of trouble if he didn't deliver, and he looked really shaky.'

'Did he now?'

'Yes, and he wouldn't say who he was afraid of. Do you know who he's working for?'

'Deary me, you make him sound like some sort of gangster. He just pops bits and pieces across the Channel to keep the wolf from the door. There is no Mr Big. He's having you on, my gullible little lady.'

'No, Richard, seriously, he was afraid.'

'The man deserves an Oscar. He just wanted to get you to feel sorry for him and carry on helping him. Now, where's that bottle of wine you opened?'

***

Charles and Veronica were on the open road, singing as they went. This really was fun. They had decided to head along the coast to Deal, a quaint historic little town with castles and fishermen's cottages. An added bonus was that Veronica had some friends there. Charles was not sure about this at first, but then they wouldn't have a clue about him, and Charles would just be passing through so if any questions were asked, he would be long gone.

The sun no longer had much warmth, but driving through seaside towns and stopping for fish and chips or pie and mash was fun. Driving the Beast, as Charles had named the campervan, took some getting used to, and they had to make sure they had water and supplies, but it was all part of the experience. For Veronica, this was living the dream. For Charles, it was an interesting interlude before he inevitably had to morph into somebody else again.

They parked on the seafront at Deal and went for a walk along the beach. Charles reached for Veronica's hand. She took his hand and smiled up at him. After years of being alone and working in that quiet, dreary pub she was ecstatic. She was no beauty and men didn't usually look twice at her, especially since she had reached 40. And here was a man she could have a future with.

After their walk they went back to the Beast, shared a pizza and a glass of wine before bed.

Bed. What would they do about bed? There were two double beds and one single.

Nobody had thought about bedding. They found some sheets in a cupboard, but they were a bit musty. There were some duvets that were fine. But who would sleep in which bed? They were as awkward as teenagers. Charles wasn't really bothered. He just wanted to get some sleep, and didn't really fancy her that much, but didn't want to offend her. She felt it was too soon to sleep together, but they were in such a confined space....

So, Charles slept in the double at one end of the van, and Veronica slept in the other.

Mandy had enjoyed her three weeks in Paris with the twins and the girls, but she was now looking forward to going home. Tindra was more than capable of coping now and was a perfect mother. To be honest, Mandy was exhausted. If only she had Tindra's energy!

Pierre picked her up and took her back to the beach house. She slept for most of the journey. Ria had missed her, and had a welcome meal waiting. Richard was out, so they sat down together and had a good chat. Ria wanted to hear all about the twins, and Mandy wanted to know how Matilda was, and if she'd missed any dramas.

Then Mandy became serious. 'Is everything alright with Richard?' she asked.

'Yes, why? He's just gone out for a drink with friends.'

'If there was something bad about Richard, would you want me to tell you?'

Oh dear, Mandy must be jealous again, thought Ria, *she's still at the mix.*

'Something bad? Like what?'

'Well, it's something that Louise told me. She and her flatmate Lizzy overheard a conversation in a restaurant…'

She went on to tell Ria the whole story.

Ria was incensed. 'What have you been cooking up between you? Don't be so ridiculous.'

She started to clear away the crockery, but Jack's terrified face kept coming into her mind. Surely it couldn't be true?

'Sorry to be the bearer of bad tidings, Ria, but don't shoot the messenger. I just thought you'd want to know.'

Ria sat back down. 'What do I do?'

'Tell him that you want no more guests or packages.'

'I've already done that.'

She told Mandy about the latest packages and how Jack had begged her.

'Well, I'm here now to back you up.'

'We can't tell him we know about the conversation in the restaurant,' said Ria.

'Let's play it by ear. Can we talk about it tomorrow? I'm so tired.'

* * *

Veronica wanted to visit her friends in Deal. Charles was not keen on small talk but went along with it.

Brian and Lin lived in a smart detached house near a park. They had been friends with Veronica for many years, but had recently moved to Deal, and she missed them. They welcomed the travellers in and were glad to see Veronica with a partner. She introduced 'Ben' and told them all about the campervan and their whirlwind 'romance'.

Charles could be very charming when he needed to be, and so he and Brian were soon chatting about Deal and its history. Lin and Brian were young retirees, and keen walkers, so after a light lunch, and as the sun was shining, they decided to take a long walk along the coastal path to Dover. It was a good seven miles, so by the time they arrived, they were ready for a coffee and a rest. It was all in a day's work for Brian and Lin, but Veronica was flagging, and Charles was almost on his knees.

They sat in a cafe overlooking the enormous harbour, where ferries and cargo ships were leaving and arriving all the time.

Charles was interested. 'Where do the cargo ships go from here?' he asked.

Brian replied, 'All over the place I suppose, but I know they go to Antwerp, Zeebrugge, Rotterdam and Hamburg. I got chatting to one of the crew last time I was here. It's amazing the amount of goods that come and go from Dover.'

'And then there are the ferries, of course, crossing the Channel. It's quite fascinating to watch,' Lin added.

Charles agreed. Very fascinating.

Charles and Veronica couldn't cope with a seven-mile walk back, so they all took a taxi back to the Beast, so Brian and Lin could have a look at it. They had a cup of tea, and the Beast was much admired. It had been a good day, and Charles was beginning to feel like a normal human being again.

Sgt Gill needed another bottle of pills. Charles Radcliffe was probably now with a barmaid called Veronica Medcalf. He discovered that she was a divorcee, no children. She didn't own a car, so that was a disappointing line of enquiry.

They knew the date she had disappeared, so that was probably the date Radcliffe had left the area. He hoped nothing had happened to the woman.

Nobody seemed to know much about Veronica except that she worked at the pub.

From his previous stops, Radcliffe seemed to be travelling along the coast from west to east, so maybe it was worth checking hotels along the route. But you'd need an army for that. He had hit a brick wall again.

Matilda was toddling now and loved to play on the beach with the dogs. Mandy took her to collect shells, while Ria and Richard had a chat.

The atmosphere in the house was tense. The elephant in the room had not been tackled yet. Ria didn't know where to start. She had to tread carefully. This was the man she loved and wanted to spend the rest of her life with. If she accused him of something that turned out to be rubbish, he might never forgive her. But did she want to be with a man who was some sort of bullying gangster? She just couldn't imagine this kind, sensitive man behaving like that.

There was a scream from the beach. Ria and Richard went running... well, walking as fast as their old legs would let them, to see what was happening. To their horror, Matilda was bleeding from a large gash on her neck. And bleeding heavily.

Mandy was holding her to calm her down and the dogs were jumping up and barking with excitement.

'What on earth has happened here?' asked Ria.

'One of the dogs ran into her and she fell on the rocks,' cried Mandy. 'We need to get her to hospital.'

Ria went ahead into the house while Richard carried the wailing child. Ria came back with a wet towel and pressed it on Matilda's neck. The ambulance arrived within minutes, and within 15 minutes they were in A&E.

But Matilda had become quiet and floppy and was soon surrounded by doctors and nurses. Ria and Mandy were frantic and were encouraged to stay out of the cubicle with Richard. A lady doctor came out of the cubicle.

'Are you the grandparents?'

'Yes, I am,' said Ria.

'Are her parents coming?'

'No, they're dead,' said Mandy. Ria flinched.

'I'm sorry. Look, this child has lost a lot of blood. We're testing her blood now. Do you know which group she is?'

'No, sorry,' said Ria. 'But her dad was group AB. I know that because it's very rare. Would she be the same?'

'Possibly. Now go and get a cup of tea. We're all doing the best we can for her.'

The three pensioners sat, ashen-faced waiting for news of the little girl they had grown to love. The girl with the blonde curls and dimples, who giggled at almost everything.

'I'm so sorry,' said Mandy to Ria. 'I was watching her, but it all happened so quickly.'

'It's nobody's fault,' said Ria as she wiped the tears from her eyes.

It was a very long hour before the doctor returned to them.

'She's fine.' She smiled. 'We had to give her some blood, and repair the wound, but she'll be back to normal in no time. By the way, her blood group is O. Did you say her father was group AB?'

'Yes,' said Ria.

'Are you sure?'

'Positive. There was quite a lot of talk about it when he was a baby as it's so rare.'

'Well, all I can tell you,' said the doctor, 'is that a man who is AB cannot father a child with blood group O. Not possible. Sorry.'

And with that, she left.

Charles decided that tonight was the night for love. The walk had put a spring back in his step and he felt sure Veronica would be up for it. After all, she had been on her own for some time. So had he for that matter.

Strangely, he felt nervous. It had been a long time since he had been with a woman. One night stands here and there in Canada, but that was it. That made him think about Tindra. He wondered if she had had her baby yet, and how she was getting on. Poor Tindra. He wasn't generally good on empathy, but he had feelings for Tindra.

Veronica stepped into the Beast with food for the evening meal. 'You looked miles away,' she said with a smile as she unpacked the shopping.

'I was just thinking,' he said.

'What about?'

'Will you marry me?'

She laughed. 'Sorry, I'm washing my hair on Saturday.'

'How about a bonk then?'

'Well, I might consider that if you're very nice to me.' She grinned.

'What if I cook dinner?'

'I'd say that would do it.'

So, when Brian and Lin went for their evening walk later that night, and they saw the Beast was rocking, they didn't knock.

Matilda was kept in hospital for observation for the night. Ria wanted to stay but was told that Matilda would be sedated, so Ria should go home and have a good night's sleep, and she could pick her up in the morning, all being well.

The three of them went home, emotionally drained, but relieved that Matilda was OK. Richard went to bed, and Mandy made hot chocolate for Ria and herself and they sat at the kitchen table. Mandy knew what was on Ria's mind.

'Bit of a shock that Matilda is not your grandchild,' she said, in her usual tactful manner.

'It must be a mistake,' said Ria.

'How can it be? If you are so certain that Charles is AB blood group and Matilda is definitely O?'

'He told me he was the father. You saw the letter.'

'He probably believes that he is the father. But the little princess must have been busy.'

'Dear God, we've stolen a child that has nothing to do with us!'

'A royal child.'

'Well actually, we haven't stolen her. She was brought to us. We have just been looking after her.'

'We must be even more careful now. We can't have her taken away, it would kill us, and Matilda. She loves us,' said Mandy.

There was a pause.

Mandy said, 'Have you tackled Richard yet?'

'Tackled him?' said Ria absently.

'Yes, about the conversation he had with Jack in the restaurant.'

'No, not yet. There hasn't been the right moment. Let's get Matilda back and all settle down, and then I'll try to approach it.'

Mandy knew that was Ria speak for 'let's just pretend it never happened because it would ruin all my plans'.

The next morning Ria and Mandy went to the hospital. Richard had other plans.

Ria asked at reception about Matilda and was asked to wait. After a few minutes, a man and a woman with a notebook approached them.

'Would you come this way please,' the man said.

They were shown into a side room where there was a desk and four chairs. They were asked to sit.

'What's going on? Is Matilda alright?' asked a frightened Ria.

The couple introduced themselves. 'I'm Dan Harvey, a social worker, and this is DC Eve Martin. We just wanted to have a chat about Matilda.'

DC Martin took over. 'We have to investigate all children that come in with injuries, and it would appear that none of the people looking after Matilda are related to her. Is that right?'

'No, it isn't right,' said Ria. 'She's my grandchild.'

'But you told the doctor that your son had blood group AB, which means that he couldn't be the child's father.'

'Yes, yes, I'm sorry I got that wrong,' said Ria. 'My memory is not what it was.'

'So, she is your son's child?' asked the social worker.

'Yes.'

'And your son sadly died?'

It was hard to say, but she said, 'Yes.'

'Can I take your names please?' said the DC.

'Maria Smith and this is Lucy Smith.'

'Are you related?'

'By marriage,' said Mandy. 'Sister-in-law.'

'And your address?'

Ria gave the address of the beach house.

'And how did this injury to the child's neck happen?' asked the social worker.

'I was on the beach with her, collecting shells,' said Mandy, 'and our dog knocked her over onto the rocks.'

'She seems to be very well cared for in general, with no other injuries or hospital visits. So, we'll leave it at that, but please keep the dog under control. Thank you for helping us to straighten that out.'

'You can collect her now,' said the DC.

* * *

Charles and Veronica sat on the beach watching the ships pass by and eating hot dogs. Charles couldn't help thinking about those cargo ships travelling to Belgium, Holland and Germany. If he could just get on one of those...

Veronica was planning her wedding. Well he did ask her, didn't he? Even if she had made a joke of it. She didn't see herself having a big white wedding, but maybe a wedding on the beach with Lin and Brian for witnesses. She would buy a cream silk dress and trim it with ostrich feathers.

Charles was wondering if he could get away for an hour or two to go back to Dover and see if he could befriend one of the ship's crew. Maybe he could be a stowaway, but that was probably just something that happened in films. The security would probably be tight. But then again, it was worth a try. He would feel safer in another country, and most people speak English nowadays.

He persuaded Veronica to go shopping with Lin. She didn't take much persuading, especially when Charles gave her £200. Charles said he was going to take the Beast to get some petrol, and Calor gas. He would park back by the beach when he returned.

He drove to Dover and parked about a mile from the harbour. He sat on a wall and watched the comings and goings of ships and people for some time. A cargo ship docked, and sometime later, its crew sauntered out of the harbour and into a nearby bar. Charles followed them. Two of them bought their beers and took them outside to sit on the wall. Charles did the same, sitting a few feet away and looking out to sea.

After a few minutes, he 'accidentally' knocked his beer over, splashing the sailor nearest to him.

'I'm so sorry, what a clumsy fool. Let me buy you a drink. What are you drinking?'

The sailor looked irritated but would never say no to a free drink. 'Beer,' he said and looked at his friend's empty glass.

'Two beers,' said Charles with a smile, and went off to buy them.

When he returned, they looked a bit happier. After all, the sailor had only had his work clothes splashed.

'Thanks,' he said. 'You didn't have to do that.'

'No problem,' said Charles. 'Are you working on the ships?'

'Yes. The NS *Holland*, over there.'

'Great ship. Where are you headed?'

'Well, we don't leave until tomorrow. There is a lot of unloading and loading to do, but then we'll be off to Rotterdam.'

'How long does that take?'

'Oh, about 10 hours usually.'

'Why, you looking for a job?'

'No, look I'll be straight with you guys. I need to get to Holland, and I haven't got time to get a passport. Is there any way you could get me onto the ship, and hide me for 10 hours?'

The two sailors looked at each other and laughed. Charles flushed. 'I would pay you of course,' he said.

'My friend, it would cost a lot of money for us to risk our livelihood.'

'How much.'

The men looked at each other.

'You're serious?'

'Yes, very.'

'Just the one trip, just you?'

'Yes, just me.'

'And if you were discovered, you would say that you boarded without any help?'

'Of course.'

The men went into a huddle and whispered to each other. Then the first one said, 'OK, two grand each, cash in advance.'

'One grand each, on arrival at Rotterdam,' said Charles.

'One grand when you are on the ship, and one grand on arrival.'

'Done.'

The men shook hands.

'Be here at 9am tomorrow wearing working clothes, and no luggage. Then do exactly as I say. We leave at 10.'

Matilda looked a little pale but was quite cheerful and glad to be home. Richard was reading a paper in the kitchen.

'Everything alright?' he asked.

'We were questioned by the police,' blurted Mandy.

'What?' he practically choked on his coffee.

'They wanted to know how Matilda was injured, and how come we were looking after a child we weren't related to,' said Ria.

'What did you tell them?' asked Richard.

'The truth about the accident,' said Mandy, 'and Ria said she got it wrong about her son's blood group. But we had to give our names and address.'

'Which names did you give?'

'Maria and Lucy Smith of course.'

'So, they were happy in the end?'

'Yes, but I nearly had a heart attack,' said Ria.

'You nearly gave me one,' said Richard. 'The last thing we want is the police nosing around.'

Ria put the sleepy Matilda on the sofa with a blanket over her, and they all spent the next couple of hours relaxing to recover. But Ria needed to talk to Richard. After lunch, when Mandy had taken Matilda out in her buggy, she decided to face the problem head on.

'Richard.'

'Yes, dear lady.'

'You and Jack were overheard in a restaurant. You were telling Jack that he couldn't leave because you had a good operation going, and his choice was jail or death.'

Richard looked as if he'd been winded. 'Where on earth did you get that from?'

'Never mind where from. What's going on, Richard?'

To her amazement he burst out laughing. 'Oh, you girls and your imaginations!'

'It's not funny, Richard. We stand to lose Matilda if you do something that puts us at risk.'

'My dear girl, Jack has a heart condition. I was telling him that I had heard of a good operation, which he can get privately, and that if he kept going the way he was, he would end up dead or in jail. He said he didn't want to end up in jail, but he didn't want an operation and wanted to leave the boating business.'

'Well, why did he look so scared and worried about what would happen to him if I didn't take the packages for him?'

'Unfortunately, he does mix with some shady characters in his line of business, but I don't think he's afraid of any of them. He just didn't want to lose face and have to take the parcels back. Which reminds me, did anyone come and pick those last two parcels up?'

'No, they're still in the hall cupboard.'

'That's odd. I'll have a word with Jack. Now stop worrying, will you!'

Chapter twenty-one

Charles drove the Beast back to Deal and stopped at a charity shop en route to pick up some 'working clothes' and boots.

Veronica was sitting on a bench by the sea waiting for him. 'You were a long time!'

'Sorry, hun, I had to go to several places before I could get some Calor gas.'

They went into the Beast, and Charles put his charity shop clothes away.

'Can you drive?' he asked.

'Yes, but I haven't for years, why?'

'I was just wondering. Maybe you could do some of the driving if we're on a long run.'

'Yes, I'd be happy to if I can. It's a bit big.'

'You can do it.' He smiled.

As they cuddled up in bed that night, he thought about what he was doing. He had a woman to cuddle, a mobile roof over his head and felt quite content. If he went to Holland, he would have nothing. He wouldn't have enough money to buy another vehicle. But he would feel a lot safer. Sometimes it was easy to forget what he had done, but he could be sure that the police had not. He never knew how far away they might be.

They would have no reason to suspect that he was in Holland. He had to do it while he had the opportunity.

'I had a call earlier from my sister,' he began.

'I didn't know you had a sister.'

'There's a lot you don't know about me. Anyway, she said my mother is ill, and I need to go and see her.'

'Oh, I'm sorry to hear that. Where is she?'

'In Hertfordshire.'

'Oh, well we could drive up there.'

'No, no, the traffic is dreadful. It will be quicker if I get the train. I'll go in the morning, stay overnight, and be back the next day. You'll be alright, won't you? You've got Lin and Brian just down the road?'

'Yes, of course. Do you want me to drive you to the station? I could have a go at driving the Beast.'

'No, it's OK, hun, thanks. I've ordered a taxi.'

So, at 8am the next morning, Charles said goodbye to Veronica and the Beast with a heavy heart. But at least he had made her dream come true. She now had her very own motorhome.

Tindra had invited her brother Hugo to come and stay and meet his new niece and nephew. She hadn't seen him for such a long time, and so much had happened. She needed a plan for the future as Lizzy would be leaving in a few weeks to go to uni.

She wanted to talk to him, and maybe persuade him to come and live in Paris. But his gap year was nearly over, and he should be off to uni soon, too.

She was also concerned about the apartment. Richard had said that she could stay as long as she liked, but that was at a moment of crisis, and she didn't know how long it would be reasonable for her to take advantage of his generosity. After all, she wasn't paying any rent. But then again, if he was into criminal activities, she needed to be careful. The police could come here for him! Probably safer if she tried to find a way to be independent.

But the babies kept her busy, so there wasn't much time to worry.

Charles met the men outside the harbour bar as arranged at 9am.

The ginger-haired one said, 'Getting you onto the ship won't be a problem. The difficult bit is getting you into the dock in the first place.' He handed Charles a small ID card. 'Walk past the security guy with us and others, and if he asks for ID show him this. It belongs to one of the men who haven't come ashore, so don't lose it. Then just stay with us and walk straight onto the ship. We share a cabin, so you can hide in there. We can bring you water and hopefully some food, but don't touch our things, right?'

'Right, thanks.'

'Good luck.'

So that was how Charles Radcliffe came to be sailing out of Dover in a windowless cabin eating a banana that he had stuffed in his pocket before leaving. Part of him felt a huge sense of relief... (who could possibly know he was on this ship?), and another part felt a sense of loss and sadness that he was leaving his home country probably forever. And he had enjoyed his time with Veronica. But now he must think ahead to how he would make a new life in Holland, and all the same old problems applied. No papers.

Ginger came back to the cabin as promised with some raw herring with onions and gherkins and some bread and sweet waffles, as well as a bottle of water.

'That's kind of you,' said Charles, wondering if he was supposed to eat the fish raw or somehow cook it.

'Will it be a problem for me to get off in Rotterdam?'

'No,' said Ginger. 'Same thing in reverse. Do you have the money?'

Charles pulled £1,000 from his pocket and handed it over.

'Thanks.'

'No problem.'

'What are your plans when you get to Rotterdam?' asked Ginger.

'I don't have any plans.'

'You're on the run, aren't you?'

Charles looked at him.

'It's OK,' Ginger reassured him. 'That's why most of us are here!' he laughed.

'If it's any help my mother runs a B&B in Hoek Van Holland. She charges about 110 euros a night, but she might do a discount for her favourite son! It would just be until you get yourself sorted.'

Charles wasn't thrilled at the idea of being in a B&B, but the guy was being helpful, and what else was he going to do?

'Thanks, that would be great.'

Ria told Mandy what Richard had said about his overheard conversation. 'So,' she said, 'it was all a big misunderstanding. Quite funny really.'

'You don't honestly believe that malarkey.'

'You're just jealous. Admit it, you don't want Richard and I to be together!' said Ria.

'Honestly, for an ex-policewoman you are so gullible sometimes.'

'You always go on about that. I was not a policewoman for long.'

'I thought you were commended for bravery.'

'I was, but it was just a fluke. I went into a post office and there was a lad with a gun. When he saw me, he turned from the counter, dropped the gun and ran out. I didn't actually do anything. By the time the papers got it, I was the big hero tackling a gunman.'

Mandy started laughing, and Ria joined in. They were old friends again.

'So how long were you a policewoman?'

'Well, I wasn't actually a policewoman as such.'

'What do you mean?'

'I was a volunteer. But it was still police work!'

They both laughed hysterically the way two friends do over nothing much at all until they could hardly breathe, and Ria needed the loo.

Veronica was on the phone to Lin. 'Charles said he would be back today, but there's no sign of him.'

'Why don't you phone him? Maybe his mother is very ill.'

'He never gave me his number.'

'Oh, well, I'm sure he'll turn up. Do you want to come over?'

'No, it's OK, thanks. I'll wait here for him.'

So she waited, and waited, and looked out for taxis, and checked train times from Hertfordshire, and waited some more. By the next day she was frantic. Something must have happened to him. He had her number. He would have called if he was OK. He had promised to update her. Brian and Lin came over to see her.

'Should I call the police?' she asked.

'I doubt if they would do anything,' said Brian. 'He's a grown man. Do you know where his mother lives, or his sister?'

'No, he just said Hertfordshire.'

'If you haven't heard anything by tomorrow, maybe it would be worth having a word with the police. Just in case he's had an accident or something. It may be that his poor mum has died and he's sorting things out. Could be anything,' said Lin. 'Try not to worry.'

But Veronica did worry. She'd planned her wedding dress and everything.

Charles wished he'd brought another banana. He couldn't face the raw herring.

He dozed off and slept for most of the journey, and when they arrived in Rotterdam it was getting dark.

Ginger and his oppo came into the cabin. His friend, a wiry man with big ears asked for the remaining thousand pounds. Charles sleepily reached into his pocket. The money had gone.

He leapt up from the bunk, 'What the fuck, where's my money?'

'Don't give us that,' said big ears.

But Charles wasn't joking. All his money had gone, not just the thousand that he was going to give the men.

Ginger grabbed him by the throat. These were men who shifted cargo for a living. He had a grip like a vice. 'We had an agreement, pal.'

'I know! I've been bloody robbed.'

'Nobody comes in here but us,' said big ears.

'Well somebody has stolen my money!'

The red mist started to gather. What would he do with no money at all? These clowns must have taken it, and now they were pushing him around.

Things had been going fine.

Why did people always get in his way?

Suddenly the monster took over. Charles suddenly had the strength of a bull. He kneed Ginger in the groin, and as big ears approached, he grabbed him by the hair and smacked his head against the wall. As he slid down, Charles kicked Ginger for good measure, and then bashed big ears over the head with a beer bottle. Then he searched their pockets. He found the thousand pounds that he had given Ginger earlier and took 560 pounds from big ears. He ransacked the cabin looking for his missing money and found the men's passports. Then he took their ID cards, locked the cabin door and went to find his way off the ship.

Richard told Ria and Mandy that he had spoken to Jack and that the packages would not be collected as the man had died, and that Jack didn't want them. He then went to have a shower.

'What's in the packages?' asked Mandy.

'How should I know?' Ria replied.

'Thought you would have had a little nose by now.'

'No, but now that you come to mention it...'

Ria went into the hall and took the two parcels from the cupboard. They sat at the kitchen table and Mandy got the scissors.

'Let's hope it's another stack of money,' she said excitedly.

'Before we open it,' said Ria. 'Let's take a guess as to what it is.'

'OK,' said Mandy, feeling one of the packages. 'I'd say it's money again.'

'I'd say it's drugs, cocaine or heroin,' said Ria, trying to sound streetwise.

'But if it is anything of that sort of value, someone would want to claim it.'

'The guy's dead.'

'Yes, but he must have been taking it to someone else. And why wouldn't Jack want it?'

'Will you just open the bloody thing!' said Ria.

It had now been three days since Charles had left, and Veronica was inconsolable.

Lin and Brian were having a cup of tea with her in the Beast.

'Maybe it *is* time to call the police,' said Lin. 'It does seem a bit odd.'

'Had you two had an argument before he left?' asked Brian.

'No, we couldn't have been happier,' Veronica wailed. 'And even if he had left me, surely he wouldn't have left the Beast. It must have cost quite a lot of money. And he didn't take any clothes or anything.'

So, the three of them walked to the police station in the High Street.

An hour later, Sgt Gill received a phone call. He had returned to his office in London when his lines of enquiry dried up on the coast.

Was he interested in a woman called Veronica Anne Medcalf?

Yes, he certainly was!

'Well she's sitting in Deal Police Station right now,' said the station sergeant.

'She's reporting a misper, her boyfriend Ben Robson. He disappeared three days ago.'

Sgt Gill was very interested indeed.

'I'm emailing you a picture of Charles Radcliffe. Will you show it to her and ask if this is the man she knows as Ben Robson please?'

'Will do.'

The picture was so dog-eared that Charles was hardly recognisable, but the station sergeant showed it to Veronica.

'Yes, that's him,' she sobbed, and Brian and Lin also confirmed it.

'Hold on to her. I'll be down on the next train,' said Sgt Gill, grabbing his coat and his pills.

He arrived less than two hours later.

Veronica and Lin were in an interview room eating cheese sandwiches with a PC.

Sgt Gill asked for some tea and some water. He was so excited to meet Veronica that he needed a chemical top up. He took two pills from the bottle in his pocket.

'Now, Veronica, where did you meet this man? I want to know everything.'

'Why, what's he done? I just want to find him.'

'So do we, trust me, we will find him.'

So, Veronica innocently told her whole story, and how he had left suddenly by taxi to go to see his sick mother in Hertfordshire.

Sgt Gill went and sat on a bench by the sea. He needed to think. Had Ria Radcliffe returned to Hertfordshire? Deal was a small town, and it wasn't difficult to find the local taxi rank. He soon discovered that Charles had taken a taxi to Dover and was dropped near the station. But why wouldn't he have gone from Deal station? Maybe it was more direct.

There was no sign of him on CCTV boarding a train that morning. So, a massive search of all CCTV of the area was launched.

Mandy carefully snipped open the first parcel and handed it to Ria.

'You open it.'

'Coward,' laughed Ria.

She pulled out some tissue paper, and then a beautiful full-length gown in ivory satin and lace. She was astonished. She turned to Mandy, who was opening the second parcel.

It was another dress, equally beautiful in light blue silk organza.

'Wait, there's something else in here,' said Ria, pulling out a card and a small box.

The card had a rose on the front, and inside it said: *I knew your nose would get the better of you!*

Will you marry me, my dear English rose? Love Richard.

Mandy also found a card. *My dear Mandy. I hope you will share your lovely friend with me. Here is a gown to wear at our wedding. I hope you will do us the honour of being maid of honour.*

'Oh my God,' cried Mandy. 'Open that little box.'

Ria opened it slowly, and inside was the most beautiful ring in rose gold with a heart-shaped diamond.

Richard was standing smiling in the doorway behind them wearing his red smoking jacket and yellow cravat. He cleared his throat.

'Well?' he said, looking at Ria.

Charles had disembarked from the NS *Holland* in Rotterdam with no difficulty. He now had some cash, two passports and two ID cards. Things were looking up. He decided not to hang around for too long in this area in case the two clowns were not far behind him. He would take the intercity train to Amsterdam, a short journey of some 40 minutes.

He now felt safe, and as though he were on holiday.

He had never been to Amsterdam but had heard about its apparently carefree attitude and ladies of the night. It was a cool, crisp day and he enjoyed wandering around the city. He didn't feel the need to constantly look over his shoulder as he had in England. He would need somewhere to stay tonight, but it was the end of the season, so it shouldn't be hard to find something.

He walked along the Prinsengracht Canal banks and admired the houseboats decked with brightly coloured flowers. Some people waved to him. A dog walker smiled. He liked this place.

Then he saw a sign on a houseboat. *Te laten, lang verblijf,* and underneath, *To let, long stay.*

A young man was cleaning the windows.

'Um, hi, do you speak English?' asked Charles.

'Certainly do,' said the young man.

'Great. I was wondering about your sign. I'm looking for a place to rent.'

'OK, hop on board. My name's Finn.'

Oh Christ, here we go again. What's my name?

'David,' said Charles, 'David Morgan.'

The boat was perfect. The outside was boxy and painted bright blue, and it had all mod cons, just like the Beast, but bigger. It was slap in the middle of town, so no transport needed. Maybe he would get a bike like everyone else.

Finn said he could provide all linen and showed Charles how everything worked.

He was delighted that Charles could move in straight away. Finn was moving in with his girlfriend on the other side of town and didn't want to leave the boat unattended.

Charles jumped onto the towpath to have a proper look at the outside of the boat.

She was called *Anna*.

Ria and Mandy stared at the grinning Richard.

'Well?' he repeated. 'I'm not going down on one knee. I'd never get up again.'

Ria went and put her arms around his neck. 'You old romantic.'

'Now that's more like it,' he said.

Mandy was puzzled. 'But I thought you couldn't get married because of having to use your real names?'

'The names we have now are our real names. I changed them by deed poll. Quite legal.'

'But even if you change your name by deed poll, your own names are still on the same record,' said Ria.

'True, but there will be no need for any alarm bells. Two old ducks getting hitched. Both English. Nobody's going to be looking for problems. So what do you say, madam?'

Ria looked at Mandy, knowing how she must be feeling.

'If you marry me, you have to marry Mandy and Matilda as well,' she giggled.

'Dear lady, I'm already married to you all, aren't I?'

'Then the answer is yes!'

They all had a group hug, and the women went off to try on their new dresses.

Ria would get Richard to place the ring on her finger when they were alone.

CCTV had shown Charles talking to two men outside a pub by the docks in Dover. Later he was seen boarding the NS *Holland* with them. So that's where he went!

The NS *Holland* was back in Dover, and Sgt Gill boarded to speak to the captain.

Again, out came the tatty photo. The captain hadn't seen Charles and had no knowledge of him being on board. Sgt Gill showed him the CCTV tape. He recognised Ginger and Big Ears right away.

'These two men are in hospital in Rotterdam,' he said. 'They were in a fight.'

'Who with?'

'I don't know. Maybe just each other.'

'Can you tell me which hospital these men are in?'

'Yes. I'll write it down for you.'

'Thanks. Are you heading back to Rotterdam?'

'Yes, tomorrow.'

'Can I hitch a ride?'

'I guess so, if you have your ID and a passport.'

Tindra was excited. Her brother Hugo was arriving today.

He had been her best friend and confidante throughout their childhood, and she missed that closeness. He was sensible and honest and sensitive to her moods.

And the biggest plus was that he knew everything about her, so she could just relax and be herself. There were no secrets.

Soon he would be off to study medicine at uni. He would make a brilliant doctor. Maybe too caring, if that's possible. He was shy with girls, but they all loved him. He was not the most handsome man in the world, but he had boyish charm and a great sense of humour. The only downside was that he had no style, and his clothes were awful. Often expensive, but just wrong. Maybe Paris would cure him of that.

Tindra didn't go to meet him at the station. It was too much hassle with the twins.

He knocked on her door at 3pm, holding a big bunch of flowers and two big teddies.

And to her astonishment, behind him stood William. She didn't know whether to laugh or cry, hug him or hit him. What was he thinking, bringing William?

Hugo gave her a hug, put down the flowers and toys and said with a flourish, 'I'd like you to meet my very good friend William, who has come a long way to see you. I'm sure you will give him a true Parisian welcome.'

'Parisians are rude, arrogant and unwelcoming,' said Tindra. 'I can give him that sort of welcome if you like.'

'Come on, Tindra,' said Hugo. 'Be nice. I want to meet my nephew and niece.'

Once she got over the shock, she remembered her manners and was polite, if not warm towards

William. She introduced them both to Lizzy, and then to the babies.

She was embarrassed to tell William that she had named their son after him. But he seemed delighted.

After they had all finished cooing over the babies, they sat down to tea and some fancy pastries from the patisserie. It was awkward. Tindra couldn't catch up with her brother with William there. And she couldn't say the things she wanted to say to William unless he was on his own. Later, she managed to get Hugo on his own in the kitchen.

'I was so looking forward to seeing you,' she said. 'But why did you bring William?'

'Sorry, sis. He begged to come with me. He wanted to see you and the babies. They are his kids after all.'

Tindra was furious. 'His kids! He gave up the right to his kids when he walked away and said he wasn't ready to be a father.'

'I know, he was stupid. I'm not defending him. But you two need to talk. He's bound to want to see the twins from time to time.'

'Tough.'

'OK, well let's not spoil this visit. I want to hear everything that's been happening.'

Chapter twenty-two

Two old ladies in satin and lace gowns looked faintly ridiculous. Their bulges were all in the wrong places, and something that would look spectacular on a mannequin looked like a shiny sack of potatoes on a shortish, plump, grey lady, and a taller blonde, but wrinkly lady, too. In fact, one such lady couldn't do her zip up. This was a great disappointment and posed a problem because Richard was waiting for the grand parade in the sitting room.

They came back downstairs in the clothes they had gone up in. Richard looked confused. 'No good?' he asked, looking disappointed.

'They're beautiful,' said Ria, 'but we thought you should wait until the day. We just remembered, it's bad luck.'

There would have to be some serious sewing going on before The Day, whenever that was going to be. Now that winter was here, it would be better to wait until spring Ria thought.

Mandy was back on the computer with a vengeance. She had paid her fee and wanted her money's worth. She had to have a word with herself about the old men. The younger ones would not be interested in her, and the older men couldn't help ageing any more than she could.

Graham's details were sent to her. The photo of him wasn't clear. He was too far away from the camera. That didn't bode well. He couldn't be very intelligent, she thought. Why would you post a picture on a dating site where you were just a dot in the background?

She must stop being so critical.

His profile read:

Interesting man, she'd be the judge of that. *Recycled teenager,* corny, *interested in Morris Dancing,* oh no, that always made her laugh, men leaping about in white trousers with bells on, waving handkerchiefs and bashing their legs with sticks and swords.

Next.

Rob. Looked like every other old man in the street, but give him a chance, she thought...

His profile:

Thank you for reading this. I know I'm an old git, and you're probably an old gittess, but we are still young inside (apart from the dodgy ticker, obviously), and I think we should at least meet for a coffee. If I hate you on sight, I won't introduce myself. If you hate me, text your friend to ring you to say your house is on fire. Don't scroll onto the next person because I know him, and he's a stinker.

Mandy laughed. A cup of coffee with him might be fun.

* * *

Charles loved the idea of living on a houseboat. It was called *Anna*, the name of his wife. It was meant to be. He had a lump in his throat when he thought of his wife. She had been his first and only love and soulmate. But in the end, she wasn't loyal to him. She started to get in the way.

Water under the bridge. This was a new day, and he had the houseboat to himself.

He went out to get some shopping and came back on a bike he had seen left outside a shop. Tomorrow he would repaint it. As usual, he sat down with a cup of coffee to think about how vulnerable he might be. How much of a trail had he left? Worst case scenario.

Veronica, being the innocent she was, might have called the police when he disappeared. He had to admit, that was not something that even occurred to him at the time. If she had, they would know that he got a taxi to Dover. Lots of CCTV, so he just might have been spotted getting on the ship.

If so, they would know he came to Rotterdam and might have connected him with the sailors. Possibly they had CCTV at Rotterdam Station and at Amsterdam. But even if they knew he was in Amsterdam, they couldn't have CCTV all the way to the houseboat, could they? He shuddered.

One minute he felt entirely safe and miles from trouble, and then, when he worked it out, he could be minutes from capture. Maybe he should change his appearance.

He looked in the small mirror above the chest of drawers. His mousy hair was neat and straight. He was clean shaven. So he'd grow a beard, and dye his hair, which he would also grow. He would buy some glasses. He would be sure not to wear the clothes that may have been seen on CCTV. Not much else he could do. His burner phone was not a problem. He had nobody to phone and hadn't given the number to anyone. But he would take the battery out, just in case.

Sgt Gill and his Dutch counterpart were at the Ikazia Hospital in Rotterdam, where the two injured seamen had been taken. He let his colleague, Bram, make the initial enquiries as he was known by the hospital staff and could speak in Dutch if necessary, although it was impressive how many people spoke perfect English.

They were taken into a side room. The injured men were Jos Jansen (Ginger) and Karl De Jong (big ears).

Sadly, they were told, Karl De Jong died of his head injuries. Jos Jansen was battered and bruised but was being discharged today.

Bram asked if they could speak to him.

They were asked to stay put, and half an hour later Jos Jansen limped into the room.

These rufty-tufty seamen were not in the habit of talking to the police. If asked about fight injuries, they usually said that they had walked into a door or fallen downstairs.

But this was different. His mate was dead, and the man who killed him was a foreigner. But he had a problem. He had helped this man sneak onto the ship and accepted a bribe to do it. He would lose his job and probably be prosecuted.

So, his version was that the man, whose name he didn't know, came onto the ship without any help. He must have had some ID so Jos thought he must be a new crew member. They had a spare bunk in their cabin, so said he could use it for his one crossing until he was allocated his own. When the two of them returned to their cabin as they reached Rotterdam, the man jumped them and robbed them of some cash and their passports and ID cards.

'But you are strong men,' argued Sgt Gill. 'You are saying that one man did this to you both?'

Jos was embarrassed. 'He caught us off guard,' he said.

'How much cash?'

'Oh, not much,' Jos said, not wanting to have to explain the thousand pounds.

So now the Dutch police had a murder enquiry on their hands.

Sgt Gill showed Jos the infamous photo. Was this the man? He looked carefully, and then nodded.

Soon the papers were onto it, and weren't shy about printing a picture of Charles, a foreigner who had murdered one of their own. But legalities meant they could only say that Charles Radcliffe was wanted for questioning.

**

Mandy plucked up courage and arranged to meet her blind date, Rob, for lunch in a nearby pub. He had to do the travelling, as he lived 15 miles away. She recognised him immediately from his picture on the website. He stood to greet her, and she said, 'Are you going to introduce yourself?'

'Only if you're not going to call the fire brigade,' he laughed.

There was no awkwardness. After the first few minutes they were both relaxed and the conversation flowed. He was a widower with two grown-up children who lived abroad and was a retired theatre director. He smelled gorgeous. Mandy told him all about her life as a theatrical agent, and it transpired that they knew some of the same people. They both missed their work but were glad of the free time they now had.

They talked about other people who had messaged them from the dating site, and he said he was definitely not a Morris dancer and had no interest in football or golf.

She, in turn, assured him that she was not like the woman he had met who was married to a feckless husband and just wanted to make him jealous.

They laughed a lot, and the time flew. They agreed to meet again for lunch the next day.

Ria and Richard had decided to get married on their very own beach in May. The only people to be invited would be Pierre and Giselle, Jack plus one,

Tindra plus one, and of course bridesmaids would be Mandy, and Matilda – who should be confidently toddling by then.

Ria, Mandy and Richard had all left their friends at home and had no choice but to lose contact with them. They would all have liked to invite them, but it would be hard to explain away their new names and a baby!

Pierre would bring Jack on his catamaran, and they would have their reception on the deck, or inside if the weather was bad. Mandy was beginning to hope that her plus one might be Rob.

William asked Tindra if she would go out to dinner with him. Hugo and Lizzy had volunteered to look after the twins. She didn't want to make a scene or continue with a bad atmosphere, so she agreed. She still had a lot of anger and hurt from her humiliation in Sweden. Her wedding having to be cancelled at the last moment, and having, for the second time, to run away and hide her pregnancy. It had all been lonely and difficult, and it was all because William was acting like a twelve-year-old, leaving her when she needed his support the most.

It was very difficult to just shake that off.

William was bending over backwards to be nice. He was only just beginning to realise how much hurt he had inflicted and how selfish he had been.

'We make beautiful babies,' he said, smiling as they sat in a booth in a restaurant.

'*I* make beautiful babies,' she snapped.

'I had a little bit to do with it.'

'A *very* little bit.'

'Tindra, please believe me. I am so very sorry for everything that has happened. It was such a big step, marriage and children. I guess I just panicked.'

'I couldn't just panic and walk away could I!'

'No. I know…. Please, Tindra, try to forgive me. I'll make it up to you.'

'How?'

'We were so happy before. We are good together. I've grown up. The babies need us both.'

'Until you decide it's all too much for you and you run away again.'

The waiter brought coffees. Tindra looked at William, and despite herself, she felt that old thrill that made her fall in love with him in the first place. He *had* grown up. He had a different look in his eyes now. The boy was now a man.

Charles was mortified to see his picture in the paper. He was praying that Finn hadn't seen it. His first instinct was to get out of the houseboat, but where would he go? His face was plastered all over the media. He might be better off keeping out of sight. Or he could try to cross the border into Germany, where presumably the press were not aware of him. Luckily, it was cold, so he wouldn't look out of place with his hood up and a scarf around his face.

He decided that it was only a matter of time before Finn, or a neighbour saw the papers, and reported him, so he would have to move on. He stuffed what he could into a duffle bag that he had found in the boat, threw it over his shoulder and set off on his bike to the central station. OK there would be CCTV, but it was a large, busy station so he would take his chances.

Trains to Frankfurt were frequent, so he jumped on the first one he could. Six hours later he was sitting in a dingy internet cafe eating bratwurst and sauerkraut. He knew little German and felt nervous and exposed.

Not so long ago he was living happily with his beautiful wife Anna in Canada. He had a good job and a lovely home. Now he was a murderer on the run with nothing. He was an educated man. How had he allowed this to happen? A huge veil of depression enveloped him. He was exhausted. The sun was no longer shining. The days were short and cold. He had nowhere to go, and very little money. On top of that, he was in a strange country.

But there was one little glimmer of hope.

When he was at uni, he had a good friend called Walter Becker from Frankfurt. He hadn't had contact with him for 30 years, but if he still lived in Frankfurt, maybe he could help. He was sure Walter would remember him as they were close buddies for two years before Walter left.

But how to find him?

He went on the internet. The only Walter Becker he could find was an American musician, who was dead.

Sgt Gill was standing beside a houseboat called *Anna*, with Finn. Finn explained how he had met the man in the photo and let the boat to him. But now he had gone, along with his things. Sgt Gill sat on the bank and ate a few pills as his twitching took on a new level.

'Are you alright?' asked Finn.

'N-n-never better, lad. Never better.'

'Where would you go from here if you were on the run?' he asked Finn.

Finn shrugged. 'If I was all over the papers, I suppose I would want to get out of the country,' he said.

'Mmm. That's what I was thinking. But which country would you go to?'

'There are planes, boats, trains… everything is easy from here. From *right* here, I guess the station would be nearest. You can get to France, Germany, anywhere.'

'Thank you, Finn. We really appreciate the call. You will let us know if you hear from him?'

'Of course.'

Sgt Gill walked to the station. He looked at the timetable. He didn't think Charles would want to go back to France. There were trains every 21 minutes to Germany. That would be his choice.

Mandy and Rob were back at the same table at the same pub. They chatted happily until Rob said, 'You remember we talked about the actor Clive Marlowe, who we both knew?'

'Yes,' said Mandy enthusiastically. She liked Clive.

'Well, I happened to speak to him yesterday, and he didn't remember anyone by the name of Lucy Smith. I described you, and reminded him where you two met, and he said that sounds more like Mandy Anderson.'

Mandy squirmed. 'Oh, that was my stage name, well, my professional name as an agent. Lucy Smith is my real name.'

'Ah, I wondered if that was the case!'

But now this man knew her true identity, and she was still wanted by the police. Had she just blown everything? After all their efforts to change their identities, had she ruined it all? Why didn't she just say, 'Oh, Clive's memory must be as bad as mine,' and laugh it off? No, she, the big mouth, had to agree that she was Mandy Anderson. Damn, damn, damn.

'Is everything alright?' asked Rob, looking concerned. 'I hope I wasn't out of line talking to Clive about you.'

'No, no, it's alright. Just seemed funny hearing my old name again.'

When she got home, she took Ria to one side and told her what had happened. Ria looked worried. 'It's so easily done,' she said. 'I've nearly put my foot in it a few times. Well, there's nothing we can do about it now. Rob's obviously not aware of the situation.'

'Oh no!' cried Mandy. 'I've just thought! If he googles me, all the old newspaper cuttings will come up.'

Richard entered the kitchen, where the girls were sitting at the table. 'What's up?' he asked.

Mandy explained.

He sat down. 'So, let's run through this. If he googles and sees the cuttings, he will see that you had disappeared with Ria and the royal baby. Have you mentioned Matilda to him?'

'Yes, I said she was Ria's grandchild, well, Maria's grandchild.'

'He won't have to be a genius to work it out,' said Ria.

'I'm so sorry, I'm so stupid,' said Mandy, on the verge of tears.

Richard sighed. 'But reports in the papers since have said that they suspected the baby had died last year of cot death. So maybe he will believe that the child is Ria's grandchild, but the ages are a bit of a coincidence.'

'What shall we do?' wailed Mandy?

'Calm down and sit tight. Are you going to see this man again, Mandy?'

'Well, I was hoping to, but I don't know now.'

'He probably hasn't thought twice about it. Just carry on as normal.' Richard smiled.

* * *

Charles went to the Frankfurt coffee bar counter. 'Do you speak English?' he asked the guy behind the bar.

'A little,' he said, without smiling.

'I don't suppose you know a man called Walter Becker, do you?'

'Yes, he was a musician.'

'No, not that one. Do you know anyone in Frankfurt called Walter Becker?'

'No. You could ask my boss. He know everyone.'

'Is your boss here?'

'Upstairs. He be down five minutes.'

'Thank you.'

His boss, a burly man in his sixties, arrived 10 minutes later.

After speaking to the barman, he came over.

'You're looking for Walter Becker?' he asked.

'Yes, do you know him?'

'What do you want with him?'

'He's my friend from university. I wanted to look him up.'

'Frankfurt is a big place. Probably lots of Walter Beckers.'

'Yes, I'm sure you're right,' said a deflated Charles.

'But I know one man of this name because I buy a few stocks and shares. He works in the stock market. Do you want his number?'

'Yes please.'

'Or maybe better that I call him and see if he knows you first.'

'OK,' said Charles.

The man dialled the number, and after a conversation in German, passed the phone to Charles.

'I'm sorry to bother you,' said Charles, 'but are you the Walter Becker that I was at uni with? I am Charles Radcliffe.'

'Charlie Radcliffe! What a blast from the past!'

'I can't believe I found you in a city of thousands.'

'Well I'm pretty famous in these parts,' laughed Walter.

'So it would seem.'

'Look, I finish at five. We could meet for a drink if you like. I'll meet you in the Manhattan Bar. Henri will tell you where it is. I'll be the fat, balding one!'

Charles laughed with relief. 'I'll be there.'

Mandy was in tears again.

Ria sat beside her in the sitting room. 'Are you still worried about that new man of yours?'

'A bit, but I'm more worried about Matilda.'

Ria put her arm around her best friend.

Mandy went on, 'It's just that the poor kid will have no one when we've gone. No brothers or sisters, no cousins, uncles or aunts, absolutely nobody, when in reality she should have a whole big royal family around her, and a life of luxury.'

Ria looked at the floor. She knew Mandy was right. She said, 'We'll be around for years yet.'

'Maybe, but let's be honest, probably not more than 15 years tops. Matilda will still be a teenager.'

'I did try to tell you this at the beginning...'

'I know you did, but I just fell in love with her, and now of course she is one of the family. I just can't bear the thought of her being alone in the world in her young teens and having to cope with our deaths.'

'For goodness sake, Mandy, you're depressing me. What's the matter with you today? We can cross those bridges when we come to them. Now come on, go and get your maid of honour dress and we'll alter it.'

Sgt Gill liked to think that he was the only one on the case, and sometimes it felt like it, but of course there were many others whose priority it was to find Charles Radcliffe, serial murderer. CCTV was a great help, but it took many man-hours to sift through hours of tapes from stations and streets.

Sgt Gill was not prepared to get on a train to Germany without something concrete to go on. Even if Charles had chosen the Frankfurt train, he could have got off at any station on that line. So, he had to wait for CCTV results.

But his hunch was right. An officer in Frankfurt had identified him coming out of the station and going into the nearest cafe. Sgt Gill was on the next train and was met by his opposite number in Frankfurt. He had now chased this damned man through four countries, but if he was honest, he enjoyed the chase.

The cafe owner, Henri, told them that the man had been in his cafe, and was going to meet Walter Becker at the Manhattan Cocktail Bar. He didn't know what time.

This was the nearest Sgt Gill had been to capturing Radcliffe, and he was more than excited.

Chapter twenty-three

As soon as Sgt Gill was out of the door, Henri called Walter and told him that the police were after his friend Charles. He had told them about the Manhattan Bar, so it was up to him what he did.

Walter was shocked. This sort of thing didn't happen in his world. He didn't have a number for Charles. He couldn't imagine that Charles had done anything serious. He had always been a good bloke at uni, one of the lads. They were all a bit mischievous, but Charles was honest and wouldn't hurt a fly.

But then, he supposed, people could change over the years. Maybe he should just not meet him and leave the police to pick him up. Or maybe he should ambush him before he got to the bar and take him back to his place to hear what it was all about. He'd just arrived in the country today, so it might be a passport or customs matter.

Poor Charlie.

Walter decided to try to catch Charles before he reached the bar. He waited across the road until he saw him approaching, five minutes early. Charles was always early.

He had seen two official-looking men going into the bar but couldn't be sure who they were. He grabbed Charles's arm and pulled him in the opposite direction and down a back street. Charles hadn't seen Walter for 30 years, so for a moment thought he was being mugged or arrested.

'Charlie, it's Walter. Come to my place, no, no, that's a bad idea. Let's go in here.'

It was a library. Charlie was totally confused. They sat in a corner away from the windows and whispered to each other.

'Look at you! You haven't changed a bit! The police were asking after you in Henri's cafe. He told them we were meeting at the Manhattan, so I needed to get hold of you before you went in there.'

'You're a pal,' said a shaken Charles, shocked that the police were so close.

'It's good to see you, Charlie boy, even if you are on the run!' he laughed. 'What's it all about?'

Once again, Charlie had to think fast. 'I got a ride to Rotterdam on a cargo ship. Two guys attacked and robbed me. I hit out in all directions trying to save myself, and apparently, I put one of them in hospital. It was self-defence, but I was in a strange country, didn't speak the lingo so decided to get out.'

'To another strange country where you don't speak the lingo,' laughed Walter.

'Maybe you should just explain that it was self-defence. I would come with you to translate if you wanted me to.'

'No, no. Who knows which way it would go. My word against theirs, I could end up in jail. I'll just keep my head down for a while until they lose interest.'

'Henri told them you were coming to meet me, so I'm sure to get a visit.'

Damn and blast. He couldn't even have a reunion with his old friend without the cops ruining it. 'I'm sorry, Walter.'

'Well, what do they say about a friend in need?'

'Is a bloody nuisance!' They both laughed, and the librarian tutted at them.

Sgt Gill waited in the Manhattan Bar with his oppo until closing time. His pills didn't mix too well with all the alcohol, so he had to be carried out.

Ria had something to tell Mandy.

'We've decided to bring the wedding forward,' she said over breakfast, while Richard was in the shower.

'Why, are you pregnant?' she grinned.

'If I was, it would be on the news! Oldest mother ever. No, we just thought we're not getting any younger, so what's the point of waiting?'

'For decent weather?'

'Yes, but the weather can't be guaranteed at any time of the year.'

'True, so when's it to be?'

'In 10 days' time. I'll have to check with the guests, of course, but the celebrant has been booked.'

'But, Ria, it will be freezing on the beach, and probably wet and windy too.'

'Which is why we're bringing everything inside. We can make the house beautiful, and still be warm enough to wear our dresses. There'll only be a few guests anyway. We never wanted a big do. It will be lovely. We'll be married, that's the main thing.'

Mandy wondered if it was too soon to ask Rob to be her plus one.

Walter was an honest man with a reputation to think of and wasn't sure that he could lie to the police. But he and Charlie went back a long way, so he couldn't drop him in it.

'I think the best thing is,' he started, 'for me to go home and when they call, say Henri phoned me and asked me to meet you at the Manhattan. But I had to work so I didn't go, and I didn't have a number for you, so I don't know if you went or not.'

'And what do I do in the meantime?' asked a forlorn Charles.

'What were you going to do if you hadn't found me?'

'Panic.'

They laughed. 'OK,' said Walter. 'I'll ask my brother if you can stay with him for a few nights on the other side of town. But no fisticuffs.'

'As if. Thanks, mate.'

* * *

The days before the wedding were frantic. Florists arrived with beautiful arrangements, and everyone pitched in with the cleaning. Mandy made a wedding cake with a little bride and groom on it, and a perfect little blue dress was found for Matilda. The dogs were bathed and were to wear blue ribbons on the day.

The guests had all agreed to the new date. Tindra had decided to bring William as her guest, leaving the twins with Lizzy and Hugo for 24 hours. She was gradually allowing herself to love William again. Truth be told she never really stopped loving him. Funny how hurt can change love to hate with the flick of a switch. But loving him and trusting him were two different things. He was a good young man and would make a good father now that he had finally grown up. And they were his children after all. So very sad that they had lost their first child.

But maybe they could now make a future for themselves in Paris. He could restore old paintings as he had done in Sweden, and she would look after the home and the children until she was able to work. All just a dream at the moment.

William had been primed about Tindra's situation. She hadn't wanted to be found, so she had called herself Louise from Denmark. He was not to call her Tindra.

Walter's brother, Hans, also worked at the Stock Exchange and lived in a large old house just on the edge of Frankfurt. He lived with his English wife, Patty. Their children had long since flown the nest, so they had plenty of room.

Patty didn't see much of her workaholic husband, so was glad of a new face to talk to. At least he didn't have to invent a new name this time! She wanted to know all about Walter in his uni days, so there was no shortage of conversation, and Charles could relax and reminisce.

Just when he felt totally at home, she said, 'I'm so sorry to hear that you were attacked on the ship. It must have been so frightening. Those docker types are usually bruisers aren't they!'

Just then there was a knock on the front door. 'I hope you don't mind; I invited a friend to meet you.'

Oh no, some nosy biddy no doubt. Why did she do that? Now he'd have to make small talk with a neighbour. The door opened and in walked a tall, stocky man of about his own age.

'Charles, this is Klaus.' said Patty. 'He is a policeman. I thought he might be able to advise you,' she said, obviously thinking this was a lovely, helpful surprise.

Charles could only bluff it out. He stood and offered his hand to shake. 'Klaus.'

Klaus stood to one side, and in walked Sgt Gill. 'Hello, Charles.'

Charles did not know Sgt Gill.

Patty continued, 'This is a visitor from England that Klaus is working with. Would you all like tea?'

* * *

360

The wedding was soon upon them.

It was a crisp, sunny day and there was great excitement. At least they would be able to take photos outside, even if they did have to shiver. They had strung lights and bunting around the garden, right down to the beach.

Pierre and Giselle turned up and brought Jack, Tindra and William with them on the cat. Mandy had plucked up the courage to invite Rob, and everyone had dressed as though the wedding was to be at Westminster Abbey. Matilda was delighted to see 'Louise' again, and there were lots of hugs and kisses.

The celebrant was a smiley middle-aged woman called Cath. She made the ceremony fun, and finally pronounced 'Maria' and Richard man and wife. Ria threw her bouquet in the direction of Mandy.

There were congratulations and champagne all round. There was a buffet, all made by Mandy and Ria. There was a whole salmon, a selection of sandwiches, bread rolls, cheese, celery, several dips, chicken drumsticks, a huge bowl of salad, and fruit scones with jam and cream. By the evening they were all full and exhausted. They sat around in the living room, chatting, and drinking, and drinking and chatting...

Problem was, William was not used to drink.

'What do you think of my beautiful princess?' he slurred to Richard. But before Richard could answer he continued drunkenly, 'Did you know

Tindra, oh sorry, Louise, is a real Swedish princess? I bet you didn't. I'm going to marry her, you know. We have babies, you should see them, they're beautiful babies, but I hope they don't die.'

There was silence in the room as the more or less still sober women listened to his rant. Tindra was in the kitchen chatting to Rob as they helped to clear up.

'Why should they die?' asked Richard.

'Our first baby died. Cot death, whatever that is.' William got up to get another drink, but fell over, grabbing the buffet table on the way down, and taking its contents with him.

He then passed out in a pile of cake, jam and twiglets.

Ria and Mandy were open-mouthed. They looked at Richard. He looked pale.

'He's talking rubbish. He's drunk,' said Richard.

'Richard, is he saying that Louise is the Swedish Princess who is the mother of Matilda?' asked Ria, who was the most shocked bride in the universe.

Mandy chipped in. 'As Richard said, he's drunk out of his mind. He probably read something about it in the papers.'

At that moment, Tindra and Rob came back into the living room. Tindra was horrified to see William lying in a mess of food on the floor.

'Oh no, what happened?' she asked as she ran to him.

'Too much to drink,' offered Richard. 'We'll get him up to bed in a minute.'

'How embarrassing, I'm so sorry,' said Tindra.

Rob and Mandy tried to help Tindra to get William to his feet.

'Before you do that,' said the bride.

'Louise, he said that you are the Swedish princess who was in the papers, who sadly lost her first baby.'

Tindra coloured and flopped onto the sofa. 'I guess I know you all well enough to tell you now. I met William when we were both working in Canada, and I fell pregnant. As even a minor member of the Swedish royal family, it would have been a great scandal if the truth had leaked out, so I went to England to have the baby. Then I got a friend to pretend to kidnap her so she could go to a safe place and avoid the backlash. It was heartbreaking but I was young, and I didn't feel that I had any choice. Later I heard that my daughter had died from cot death.' She welled up.

Richard and Giselle tried to comfort her.

Mandy beckoned Ria to the hallway.

'This can't be happening,' said Mandy. 'Do you believe her?'

'Yes, I do,' said Ria.

'What are we going to do? If we tell her about Matilda, she'll take her away, or even call the police.'

'If Matilda is her child, she will be entitled to take her.'

'But do we have to tell her? She thinks her baby's dead, and she has twins now and a fiancé. Why don't we just keep quiet. She never needs to be any the wiser?'

They called Richard into the hall for his opinion. 'We've known her all this time and had no idea. Thought she was a little backpacker. We have to break it to her that her daughter is here.'

'No, Richard!' cried Mandy.

'We can't lose our baby,' said Ria.

Pierre and Rob helped the semi-conscious William to his bedroom, undressed him and tucked him in.

'Let's sleep on it,' said Richard. 'She'll still be here in the morning. What a day this has been!'

Sgt Gill sat down with Patty, Charles and Klaus. He was now thoroughly enjoying the cat and mouse game. His man was right in front of him, and he didn't have a clue.

'Charlie has a legal problem,' said Patty in her best voice. She was thrilled to be involved in a drama as her life usually involved making cakes for charities and growing tomatoes. 'The poor man was set upon by thugs and robbed. Tell them, Charlie.'

'Sorry to hear that,' said Sgt Gill. 'How awful. Tell us about it, Charlie, maybe we can help.'

'I will,' Charlie smiled, 'I'd be glad of your help, but it's a bit of a long story so I must pop to the bathroom first, if that's OK. It's all the tea I've been drinking.'

'Of course,' said Klaus.

Patty came back in wearing an overwhelming perfume, with another pot of tea and some homemade lemon drizzle cake. Charles went past the bathroom, out of the back door, over the garden fence, and hopped straight onto a passing bus.

William stayed in his room with the world's worst hangover. The others came down to breakfast except Richard. He had been so exhausted by the wedding day that he had gone into a deep sleep, and Ria didn't like to wake him.

They all chatted politely over a full English, while Ria fed Matilda in her highchair, and Tindra talked about her twins, and said she would love everyone to meet them next time. It just would have been too much to bring them to the wedding. She showed pictures on her phone and then came across a picture of her first daughter when she was hours old.

She passed it to Mandy. 'That was my first baby,' she said, with glistening eyes.

Mandy was immediately taken back to the day when she first saw this child on her doorstep. Tears started to fall.

'Oh, I'm so sorry, Lucy. I didn't mean to upset you,' said Tindra.

'I'm not Lucy. I'm Mandy. And this child was left on my doorstep in Hertfordshire last spring. Ria and I have loved her and looked after her ever since. It would appear that our Matilda is your daughter.'

'But... but my daughter died.... cot death,' Tindra stuttered.

Ria said, 'We told Charles that because he wanted to give the baby to an orphanage.'

'You know Charles?'

'He's my son. That's why his baby was brought to me. But as it turns out, he is not the father.'

'No, William is.'

'So why did my son believe the child was his?'

'I'm so sorry, Maria. There was a lot of partying in Canada. I was young and stupid.'

'I'm Ria, by the way.'

Tindra went to the highchair and lifted her daughter onto her lap. 'She is so like my little twin Alice,' she said.

She looked at the distress on the women's faces. 'I expect you think I'm going to take her away?'

'Are you?' asked Ria tearfully.

'I don't think I can manage three babies, and I don't know how I would account for her. If you are happy to keep her, I would love to spend some time with her in the holidays, and maybe she could come to stay with my family and get to know her dad and her brother and sister. I know she's very happy here, and well looked after.'

'And when we are no longer around,' started Mandy, but Ria tried to shush her. 'When we are no longer around,' she persisted, 'Matilda would have a real family, and not be left on her own.'

They all hugged, including Pierre and Giselle, who had stayed the night.

Then Giselle, who never said anything, said quietly in a strong French accent, 'I too have some news.'

Everyone looked at her. They had forgotten she was there.

'I am also to have baby.' She smiled and patted her belly.

'That's wonderful, Giselle,' said Ria. 'Congratulations, both of you.' Pierre looked very pleased with himself.

William staggered in in his pyjamas, holding his head. 'What's all the noise about?' Then he gave Tindra a peck, turned to the others and said, 'Sorry about last night. I never drink as a rule, so I overdid it a bit. Sorry.'

'Just a bit,' said Mandy with a smile. 'Do you want some breakfast?'

He took one look at the greasy plates and ran from the room. They all laughed.

Ria said, 'I'd better go and get *my husband* and tell him the glad tidings.'

Mandy gave her a genuine best friend smile. She was happy for her.

As soon as she entered the bedroom, Ria knew. She sat on the bed for five minutes and told the old rogue how she loved him and would miss him.

Then she went back down.

She sat at the table and said nothing.

Richard was dead. She knew it was coming, that's why they brought the wedding forward. But she had lost the love of her life.

It was a huge shock to almost everyone else. The weekend had been a roller coaster of emotions. And now they had a funeral to arrange. Pierre went up to say farewell to his father. He was not surprised. He had taken him to numerous doctors in the past few months, but it was still a painful blow. What an end to a wedding party. At least they had managed to get married.

Sgt Gill is probably still twitching his way around the globe, trying to lay his hands on Charles Radcliffe. And people are probably still inducing the red mist by getting in Charles's way.

The last sighting of him was by Veronica in Spain, who was charging around Europe in her campervan, with Brian and Lin on board.

She was sure that she saw Charles sitting on the pavement dribbling into his long beard, begging, and gabbling incoherently about royal babies and policemen's balls. But then again, it could have been someone else. Maybe it was Sgt Gill. It was hard to tell.

Once Ria and Mandy had recovered from a period of mourning, they loved their lives at the beach house with Matilda and the dogs. It was exactly as they had imagined it would be when they bought the house.

Rob had moved on to a younger model on the dating site, but by then Mandy had lost interest anyway. He was sex mad, as it turned out, and she was no longer interested in all that messy business.

Matilda went to Paris regularly, where Tindra and William and the twins had set up home. They had married back home in Sweden, where, with the help of Hugo, they had mended bridges with their families. There was great publicity, and the nation had taken the new royal twins to their hearts.

One day Tindra and William would have to come clean about Matilda, but for the moment she only visited them in Paris, so no explanations necessary.

This gave the ageing women a break, and the chance to go to the theatre or a film.

Sometimes they would go to a tea dance, or treat themselves to a pub lunch, or a posh dinner. And sometimes Mandy would work on the novel she had always wanted to write, now that she had a true crime story.

Ria was thinking about all this as she was hanging out the washing on this beautiful spring day. This time she was not on autopilot. She noticed her beautiful surroundings, the smell of the flowers in the garden and the sound of the waves on the beach, and she felt truly content.

And as she returned to the house, she realised that she wasn't shuffling any more.

About the Author

Suzanne Shearing is a retired journalist, stage school owner and film maker.

Starting on her local paper, the *Welwyn Hatfield Times*, as a cub reporter, she progressed to evening and national publications, writing news and features, as well as a local column.

In 1995 she had a change of career, due to her love of the theatre and film. After attending drama school, she opened a stage school, which soon became the most successful part-time stage school in Hertfordshire, with 300 young students and 14 teachers of drama, dance and singing.

When she retired, she started writing scripts, and made two feature films, *No Smoke* and *Archie*, which have been distributed throughout the world, and a short, *Nobody's Child*. *No Smoke* was an official selection for the International Marbella Film Festival.

Two Old Ladies and a Secret Child is Suzanne's debut novel, something she thought she would never achieve. Writing 80,000 words is not easy for a journalist who has been trained to keep everything short and sweet!

Suzanne lives in rural Hertfordshire with her pups Rusty and Rocky, and with her son and his family nearby.

She is working on her next novel with great enthusiasm, having discovered that fiction is so much more exciting than facts!

Suzanne would love to hear from her readers.

sueshearing@aol.com
www.suzanneshearing.com
Facebook – Two Old Ladies and a Secret Child

CPSIA information can be obtained
at www.ICGtesting.com
Printed in the USA
LVHW032007280121
677755LV00002B/139

9 781839 753350